The endless surf dragged at the sands as if grasping at the land with white-knuckled, desperate fingers. As if something or someone longed to free itself from the sea and pull itself onto shore in the long night. Juliana watched with detachment, the small child in her dream crouching among the tumble of boulders marking the water's edge. Now the woman—for suddenly the child was grown to a young woman—trembled. Her eyes stared unwaveringly at the rough track that entered in the center of the curve of the beach.

One slender hand held to a boulder for balance, the other caught at the collar of her shirt. A sheen of perspiration clung to her cheekbones and darkened the damp curls about her face. She grasped at the rock, pushing forward, then sinking back out of sight. Again and again, she rose in a crouch, then shrank down into her hiding place, sheltered from the sight of anyone on the track.

The gleam of moonlight striking an object on the beach broke the woman's concentration. Suddenly decisive, she pushed away from the safety of the boulders and staggered through the ragged edges of the surf to the thing that lay exposed in the wet sands. Juliana's breath came in gasps; she panted as though it were she who ran through the surf and came to a halt before the half-buried metallic object that threw back the shifting moonlight. Casting a frightened glance along the still empty track, the woman dropped to her knees and dug at the small, heavy thing. Wet fingers wiped the smooth surface clean, then she stared at the face of the tiny golden mask dwarfed by the palm of her hand. Her hand. Juliana's own hand.

Even as her fingers closed about the worked gold piece, Juliana's head snapped up. Pounding hoofbeats resounded from the trail. Rising, she stumbled back a step. One horse, dark, powerful. One rider. Juliana cried out. The face of the rider was the face of the mask! Anchored to the spot, she swayed, the hand with the golden mask cupped to her breast, the other extended. The rider reined in sharply some yards away. One hand rose slowly to the mask. Juliana's heartbeat thundered in her ears like the wild crash of the surf behind her. Now the mask was lifting free; another moment and the face would be revealed. A wild cry rent the darkness. The mask dropped down and the great horse wheeled, carrying away its rider.

Juliana's anguished cry echoed the scream of the gull that had awakened her. Her heart still pounding as though she had in reality run through the wet sands, she sat up slowly, grasping at the fragments of her dream. Already it was too late; the masked rider was fading. Tears gathered as she tried to blink them away, but first one, then another and another escaped to spill down her cheeks. She sat sobbing on the beach, grief tumbling from her as fresh now at twenty-two as it had been when she was a child awakened from her sleep by the same nightmare. The face behind the mask was never revealed, nor could she ever put a name to whose face it was that she so longed to see.

When the sobs subsided she took several deep breaths, then made her way to the shore edge and dipped her handkerchief into the water; the cold cloth stung against her reddened cheeks. Retrieving her hat and book, she pushed the damp curls from her face and determinedly pinned the wide-brimmed straw boater in place. Her glance swept along the rugged coastline of Point Lobos, where white water marked the grave of the schooner *Altamira*, then along the cluster of cottages forming the Portuguese fishing village with its single quay where a boat was putting in. Lastly, she let her gaze rise along the cliff above her to the imposing tower of the Point Lobos lighthouse and its attendant outbuildings. Her attention swept back to the docking ship.

As Juliana strained to make out the ship's markings, she gathered up her skirts and headed for the path that would bring her out to the rear of the keeper's house. If the ship had brought the Lighthouse Service district inspector, every last inch of the keeper's buildings, grounds, and person would be subject to minute inspection, including the keeper's family. Her family, Bernard and Faith Russell, the present keeper and his wife, had driven into Santa Rena for a rare holiday on the occasion of their sixteenth wedding anniversary, leaving the Point Lobos station in the hands of Bernard's very capable first assistant, John Pevie, and Juliana herself. Assured by Pevie that the station was shipshape and nothing needed her immediate attention, she'd slipped away for an hour to read her book, John L. Stephens' *Incidents of Travel in Central America, Chiapas, and Yucatan*. For a while she had been transported far away from the light station; now she pushed away the restless urge to widen her world that the book evoked and scrambled up the last few feet of the cliff path to the gate.

Running across the enclosure that held Lilly, their cross-eyed Guernsey milk cow, she let herself in through the far gate past Faith's tidy vegetable garden and raced in through the kitchen door of the keeper's dwelling.

Pevie called out from the porch.

"'Tis only the regular supply ship with the mail, me beauty. No need to panic." A deep undercurrent of amusement colored his words, and Juliana breathed a sigh of relief, dropped her book on a table, and joined Pevie.

John Pevie stood six feet two with broad shoulders, a shock of neatly trimmed wheat-colored blond hair, and a luxuriant, well-groomed moustache the envy of half the young men in nearby Santa Rena and admired by most of the women—old and young. His blue eyes, the color of turquoise blued by the sea, lost their twinkle of amusement as he took in Juliana's flushed cheeks and the slight puffiness that lingered about her eyes. Her thick black hair was twisted in a loose braid, with fine wind-teased strands curling about high cheekbones that graced a heart-shaped face. In contrast to her hair, dark brows framed deep blue eyes, far-seeing eyes now as they focused beyond him on the careful upward progress of the approaching seamen from the U.S. Lighthouse tender. Her neck rose slender, one strong, sturdy fingered hand still gripping her collar. At five foot seven inches she seemed taller, with head held high and shoulders back, emphasizing the slender waist and well-proportioned bodice. Now a tiny sigh escaped her and the wrinkle between her brows smoothed out. The generous mouth relaxed into a grin.

"I'll wash up, then see to lunch, Mr. Pevie. There'll be coffee and pie for the crew if they want to join us."

Her grin belied the formality of her address.

"Do you remember, Juliana?" Pevie asked and laughed as Juliana turned away to the kitchen.

"Aye, Pevie," she responded. "I remember. You were only twenty when you came to Point Lobos eight years ago. Starched collar, pressed uniform." And, she recalled, with all the intensity of a young man who came from a long line of keepers.

"Well, now," he said and grinned again, "'Tis true, I was terrified I'd make a fool of myself in front of the legendary Bernard Russell—keeper of his first light station at the tender age of twenty-three! And you, Miss Russell, as I recall, were all legs and arms and barely fifteen, but desperate to keep your dignity and seem older."

Juliana rolled her eyes. They had "Miss Russell'd" and "Mr. Pevie'd" themselves for weeks, until the afternoon when they had been put to painting the white picket fence that surrounded the complex of lighthouse structures. Each on their fierce dignity under a blazing July sun, until John Pevie wiped his brow with the back of his hand and smeared a glob of white paint across his forehead. Juliana whooped with laughter as Pevie's predicament slowly dawned on him. She had doubled over laughing, and when she'd straightened, stepped back squarely against the newly-painted fence so that the back of her dark work skirt was suddenly striped with white. This proved the undoing of John Pevie in turn, and he'd roared until they were both laughing, tears streaming down their faces. Under control at last, they finished the fence. But the ice had been broken between them and an easy comradeship replaced it.

She laughed, remembering. "I'll put the coffee on, Mr. Pevie."

Pevie watched her go, his brow furrowed. At least he'd made her laugh.

Brighty Severn held out his coffee mug for a refill with gnarled hands while Jasper Taylor polished off the last bite of a generous slice of pie. Brighty took a long sip of the steaming brew, then set his cup down and flexed the stiffened fingers of his left hand.

"Bad weather on its way," he announced.

Jasper nodded sagely, his eyes wrinkling almost shut. "Aye," he agreed, his fine hair flying as he nodded again. "Brighty can feel the changes coming in his hands. Never been wrong yet."

His older companion glanced out to sea, where the day seemed unchanged from the morning's calm, and massaged his hands as if to rub away the aches in those swollen joints. Juliana suppressed a groan; she had lived around sailors long enough to accept such pronouncements and to act accordingly.

Across the table, Pevie pushed back his chair. "Then I'd best be making sure the station's battened down." He rose, as did Brighty and Jasper.

"We'll try to run before the storm to San Francisco." Brighty shrugged. "I reckon we'll make it if'n we leave now."

"And if we don't run across another o' them pleasure boats in trouble," Jasper added with relish. "Seems like we're rescuing city sailors from San Francisco Bay nearly every other voyage up north."

"Durned fools." Brighty tipped his hat. "Never think o' the trouble they cause other folks what's got their own business to take care of." He shook his head. "Thank you for the pie, Miz Juliana. Don't you worry none about your folk. Mr. Russell'll stay put in town till the storm blows over."

"I daresay you're right, Brighty." Juliana tried to smile. "Tell the Pattersons hello, will you?. Faith said to remind Alice Patterson that Bernard still needs a second assistant keeper. He's hoping her nephew will apply after the new baby comes."

This set Brighty and Jasper off on a tangent, as she had known it would, rehashing the last second assistant keeper at Point Lobos.

"Robbie Griffith deserved to be cut," Jasper was heard to offer as he and Brighty disappeared down the cliff path, "what with him sneaking a bottle into the fog signal building."

Juliana let herself into the pasture and coaxed the stubborn Lilly into her shed. Next she made her way to the fog signal building to check that the firebox was fully stacked with cordwood.

The fog signal was a steam-driven whistle with water piped into the boiler from a well south of the lighthouse. The firebox needed an entire cord of wood to keep the steam boiling for just ten hours—not an unusual length of time when the fog rolled in early and stayed. A timer produced the distinctive Point Lobos fog signal of whistle blasts five seconds long, separated alternately by ten and twenty-seven seconds of silence. Juliana hated the fog signal and not because it sounded, as Faith Russell described it, like the lowing of a bad-tempered Lilly. It was inordinately troublesome, requiring a lead time of three-quarters of an hour to get up enough steam to run the whistle; it was consequently kept loaded and ready to light, as it was now. Worse, however, it was prone to breaking down. Minerals from the well water often created havoc with the boiler's tubes, while the equipment in general was constantly in need of repairs or replacement parts, to the despair of the normally stoic Bernard.

A large bell remained mounted in the fog signal building in case of emergency. This had almost been pressed into service once or twice that Juliana could recall, but last minute finagling by the keeper or his assistants had always managed to get the fog signal up and running. There was talk of building a rain shed and storage tanks to bypass the well water now used for steam, as had been done at a sister lighthouse farther south along the coast. Fervently, for Bernard's sake, she hoped so.

Juliana gave the shed one last glance and moved on. Pevie would see to the oil house next to the tower where the oil supply for the light was stored. She checked the keeper's workshop and the storage sheds. Already the wind was picking up, with little whitecaps foaming on the waves in the bay below. Making her way toward the keeper's quarters, she paused. The two-story clapboard house had a pitched roof with chimneys at either end and a broad porch across the front of the double dwelling. Behind it the white masonry tower of the lighthouse rose one hundred fifteen feet into the air.

A shiver of wind sent her hurrying up the steps to the porch. *Better check the unoccupied keeper's quarters.* If Stewart Patterson, Alice Patterson's nephew, did come to Point Lobos, he would find ample quarters for his growing family. Point Lobos had always had at least two keepers since its lighting back in 1872. Pevie, as a young bachelor, had taken up residence with the Russells because the second's quarters had been filled at the time by a keeper who had since retired from the service. Pevie, now promoted to first, remained unmarried and still lived with the Russells.

As Juliana checked the windows one by one in the downstairs rooms, the thought crossed her mind that Bernard might soon retire from the service. At that, a second helpless thought reared its head. Although never expressed in so many words, she knew it would greatly please her adopted family if she and Pevie made a match. A certain amount of isolation was built into the life of the keepers and their families, so that Juliana had not met many eligible young men. John Pevie was handsome, personable, and would make some lucky woman a fine husband. But not her! Pevie was like an older brother to her. She shook her head, dismissing these vague worries. Content that the unoccupied quarters were secure, she made her way to her own side of the dwelling.

The sky was darkening now, and Juliana made a determined effort not to think about the oncoming storm. A sudden foreboding, perhaps brought on by the unexpected recurrence of her youthful nightmares, tensed her muscles and made her hunch her shoulders against the signs of imminent fury. As if the storm was about to wreak havoc on the precarious peace of her life at Point Lobos. As if, a whisper of foreknowledge chilled her, the terrified child she had once been was only hidden beneath the surface, and old truths and dangers were about to drive that terror into her present.

"Really, Juliana Russell," she scolded herself, "stop acting like a ninny!"

Bringing in potatoes from the root cellar, she set herself the task of preparing supper. If a heavy storm blew up, they'd need the food to keep them at their watch. Carrots and peas she'd picked from the vegetable garden, along with some baked potatoes, would go well with the fish she'd purchased that morning from the Portuguese fishing village below. Keeping her mind on her immediate tasks, Juliana decided on fresh biscuits to go with tinned peaches from the larder. A pot of strong coffee was brewing as the first assistant came into the kitchen, his face grave.

"If the storm doesn't break soon, there'll be fog rolling in, mark my words." Pevie moved to the cupboard and took down plates and cups. Juliana stifled a groan; Pevie flashed a rueful grin at her. "Aye, well, just pray, me beauty, to whoever is the patron saint of troublesome machinery, that the fog signal holds up 'til the fog blows on by the point." He poured the coffee and helped Juliana set out their supper.

"Mmm, Miss Russell, tis a smell to warm me heart!"

She managed a tight grin in response, and he sent a shrewd glance her way. "Eat up, Juliana. We'll manage, don't you be worrying!"

After washing and drying the supper dishes, they retreated to the front porch where Pevie swore softly under his breath. The first thin fingers of fog were already sliding across the bay below.

"I'll see to the fog signal, Juliana. Then we'll light the lamp."

Juliana pulled her shawl more tightly about her and nodded. A quarter of an hour later she heard his steps ring out on the spiral iron staircase below her. Pausing at the window on the second landing, she rested her palm against the wall. At nearly five feet thick, the massive walls had withstood many storms in the decades since the tower had been built, but Juliana was well acquainted with the fury of a storm-tossed sea. She never took safety for granted at such a time. Bernard's assistant joined her on the landing and without comment on the thickening fog below, they continued to climb.

Pevie had long ago ceased to take notice of the trousers and thick jersey Juliana changed into at times like these. She had been required on more than one occasion to assist the keeper and his staff in securing their boat in its slip in the bay, and once she'd helped get the survivors in when a steamship had wrecked off their coast. *And through no fault of Bernard's,* she reminded herself fiercely now. The light and the fog signal were operating smoothly at the time, but the steamer's first mate had mistaken the Point Lobos signal for that of their sister lighthouse farther south. He'd thought himself safe as he brought his ship close in to shore, then the rocks just beyond the bay had ripped the steamer's bottom out and snagged her high and dry. Luckily, all the passengers and crew were rescued, and two weeks later—before all but the most cursory of salvaging efforts could begin—a second savage storm plucked the steamship from its perch and sent it to the bottom of the bay. She hoped fervently that this night would see them free of any such disasters.

Up past the final landing they reached the watch room. There, the first assistant keeper took up a *lucerne* as Juliana set a match to it, then opened the Fresnel light to expose the lamp at its heart. Everything had been cleaned and prepared so that the lamp stood ready to be lit at any moment after ten o'clock every morning. As Juliana kept one eye on the windows, praying the fog would lift, she sent a silent prayer heavenward: *Please, don't let anyone be caught in the storm.* Pevie's steady arm thrust in the metal *lucerne* with its lighted wick, which he touched in turn to each of the five concentric wicks. *Please,* she prayed, *please let this night pass without incident.*

When the wicks were all equally ablaze, Pevie withdrew the *lucerne* and closed the light, handing the extinguished *lucerne* to Juliana.

"Don't be worrying so, Juliana." He flashed a grin at her. "Most folk have sense enough to stay put or put into port when the seas start raging."

While she made sure that the lucerne was completely extinguished, Pevie turned to the clockwork mechanism of the light. Once the weight was properly engaged, the twenty-four flash panels of the light would rotate on wheels so the light from the lamp flashed in a set pattern. Completing one rotation every four minutes, the Point Lobos light was set to a pattern of one flash every ten seconds.

As the mechanism engaged the wheels and the massive light began to turn smoothly, Juliana looked out the wall of windows. A break in the fog revealed the choppy seas of the bay and the twinkle of lights that marked the Portuguese settlement below. No need to worry about that quarter; the Portuguese fishing community knew when and how to ride out a storm. No; it would be the unwary, the inexperienced sailor who'd find himself in need of help. She glanced away from the view and looked at her companion.

"Pevie?" A quiver of unease ran up her back. Pevie stood motionless and held up one hand.

He shook his head, running a hand through his thick shock of hair so that it stood on end.

"'Tis nothing, I'm hoping. I thought the fog signal sounded out of sync, Juliana. It seems to be on at the moment, but...."

"...you'd better check the machinery," she finished for him.

"Right." He nodded, clasped her shoulder briefly. "I'll be back in a tick, me beauty. You know what to do." His broad shoulders disappeared down the stairwell.

Juliana paced the watch room, arms folded tightly across her chest. The steadfast flash of the light reassured her, as did the patterned bellow of the fog signal. Straining her hearing, she listened hard and counted as she did so. Five seconds for the first blast, ten seconds of silence, a repeat of a five-second blast followed by a long twenty-seven seconds of silence once more, then a third five-second sounding of the foghorn. And now the pattern should be repeated exactly. Still pacing, she counted the interminable seconds through the fog signal. One thousand twenty-four, one thousand twenty-five, one thousand twenty-six, one thousand twenty-seven. Then the blast. Had there been the slightest hesitation before the blast began? She lost the count in her momentary agitation and willed herself to patience. One… she picked it up at the next blast and counted through two entire sequences. At the last, Pevie climbed into the watch room, bearing a tray with a pot of strong coffee and two pieces of pie.

"It seems to be okay, Juliana. For now. Here," he indicated the coffee and apple pie, "take a break. I'll watch. 'Tis going to be a long night, if I'm not mistaken."

Juliana noted that the hands of the watch room clock marked seven-thirty. Yes, indeed, a long night. She helped herself to coffee and let her thoughts stray far from the confines of the tower. She'd often kept Pevie or Bernard company through parts of nights just like this one, and on clear nights, too, when the stars hung so close in the sky she'd been tempted to stand on her toes and reach for one. Other nights she and Bernard sat together in companionable silence and watched ships pass beyond the bay. Where did they come from and where were they going? She would question the keeper. Bernard Russell's deep, slow voice would weave stories out of the darkness of exotic ports and cargoes bound across the high seas to San Francisco and Los Angeles. Hadn't he ever wanted to ride one of those ships to sea and back again, she'd asked him once. No, had come the answer. He was a solid man, with a still, calm center. Faith and family were one center of his world, the lighthouse service the other. Capable and content, both his worlds melded at Point Lobos.

But Juliana's eyes followed the silent passage of the ships until their lights were lost far out to sea. She longed to travel beyond the circumscribed confines of her world and search out... what? With an involuntary shake of her head, she acknowledged the restless, rootless longings that she tried hard to suppress. Faith and Bernard Russell had plucked her from the sea when she was but eight years old, Faith a new bride barely eighteen years old and Bernard a trusted keeper in his second year at Point Lobos. Since that time they had become her family with every small wordless comfort and gesture and act of love given through the years.

Her natural parents had perished in the storm that had brought her so fortunately to the Russells. If she searched the world over, she would not find again the two who had brought her into this world. But sometimes, like the faintest whisper from the past echoing in her dreams, she would wake slowly and hear a sweet, deep voice lulling her. Or, other times, she jeered at herself, there would be a woman, pale hair brushed smoothly away from a blur of a face, bending over her. As if one fragment was any more real or remembered than the other. Her birth parents had been small, dark-haired people, their bodies pulled from the sea and buried in the churchyard in Santa Rena. So her dreams were only that, and they shamed her because she dearly loved her friends.

Faith Russell had coaxed only her first name and age from the quivering, terrified child rescued from the bay. When told her parents had perished in the storm, she had become hysterical and vehemently denied this fact. Nor could she ever be persuaded to visit their graves in Santa Rena. Faith had long ago found that any attempt to discuss Juliana's past brought on more nightmares. She learned to let the past lie.

Now, Juliana's fingers itched for her sketchbook to occupy her mind as well as her hands. But, the Lighthouse Service demanded all one's time and energy. There were precious few idle hours during the long days, and she had come to terms with that fact as best she could this past year, putting her sketchbook and watercolors away. Her family had not asked her to do so, but she was no longer a child and would not jeopardize Bernard's livelihood by adding to his burden of care. She had come also to realize and to accept that neither was she likely to find a more traditional means of support, a husband, as isolated as she was at Point Lobos. No, she would have to take care of herself and not depend solely on her friends.

It was in the back of her mind that one day soon she might seek a paying position in the service for herself; women keepers weren't all that unusual. If she lived frugally as a keeper for a few years, perhaps she could put enough money by to allow her to travel and return to her watercolors. Only... she sighed. When the money ran out, what then? She harbored no great illusions that she would become another Winslow Homer or Albert Bierstadt and find her efforts in great public demand. What she loved best was to work with her watercolors outside, making rapid fluid sketches of the light tower, the fishing boats, nets draped over rocks to dry, a handful of pebbles whose textures and details caught her eye. But there was no livelihood in such whimsy.

"Damn!"

Juliana started from her reverie. Her companion swore again and she joined him at the window, sucking in her breath sharply. Pevie pointed at a ship's lights dancing in the bay below them, visible in the intermittent breaks of the fog. The forlorn sailing yacht rode low in the water, her mainsail flopping uselessly from side to side.

Pevie's glasses raked the decks. "She's still manned." He headed for the stairwell. "Let's go, Juliana!"

Juliana's thoughts raced. Getting their lifeboat launched from its slip would be tricky with just the two of them. Grabbing a sou'wester and pulling on her boots, Juliana stopped to fill two large kettles with water and set them on the stove next to the large pot of coffee Pevie had made earlier. As she worked, she spared a thought for those unfortunate voyagers trapped on the yacht.

Outside, the wind tore at her rain gear, buffeting her back one step for every three she took. Pevie's arm steadied her as they clambered down to the beach and the boatslip.

"Stand by!"

They lowered the boat nearly to the water's edge, then Pevie climbed in. Juliana paid out the lifeboat's rope until the rough seas took the boat, Pevie's muscles straining at the oars as he turned it toward his partner. Juliana was already wading out, flinging herself into the spray and flopping into the boat where she righted herself as Pevie headed them toward the open bay and the battered sailing yacht.

Juliana tucked her chin down and manned her oars, trusting in Pevie to set their course. As had happened before in such emergencies, she spared no thought for what they might find on the yacht. One thing at a time. If there were survivors, their only hope of safety lay in her hands and Pevie's, and there was no time at all for doubts. They would do what must be done. After an interminable amount of time, blinded by the fog and with a sense that they were heading well out into the open seas, Juliana at last felt their boat bump the yacht and she scrambled forward as Pevie brought them around. Her task was to climb aboard and guide the survivors to safety. Pevie's strength was needed to keep their lifeboat alongside and ready to take on passengers.

Juliana grabbed at the rigging and clambered stiffly aboard. Getting her breath under control, she ducked beneath the swinging mainsail and looked about for the luckless sailors. The far side of the yacht was already listing, filling up as water washed over the sides. Even if she had help, the yacht was clearly destined for the bottom of the bay. But where were the survivors? She grasped the wheel to steady herself. The door to the hold snapped miserably to and fro. Juliana hesitated, dreading a descent into the unknown confines of the yacht's hold. Lurching her way over to the door, she found the galley steps awash. If anyone had been trapped below, they were beyond her aid now.

A bobbing blur of light caught her eye among the waters that threatened to engulf the vessel beneath her feet: the yacht's lifeboat, rising as the incoming water crept higher and higher. It was unsecured, and Juliana made a determined plunge for the small emergency craft. Inside lay a dark, huddled bundle, surely one of the ill-fated vessel's crew. And alongside, half-draped over the side, was a second sodden, motionless figure. Splashing through the flooding seas, Juliana grasped the man and shoved him into the lifeboat.

Quickly she ran her fingers along the side and was relieved to find the oars intact and ready. Without further thought she climbed in, shipped her oars, and winced as the light craft was pulled away from the mother ship. As carefully as she could, she struck out away from the sinking yacht and carried her craft around to the shore side where Pevie stood off the vessel, his head turning toward her as she came into view. As she approached the lighthouse boat, she scrambled forward and flung a line to Pevie, who made the smaller craft fast, then steadied her as she came aboard. Together they bent over the oars to take themselves and what was left of the yacht's crew—dead or alive—back to the safety of Point Lobos.

Shoulders on fire as she hunched over the oars, Juliana risked a glance at the lifeboat they pulled alongside and saw the figure she'd pushed aboard now lay next to the other dark lump. At least one of them appeared to be alive. With grim satisfaction she applied herself with renewed determination to her oars. Then came the scrape of the beach beneath them, Pevie already leaping out as rough hands grasped the sides of both boats and hoisted them beyond the pull of the waves. *Senhor* Coelho and the other able-bodied Portuguese fishermen must have seen them coming in.

Juliana was lifted from her seat and made her way to the two inert survivors. The one she'd hoisted into the lifeboat moaned as she turned him onto his back. No need to feel for a pulse; he was alive! She knelt beside his companion. Beneath the lights one of the fishermen held close, the face was white, as if the seas and rain had leached all color from it. A great livid bruise swelled along the left side of his face. Her fingers probed at his throat; to her relief the unmistakable pulse of his heartbeat throbbed beneath her fingertips. At least for the moment, this one too had survived.

Having secured their craft and the yacht's, Pevie helped the fishermen lift the bodies onto the blankets they'd fetched. He carefully guided the men up to the light tower, Juliana hurrying ahead as fast as she dared on the rain-slicked path. Inside she directed them to place the makeshift litters in the kitchen where the stove radiated a welcome warmth, then set out mugs and motioned for the men to help themselves to the hot coffee simmering strong and black on the stovetop. They drank quickly, murmuring their thanks, then took themselves back down to their families in the village, where she knew there would be a great deal of intense speculation about the survivors, their yacht, and the chances of salvaging the boat and what was on it.

As Juliana filled hot water bottles from the steaming kettles, Pevie brought in cots and dry blankets and set them up next to the stove. He had, Juliana noted, taken time to get out of his wet things. Fetching towels and nightshirts, she went to change out of her own wet clothing while Pevie stripped down their charges. When she came back, wearing fresh trousers and a thick cast-off sweater of Bernard's, the sleeves rolled up, Pevie was packing the last of the hot water bottles about the young man with the bruised face.

Pevie's grave features relaxed when he saw her.

"Come, me beauty, I'm in need of your assistance with this fine gentleman." He nodded at the other cot. "'Tis his shoulder, I'm thinking. It may be dislocated. If you would be so good, help me hold him up?"

As she stepped past Pevie to take up her position, Juliana's eyes widened as she saw that the patient's eyes were open, dark with pain and something else, an air of bewildered recognition. Pevie noticed that the man was awake. He addressed his remarks to the fellow as Juliana lifted him and braced his back against her.

"Congratulations, good sir," Pevie said briskly. "You've come through your escapade with only a nasty bruise on your shoulder. Mainsail gave you a bit of a knock, did it?" The man winced as Pevie's fingers probed, but he made no sound. "Don't worry, we'll fix you up and have the doctor in to look at you as soon as the weather permits."

He continued to probe the shoulder. "'Tis the Point Lobos light station where you've fetched up. I'm John Pevie, first assistant keeper, and this," he indicated Juliana with a nod, "is Miss Juliana Russell, daughter to Bertrand Russell, head keeper of our light station."

As the man glanced up at Juliana, Pevie's large, capable hands smoothly snapped the shoulder back into its socket; the man's eyes rolled back in his head and he slumped against Juliana. She lowered him gently to the cot once more, studying his features with interest. The thick black hair straightened as it dried. Fine, dark brows marked a strong forehead, and high cheekbones were brushed by long black lashes and dusted with the faintest sprinkling of freckles, faded now, as if they had been outdone by his deep tan. His jaw was squared, his mouth relaxed; his eyes, seen moments before, a dark gray with lighter flecks that had sparkled in the lamplight. Now she toweled away the sheen of perspiration that glazed cheekbones and forehead and propped an extra pillow behind his newly mended arm to make sure he didn't turn onto it in his sleep and cause himself further pain.

That done, she found Pevie refilling the water bottles tucked about their other charge. This second survivor had straight blond hair, very light and streaked as though he'd spent some time out of doors, which fell back from the bruise and brushed the collar of his borrowed nightshirt. His features were even, unremarkable in repose. He seemed years younger than his companion, hardly more than a boy.

She glanced up at Pevie. He shrugged.

"Nothing appears to be broken, Juliana. Probably 'tis the blow he took on the head has him out for the time being. All we can do is keep him dry and warm, and when he regains consciousness, get some warm broth into him."

"When," Juliana repeated with a smile, laying her hand on Pevie's forearm. "You are always the optimist, Mr. Pevie."

His blue eyes twinkled as he returned her grin, then he sobered.

"I'm off to the tower for the rest of the watch. If you need me...." he let his glance finish the sentence for him.

"Rest if you can, I'm thinking."

Juliana moved quietly about the kitchen, one eye on her charges as she brewed tea and set a pot of broth to simmer on the stove. After refilling her kettles, she at last picked up her book and settled herself in Faith's rocker with a fresh cup of tea. Her glance strayed more and more frequently to her patients. Had there been others on the yacht? She sighed and renewed her concentration on Stephen's travails in the Yucatan. Perhaps half an hour later, she sighed again. It was no good; she hadn't finished three pages.

"Miss Russell?"

Startled, she looked up as the book slipped from her grasp.

Those dark gray, luminous eyes watched her steadily as she rose and went over to him.

"William Jordan McKenna at your service, Miss Russell." His voice was deeper than Pevie's, steady in spite of the pain pinching his nostrils. "May I trouble you for a glass of water?"

"Perhaps some coffee, Mr. McKenna?" At his nod, she fetched a large mug of coffee, then helped him sit up, steadying the mug as he held it awkwardly in his right hand and drank. He grimaced.

"I know it's sweet," she told him, "but the sugar is good for the shock you've had tonight, Mr. McKenna."

"Will." He lay back against his pillows, his eyes bright. "Call me Will, Miss Russell. Circumstances have contrived to make us friends."

Now he was teasing her. Her cheeks flushed.

"No, no," he protested, "I make it a habit to include among my best friends all those who save my life." He produced a faint grin and held out his uninjured arm. "Friends?"

She took his hand and tucked it firmly under his blankets.

"Rest, Mr. McKenna... Will." He winced again. "You've come through quite an ordeal. Lie down, please."

"Yes, Miss Russell." But still he hesitated, straining to look over her shoulder. He nodded at the still form of his companion. "How's Jimmy? Mr. Dutton?"

"He's not regained consciousness, Mr. McKenna, although—" Will moved convulsively to sit up "—he appears to have suffered no broken bones. I think he's resting easier." This much was true, for his breathing was coming more naturally. "As long as we keep him warm and immobile, I think he'll mend." She hoped this was truly the case and kept her voice calm, her tone soothing. "Was there anyone else aboard?"

Will McKenna gave her a long, measured look, then shook his head.

"Only Jimmy. just Jimmy and me. We were heading home—to San Francisco." A yawn escaped him. "Sorry."

Finishing his cup of coffee, he slipped silently down into his blankets. Within moments his long lashes swept his cheeks again as he dropped off to sleep. Juliana waited a moment, but he didn't stir again. Who was this Will McKenna? And Jimmy? Just two rich young men with a yacht and time to sail her? She shook her head and went to check the water bottles on young Mr. Dutton, then filled a thick mug with coffee and set off for the light tower. As soon as she saw to Pevie, she decided, she'd settle herself for a nap.

A short time later, Juliana wearily put away the tray and stretched her aching shoulders. With a start, she saw that it was just gone midnight. With any luck at all, the worst of the night had passed. As she straightened her back, her glance swept the *AlyceGee*'s survivors. Will McKenna slept easily now. She leaned over James Dutton, laying her hand on his brow as she did so. His forehead was warm to the touch; not feverish, but no longer clammy with shock. A good sign, she thought. As she removed her hand, her patient stirred beneath her touch. His eyelids fluttered open and a hand grasped at her arm. Blue eyes stared into hers, widening in recognition.

"Lucy!" he whispered with a strange little smile of affection. "Lucy Katerina!"

Her arm jerked convulsively, and his hand dropped away.

"No, no, Mr. Dutton," Juliana whispered, her throat tightening. "I'm Juliana. Juliana Russell. Here." She turned away, then came back to him with a cup of broth and a spoon, the broth threatening to spill from the trembling of her hands, "let's get some of this broth into you."

Seating herself on the edge of the cot, she turned the bruised face gingerly toward her and spooned the warm broth into her charge until a scant half cup was consumed. His hand crept back and held her sleeve as his eyelids dropped lower and lower. Setting the unfinished broth aside, Juliana gently unhooked his fingers and smoothed his blankets over him.

"Lucy." The barest sigh escaped him as he slipped into sleep, that same lingering smile turning up the corners of his mouth. She was left to watch him sleep and wonder at that odd little moment of panic that had overcome her. Pressing her fingers over her eyes, she rubbed them tiredly. It had been an extraordinary night, and while the rain seemed to be abating, she knew that the fog still sat over them as thick as ever. It was nerves, she reprimanded herself. Just nerves.

CHAPTER TWO

After James Dutton had roused himself again and been helped to take more broth, Juliana dozed sleepily in a rocker wrapped in a quilt. How quiet the station was with Faith and Bernard gone. Perhaps it was the fog, muffling the common night noises. Quiet. Juliana's eyes jerked open in sudden, horrified understanding. Too quiet! She groaned aloud. The fog signal had stopped! As she struggled from the quilt, she heard Pevie clattering down the last few steps of the light tower. He paused long enough to pull on his oil coat and grab the lantern she thrust at him.

I'll check the signal building, Juliana, and let you know if I need you."

She nodded and turned an anxious face on her charges. Will McKenna propped himself up with his uninjured arm.

"What do we do now?" he asked, his gray eyes taking in the sleeping form of his friend.

"We wait," Juliana replied, running a hand down the loose braid that fell over her shoulder. "Pevie's a fair hand with the machinery, but I wish Bernard were here!"

On her words Pevie stamped the water from his boots on the porch and hurried in.

"The box is full, , but the blasted machine won't go. It'll take me a while to tinker with the system and see if I can find the trouble. I'm going to need you."

"Oh, Pevie!"

"I know, Juliana. Don't worry, I'll get the signal back in working order as soon as I can."

Will McKenna swung his feet to the floor.

"If you'll find me some trousers, Miss Russell, I think I can manage to assist Mr. Pevie. You won't have to leave Jimmy, then.

Pevie's eyes met Juliana's even as he reached for the clothing drying by the stove.

"We can try. If I can fix the damage, you won't be kept at it long. If I can't, then we can take turns until the fog lifts."

As Juliana turned her back to gather her boots and slicker, Pevie dropped an oiled jacket around Will McKenna's shoulders. The other man was nearly of a height as him, but slightly built. He frowned as he saw Juliana's preparations for venturing out in the rain.

"But why?" he began, and Juliana finished quietly for him.

"We're responsible for the safety of everyone within sound of the Point Lobos signal, Mr. McKenna. Your friend is resting peacefully. There's nothing more we can do for him. Someone needs to sound our temporary fog signal until Pevie repairs the mechanical one." She looked meaningfully at his shoulder. "It's a task needing two hands."

She was already on her way out the door, Will behind her, and Pevie following with a second lantern. Entering the fog signal building, Juliana pulled a thick scarf from her pocket, folded it into a narrow band about her ears, and then tied it at the back of her neck. Pevie handed Will the lantern and directed him to the machinery. Juliana picked up a wooden mallet from a shelf and stooped to pull the canvas from a large bell. Folding the canvas into a thick rectangle, she put it down close to the bell and knelt on it.

Hefting the mallet's weight, she struck the bell, then hit it again, and again, and twice more, the force of the impact jarring all the way through her shoulder blades. Five peals, then ten seconds of silence. She counted out each second, readied her hammer, and swung once more for five peals, then began the long twenty-seven seconds of silence before the next set of five strokes.

As Juliana counted, Pevie worked his way along the steam machinery. Will braced the lantern atop the pipes awkwardly with his good right arm. There, begin; she swung resolutely on the count. Five strokes. Ten seconds of silence. Five loud strokes that reverberated throughout the small shed and threatened to deafen her through the thick folds of her scarf. Now twenty-seven seconds of silence again. She counted them to herself, biting her lip as she concentrated and blocked out her sight of Pevie, who'd arrested his progress and was now tinkering with the workings of the mechanical whistle. Will's set face, turned toward her, blurred as she forgot everything and focused all conscious thought on the fog signal cycle. She pushed away the pain and swung, fire burning from her shoulders along the aching muscles of her upper arms each time she tightened her grip on the mallet and swung. Pushed away the damp discomfort of the canvas beneath her trousers, and counted nine, ten, then felt the wooden mallet making contact with the bell once more and the tone sound, tolling five times across the bay. Ringing out its warning, its code of identity to the ships riding out to sea and depending on the Point Lobos station to keep them clear of the treacherous coastal rocks, to keep them on course when they could not see the stars for the fog.

Over and over she beat the bell while Pevie struggled to fix the machinery. She lost all track of time, perspiration beading her forehead and running down the hollow of her back. In a half-stupor, she found herself counting out loud.

"One-thousand twenty-?" Juliana's breath caught raggedly. Where was she in the count?

"Five. One-thousand twenty-six, one-thousand twenty-seven," a strong, clear voice finished for her, and her hands swung without thought. Juliana opened her eyes and met the gaze of Will McKenna. Strength seemed to pour into her, infusing her weary limbs with renewed energy. As she straightened her slumping shoulders, she heard Pevie's strained voice over the bell.

"Hang on, Juliana, my lass. She's slipped a cog and lost a pin this time. We've just about got the cog replaced. Will here spotted the pin. When I pop it in, she should take off."

And then Will's voice lifted and filled her mind with the count; she followed and swung on the mark, her body repeating the cycle of strike five times, resting ten or twenty-seven seconds, then five more steady, measured strokes upon the clanging bell.

The first blast of steam arrested her in mid-strike. She sagged to one side with numbed relief, her stiff fingers loosening their hold. The mallet clattered to the ground. Only the large metal bell kept her from sprawling across the floor.

"Come, come, Miss Russell." Pevie's voice sounded in her ear as he ducked his head beneath her arm and pulled it across his shoulders. His other arm around her waist, he supported her to a standing position. Leaning against him until the trembling in her knees lessened, Juliana allowed him to walk her slowly about the building for several turns until her stride steadied.

"Okay now?" He hugged her shoulders briefly at her nod. "Then go up and see to the lad. I'll fill the firebox and watch this cantankerous contraption for a few cycles."

Will McKenna, his eyes dark with weariness, lifted his lantern with his good arm and held the door for her with his body. As they stepped outside, the chill struck at them and they moved closer together, shoulder to shoulder, as they hurried as best they could along the path to the keeper's quarters.

Inside, the welcome warmth of the kitchen enveloped them. Will McKenna lowered himself with a stifled protest onto his cot. Juliana checked the sleeping figure on the other cot. Mr. Dutton had not stirred in their absence, but his hot water bottles had lost their heat. The kitchen remained warm enough and his blankets heavy enough to wrap him in comfort until she could lift the steaming kettles from the stove. Stumbling to the rocker, she sank onto her abandoned quilt and closed her eyes. Distant clinking sounds came to her, but all that mattered was the clear, steady call of the fog signal. Her weary body refused to get up and she sat with her eyes closed. Then a delicious aroma assailed her nose.

"Open wide, Miss Russell."

Her tired eyes struggled open. Not Pevie. Pulling a chair to her side, Will McKenna held a steaming cup of coffee before her with his uninjured hand.

"Can you manage as you did so steadfastly in the shed, or shall I do the honors?" he asked with the faintest of smiles.

She flushed, managing to take the cup from him without spilling the hot brew, and sipped. A strange, soft glow coursed through her; how much of it was due to the hot beverage and how much to his praise, she couldn't sort out. When she had the strength to summon words again, she nodded at the still form beside them. "What happened out there to you and your friend, Mr. McKenna?"

The gray eyes sobered as they stared past her to his injured companion, then Will turned his thoughtful gaze to Juliana.

"The *AlyceGee* belonged to Jimmy's great-uncle. The old man got her as part of a shrewd piece of business, but no one in the family ever made much use of her until Jimmy grew up. He rechristened the yacht after his mother and sails her every chance he gets. He's an artist; he liked to anchor her off the coast wherever he fancied, then take the dinghy to shore to paint."

He cleared his throat before continuing. "Jimmy was spending some time on the *AlyceGee*, painting near Monterey, when he wrote to ask if I were free to sail her back to San Francisco with him. He didn't have to ask twice! I'd recently been laid up with a fever and was itching for some fresh air and activity. When the storm hit, we had the *AlyceGee* well in hand until I lost my footing and the mainsail caught me, slamming me into the railing. And very nearly went over, as well as knocking my arm out of place," he added lightly, although Juliana saw his eyes deepen as he relived that moment of near death.

"That's when our bad luck tripled. Jimmy lunged to my rescue, but the mainsail swung back and caught him off guard. It's a wonder we didn't both go tumbling overboard. By that time the *AlyceGee* was well within the bay. When she started to take on water, I dumped Jimmy into the dinghy— and then I guess I passed out. Then you and Mr. Pevie came along to dump me in after him, and don't think I'm not grateful!"

His sudden grin caught her unawares. She ducked her head and made a pretense of sipping her coffee. Will's good hand touched her arm, and Juliana looked up quickly.

"I'm doubly in your debt, Miss Russell. For my life and for Jimmy's. If ever I can repay you, you need only tell me how."

Uncomfortable, Juliana nodded to her teacup and tried to speak lightly in turn.

"Thank you, but I'd say we're even, Mr. McKenna. This cup of coffee has restored me. Now," she said as she gathered herself up, "I'd better see to Mr. Dutton's hot water bottles. If I were you, I'd try to get some sleep."

With morning the fog lifted, leaving behind a placid glassy bay with no hint of the *AlyceGee*. The yacht had gone down in the night. Juliana shuddered as she stared out to sea. Sunlight washed through the windows, promising a bright, full day ahead. Moving as quietly as she could, she lit the stove and started bacon frying, then measured flour for a batch of buttermilk biscuits. Above her, she could hear Pevie moving about.

"Good morning, Miss Russell." Juliana started, then turned about to find Will dressed and stretching gingerly. "You're an early riser." He spoke softly so as not to disturb his sleeping companion.

"Needs must, Mr. McKenna," she answered, slipping the pan of biscuits into the oven. "The Lighthouse Service has strict rules. One of them is that the light must be extinguished at daybreak. And, equally important, every bit of the Fresnel must be cleaned, polished, and ready to light by ten o'clock sharp every morning."

"'Fresnel'?" he repeated.

"That's the lens, Mr. McKenna. A first-order Fresnel." It was Pevie speaking, answering as he stepped into the kitchen, buttoning his jacket. "A glass beehive lens six feet tall with a single lamp in the center. It's mounted on a revolving base, and every brass piece and glass facet will be polished until it shines!"

"And the lamp made ready for lighting," Juliana finished, "in case of inclement weather." She sought Pevie's eye as she reached for a shawl hanging by the door. "Will you help me with Lilly this morning, Pevie? You know how she is after a storm."

With a nod at Will McKenna, she indicated the door to the hall.

"There's hot water in the bath, if you can manage a wash. We'll be in shortly."

Pevie glanced at his friend and raised a brow as they walked toward Lilly's shed. "Well, Juliana, me beauty? What's the matter that you feel the need to malign our sweet Lilly?"

In spite of herself, Juliana giggled, then sobered, her brown eyes troubled as they met Pevie's glance.

"It's young Mr. Dutton, Pevie. He hasn't roused this morning, and I'm worried. I think you should go for the doctor. I'll tend the light."

Pevie attended to her words with pursed lips as he opened the stall door for a slightly cross Guernsey. Lilly lowed and swished her tail into Pevie's face as he elbowed her aside and sat on the milking stool. He sighed.

"Pevie?"

"It's not that I don't trust you, Juliana, to do your usual fine job, but that I don't much like leaving you with the added burden of Misters McKenna and Dutton." He shrugged. "I'll do the honors with Lilly, then grab a bite of breakfast and be on my way." He patted her shoulder. "Run along in. With any luck young Dutton will be awake and asking for room service."

Re-entering the kitchen, she caught sight of Will McKenna standing over his friend. Something in his stance arrested her in the doorway. With a hesitant gesture, Will smoothed the damp strands of hair back from the younger man's brow. He looked up to meet Juliana's gaze; his own told her that he was aware of the seriousness of his companion's condition.

"Mr. Pevie will go for Dr. Rufton in Santa Rena as soon as he's eaten, Mr. McKenna." She joined him beside her patient. McKenna's cot, she noted, had been neatly folded up, the bedding also folded and stacked upon it. "Your friend seems to be sleeping. I don't think he's still unconscious, but I'm sure you'll agree that he should be seen by a doctor?"

Will McKenna fingered the dark stubble on his chin.

"Yes, of course, Miss Russell."

Juliana set the table, then took the pan of browned biscuits from the oven. Pevie came in at the back door with *Senhor* Feira from the fishing village.

"I thought perhaps we could remove our patient to the front parlor, Juliana, where he's less likely to be disturbed by our comings and goings. *Senhor* Feira and I will transport him in the cot, if you'll make the parlor ready?"

"Of course. Mr. McKenna, help yourself to coffee, we'll only be a moment."

With a fresh fire lit in the grate, the chill of the little-used parlor soon dissipated. Juliana pulled the shades to dim the light in the room. Pevie and his assistant easily handled the cot with its burden. Neat and quick in his movements, *Senhor* Feira was quiet and somber in mien. His black eyes missed nothing, but when Juliana thanked him for his trouble, he only nodded and quickly took his leave.

James Dutton stirred once, but didn't otherwise rouse as he was moved. His companion waited for them at the kitchen table, drumming his fingers against the side of his cup.

Pevie tucked into his breakfast with a will, while Juliana forced herself to eat something. Will McKenna barely managed a bite, although he accepted a second cup of strong black coffee.

When Pevie finished, he grinned at Juliana.

"Sorry to leave you with the dishes, me beauty, but I'd best be off." He gave a nod to Will. "It's an hour and a half walk into Santa Rena, Mr. McKenna, but I daresay we'll make better time on our way back. I leave the station in your hands, Juliana."

With another quick grin and a mock salute, he grabbed his hat and was gone.

Taking a deep breath to steady a sudden nervous spasm in the pit of her stomach, Juliana began to clear the table. Will McKenna rose.

"Let me," he suggested. "I know you've plenty to do elsewhere. I'd be happy to wash up."

The light playing across those gray eyes made their expression hard to read, but her mind was quickly made up.

"Thank you, Mr. McKenna. That'd be a help, if you're certain you won't do injury to your arm."

"Not at all." He grinned, his dark eyes lightening.

"I'll be in the tower if you need me," Juliana told him, an answering grin tugging at the corners of her mouth. "It'll take more than an hour to attend to the lens." As she went up the steps into the tower, she could hear him whistling. The mute appeal in those gray eyes had decided her. An entreaty to allow him to keep himself occupied while they waited for Pevie and the doctor.

Once in the watch room, she pushed all thought of the injured young man and Will McKenna from her mind, giving her full attention to the care and cleaning of the lens. Bernard's and Pevie's livelihoods depended on how well she performed this task: the United States Lighthouse Service allowed no margin of error. Working without respite, she cleaned and polished the glass until there wasn't a streak or a speck marring its surface. Then she turned her attention to the brass work and became so engrossed that when a voice spoke behind her, she jumped and found Will McKenna's sharp eyes taking in the watch room with interest.

"You're a hard taskmaster, Miss Russell."

"The light demands no less, Mr. McKenna. Has there been a change in Mr. Dutton's condition?"

The instant shake of his head reassured her.

"No, I looked in on him, but Jimmy didn't awaken. He seems to be sleeping, but he stirred slightly. I finished my chores and thought I'd come up and assist you, if there is aught I may do."

It was her turn to shake her head.

"I've just finished, Mr. McKenna. The lamp is ready to light." She checked the watch on its grosgrain ribbon about her neck. "And right on schedule. I'm afraid you've climbed all this way for nothing."

His gaze moved beyond her to the wide view seaward.

"On the contrary, I've always wanted to see what the world looks like from a lighthouse. Many times I've sailed right past this very tower and watched the sea spray on the rocks from offshore."

"On the *AlyceGee*, you mean?" Juliana asked as Will went to the window.

"Often Jimmy and I sailed this route when I was still at school. But other times I've sailed to southern ports. From Los Angeles to Buenos Aires."

"Have you?" Juliana turned toward her companion, reached out as if to touch him, then hugged her arms to herself. "What's it like to travel so far?"

His sharp eyes caught the eagerness behind her question, the hunger to hear about the larger world.

"Not so wonderful, Miss Russell, when you're sharing a cramped steamer cabin with a seasick parson and the hold of the steamer smells like dead fish. But," he grinned as her mouth twisted in commiseration, "when the sea is calm and the stars bloom like crystals, one feels a great satisfaction to be on the ocean."

Juliana smiled. "Dead fish or not, it sounds wonderful to me." She turned away from the window, "We'd better go down," she said and moved towards the stairs reluctantly, but not before he caught the faint sigh of longing that escaped her. "We shouldn't leave your friend alone."

As they reached the landing with its landward window, Juliana stopped short.

"A buggy! Someone's approaching the station!"

Descending quickly, she flung the outer door open and stepped onto the porch in time to greet Pevie and the doctor.

"G'morning, Miss Russell," Dr. Rufton said in his gravelly voice. "I was on my way for my monthly visit to the fishing village when I met Mr. Pevie. I hear you've spent a busy night. Come, show me this young man, this James Dutton."

Taking Juliana by the arm, he turned her about, his keen eyes—blue-green beneath bristling brows— missed nothing, not the circles under her eyes or the lean figure of Will McKenna alert behind her. The doctor summed him up with a quick glance.

"You must be the second fella Mr. Pevie mentioned. A Mr. McKenna, eh? Looks like you'll do for now," he remarked, extending a hand for a brisk shake, "but I'll have a look at that arm after I've seen to your friend."

His frank appraisal and no-nonsense air of competency visibly reassured Will, who followed the doctor and Juliana into the parlor. Dr. Rufton checked his patient's vital signs, gingerly prodded the livid bruise on James Dutton's face, then probed his scalp for bumps and contusions. Removing his stethoscope, he gestured for them to follow him from the room and cleared his throat.

"He'll mend," the doctor announced abruptly. Will McKenna's shoulders sagged with relief. He cares deeply about his friend, Juliana thought and focused her attention on the doctor with difficulty.

"His system has suffered a profound shock. He has a slight concussion. Wouldn't be at all surprised to find he has some memory loss when he wakes up. Temporary, temporary," he insisted as Will made some movement of protest. "Concussion and the shock would explain why he's sleeping so long. I hate to impose on you like this, Miss Russell, but in my opinion he shouldn't be moved for a few days. He'll need to be watched for a day or so, to make absolutely sure that he's recovered. I don't think he'll be in any pain, just sleep a great deal.

"Now," he spoke crisply to Juliana, "Mrs. Russell is a wonderful hand at nursing. I understand she'll be home shortly. You, sir," he nodded decisively at Will, "come along into the kitchen and let me see to that shoulder."

After the doctor pronounced his second patient well on the road to recovery, it was decided that Will McKenna would accompany Dr. Rufton on his return to Santa Rena, where he could wire James Dutton's family and his sister, Marthe, with whom he presently shared a home. He would take a room in Santa Rena until Dr. Rufton gave his patient permission to travel.

With the house quiet and James Dutton still sleeping, Juliana threw herself into the day's chores, turning out bedding in preparation for the Russells' return, beating rugs, sweeping, dusting, and putting a vegetable and beef-laden stew to simmer on the back of the stove. For lunch they could have the stew and fresh bread with cheese and Faith's pickles. There was cold cider in the cellar. Pevie informed Juliana that he'd take his lunch to the beach where he would inspect their dinghy and the one from the yacht for any signs of damage after the storm.

Giving the stewpot a stir, Juliana glanced once more about the tidied kitchen, then took her mending bundle along to the parlor. She settled herself in a chair pulled close to the windows and let her mind drift as she repaired a rent in the sleeve of one of Bernard's work shirts, and tightened and replaced several loose and missing buttons.

At length, her hands stilled in her lap, she recalled Will McKenna's words, that he'd been all the way from Los Angeles to Buenos Aires. There had not been time to ask why, nor even to discover what he did for a living. Perhaps he was independently wealthy and simply adventured about the world. By his demeanor and clothing, he was a gentleman certainly. Equally true, she observed, for young Mr. Dutton—her glance flicked across him as he stirred without awakening—with a yacht at his disposal. Her thoughts returned to Will. Somehow, given the intelligence evident in those gray eyes and the determined set of the chin, she felt sure that he was no idle gentleman. She felt a hot blush creep along her cheeks as she recalled his gaze meeting hers the night he'd one-handedly made her tea after their ordeal in the fog signal building. Pushing aside her mending, she reached for her book. Better to lose herself in Mr. Stephen's *Incidents of Travel* rather than indulge in idle thoughts.

She turned her imagination to conjuring up the exotic world of mysterious ruins recorded by the author. Great, hot bursts of color, as intense as the heat must have been, wove into vivid shapes of forest and villages and sea and crumbling towers encrusted by jungle growth. How remote and primitive it must have seemed! Into her reverie slipped the image of a small gold mask, its features grinning with the lipless grimace of death. Panic began to rise in her, her breath quickening.

"Lucy! Lucy Katerina!"

Her head jerked about at that whisper, her book spilling from her lap. James Dutton's sleepy eyes met her own. Quickly she retrieved her book and went to his side.

"No!" She spoke sharply. "You're mistaken." Forcing her voice to be milder, she continued, "I'm Juliana Russell. There's been an accident, Mr. Dutton. You're at the Point Lobos light station near Santa Rena."

Her patient stared at her, his confusion and bewilderment obvious, his eyes blinking as he struggled to come fully awake. Her own moment of uneasiness averted, she repeated, quietly this time.

"You've had an accident at sea, Mr. Dutton, but you're safe now at the Point Lobos light station."

"Point Lobos?" He frowned, his voice wondering, faint. His hand crept to the great bruise on his face and he winced at the touch. "An accident, you say, miss... miss... I'm sorry," he said, looking abashed. "I'm afraid I didn't catch your name."

"Russell. Juliana Russell," she supplied rapidly. "You've been here since last night. The doctor from Santa Rena has come and gone this morning. He says you'll mend with a bit of rest."

"Thank you, Miss Russell." James Dutton met this piece of news with a half-chagrined smile. "I'm afraid I don't remember. I was... sailing the *AlyceGee* home, that's right. That much I do remember." He seemed to be wandering, almost talking to himself. "It had been a wonderfully productive trip, but I needed to talk to Henry. I shipped my canvases home, always do, y'know." Juliana let him talk, afraid to leave him. "Ever since that time, well, you don't want to hear all the details, but that storm was unexpected, too. It swept a particularly vicious wave aboard, swamping one of my better efforts.

"So now, don't y'know, I ship the lot of them home ahead of the *AlyceGee*. Well, and I had Will to help me. Good old Will," he went on fondly, his voice gaining in strength and animation. "My best friend and most honest critic! His father, Dr. McKenna, took care of the old man, y'know, so I've known Will forever." He laughed at that, inviting her to join in the joke, then suddenly sat straight up, his face gone white as the linen he wore.

"Oh my Lord, Will!" Huge anxious eyes fixed upon her, the words spilling from him even as he threw aside the covers and tried to get up. "He was sailing home with me. Came down on the train to join me. My dearest and best friend," he repeated as Juliana tried with difficulty to restrain him.

"Please, Mr. Dutton, please! Will McKenna is fine. He's alive and well!"

Clutching her hand, the younger man fell back against his pillows as Juliana's words sank in.

"He's alive!" Tears beaded his eyelashes and filled his eyes; he covered them for a moment as he regained his composure. "Thank God," he said at length, quietly but vehemently.

"He's gone into Santa Rena with Dr. Rufton," Juliana informed him, "to notify your family." She bit back the news about the *AlyceGee*. If he did not ask outright, let his family and friend break it to him. Although, judging from his reaction, the things that mattered most to this young man were still in his possession—his friend and his paintings, and in that order, too, unless she badly misjudged him. She found herself liking her storm-tossed patient, his blue eyes shining with relief, and smiled at him. "Let me make you comfortable, then I'll bring you a lunch of hot stew and fresh bread."

"Thank you. Thank you for everything, Miss Russell."

With her patient fed and asleep once more in spite of his best efforts to remain awake, Juliana stole a few moments to work in the garden, weeding the sweet peas and the snap beans just beginning to vine along the rows. The sun warmed her after the storm, and she found her thoughts returning to James Dutton. Who was Lucy Katerina? His wife? Sister? A sweetheart? It could not matter to her, after all. What mattered was her response. Why should it so bother her to be mistaken for someone else? It troubled her, now, and she sat back on her heels. Was it because in a real sense her true identity was lost to her? Juliana Russell was the person she had become, the identity she had worked so hard to establish. Her adopted family had given her their name and with it her identity, and, she realized, irrationally, she was afraid that someday that self would be ripped away, exposed as false, leaving her with no ties, no knowledge of who she truly was.

Juliana shook her head to clear her mind. Her life was real, she was real, her family real as well. No, whoever she had been born, that life had no power to touch her in the present. She was rooted in the years of love and security bestowed upon her by Faith and Bernard Russell. No matter what happened, that knowledge would sustain her. No matter what. The vehemence of her thoughts startled her, as if, the unwelcome thought came to her, as if someday soon she would have need of just such reassurance.

CHAPTER THREE

Henry Bennett Dutton was looking grave as he held his sister Sarah's arm and waited for Will McKenna to alight from the livery buggy. Clearly, Juliana saw, his was a face unused to sober expressions or thought—ruddy, smoothly unlined, his mouth seemingly held to a stern line against its will. She noted the care he took to guide his sister, then she let the curtain fall and turned to her patient. James Dutton's great bruise was spectacular now in shades of red and purple and yellow, but his appetite was returning and his face, where it was not bruised, had lost the pasty white hue of shock. She smiled.

"Mr. McKenna has arrived with your family, Mr. Dutton." As she turned to go, he spoke.

"Please stay, Miss Russell. I want them to meet you."

"I'm needed in the kitchen, Mr. Dutton. We've no help to serve the tea." Juliana's fleeting grin robbed her words of any sting. "I'll meet them then."

From the kitchen she heard the cries of joy and dismay that greeted James Dutton's appearance, then the quick step of Faith behind her. The keeper's wife barely reached Juliana's chin but for her pompadour of glossy chestnut hair, graying early. Her brown eyes noted with approval the thin slices of oatmeal bread, studded with apples and raisins and nuts, that Juliana was carefully fanning on a plate. Only the quick pat at her hair and the fact that she was wearing her best shirtwaist and shawl on a weekday betrayed any hint of nervousness.

"We'll give them some time alone with their brother," Faith decided, "then we'll serve tea. Bernard and John will join us."

Juliana lifted a brow at Faith and without comment began to pile a second plate high with delicately flavored lemon cookies and divinity. Faith laughed.

"Now, Juliana! But I daresay it will be eaten. Henry Dutton looks to be a man who enjoys his food, and John won't say no to seconds."

Her assessment proved accurate as Henry Dutton accepted coffee over tea and gave high praise to Mrs. Russell's sweets. Pevie, on the other hand, ate very little, and when Bernard Russell turned aside the Dutton's gratitude by pointing out it was his duty to care for those rescued from the sea, a rescue moreover handled by his first assistant, Pevie demurred.

"All I did was man the oars, Mr. Dutton. 'Twas Miss Russell who climbed aboard the vessel and loosed the lifeboat and its cargo."

Everyone looked at Juliana, who flushed under the astonished scrutiny. Will McKenna was watching her, too—as he had all through tea—with a look she couldn't fathom. Now he was frowning at her.

James Dutton's face broke into a wide smile.

"Then I am doubly indebted to you, Miss Russell, for saving my life and that of Will, and for your fine care of me since."

Sarah Dutton reached over to grasp her brother's hand, as if to reassure herself that he had in fact survived his ordeal. Her voice was low and sweet, but quite firm.

"Your courage and resourcefulness have given us back our dear brother and our friend, Miss Russell." Her glance lingered on Pevie. "I am equally certain that you downplay your true role in their rescue, Mr. Pevie. My brothers and I are forever in your debt. I am sure there's no token of our gratitude that you would accept, so please accept our heartfelt thanks."

"Yes, yes," Henry echoed his sister's words. "Don't know what we'd do without young Jimmy here." His voice was slightly gruff, and he looked embarrassed, but Juliana recognized the deep emotion he was trying to hide and looked at the three siblings with respect and a kind of envy. There was no doubting their closeness and affection for one another. She answered lightly.

"I didn't do any more than anyone else would've, Miss Dutton. You're very kind to think so highly of my efforts. In fact, I merely finished what Mr. McKenna had already begun. More tea?" she inquired with a nod at Sarah Dutton's empty cup.

"No, thank you," Sarah replied, starting to put her cup down on the edge of the table. Henry unobtrusively guided her elbow so his sister set her teacup squarely on its saucer, all the while talking to divert attention away from her.

"We spoke with Dr. Rufton in Santa Rena. He'll drop in on Jimmy in the morning and thinks in all likelihood we'll be able to relieve you of your burden and cart our younger brother away with us. What say, Jimmy? Are you ready to cease being waited upon hand and foot and return home?"

"I hope I haven't been that demanding, Mrs. Russell." James Dutton's bright eyes were turned upon the keeper's wife as Bernard stood and spoke.

"No trouble at all, Mr. Dutton, and you may be certain Dr. Rufton won't allow you to travel unless he finds you well on the mend. If you will excuse me, I must see to the station. Coming, Mr. Pevie?"

Pevie started, his blue eyes blinking rapidly.

"Yessir!" He turned to their company. "Miss Dutton," he nodded at Sarah Dutton, blushed, and hurried after Bernard.

Stacking cups and saucers on a tray, Juliana also stood. "I'll look forward to seeing you both tomorrow," she smiled diffidently, "with Dr. Rufton." Gathering up her tray, she made her way to the kitchen, put down her tray, and half-turned as a footfall sounded behind her. "I'll see to the dishes, Faith," she said, then stopped.

Will McKenna, carrying the second tray, stood staring at her, still with that suggestion of a frown that was beginning to irritate her. She reached to take his tray and for a moment their eyes met, his searching her face. He opened his mouth, but didn't speak. Juliana snatched the tray from him and plunked it on the table, the cups rattling in their saucers. His stare reminded her that her hands were calloused from her chores, that her hair was not perfectly curled and coiffed, and that her skirt was dark serge, not the beautifully tailored pale gray silk that set off Sarah Dutton's tiny waist and fragile features.

Horrified at her thoughts, Juliana kept her face averted as she cleared the tray.

"Thank you, Mr. McKenna. It was kind of you to help." She risked a glance in his direction as he said nothing, and saw that he was staring out the window where Pevie, jacket discarded and shirt-sleeves rolled above the elbow, was splitting wood for the fog signal firebox. If anything, Will's frown was even more pronounced. Pevie was an attractive figure of a man, Juliana admitted, and Will could well worry if he entertained thoughts of Sarah Dutton's affections. Not, of course, that such a lady would ever consider a working man in that light. Juliana moved between Will and his view of Pevie, placing the dirty dishes on the sink board. His gaze suddenly focused on her.

"Have you ever been to Italy, Miss Russell?"

Juliana stared at him in bewilderment.

"No, never. I've never traveled farther than our sister light station to the south. Why do you ask?"

"Why, because it's a beautiful country, Miss Russell." He smiled swiftly, and she knew his thoughts were far away, and whatever he was thinking, it was *not* that Italy was a beautiful country. Suddenly his frown relaxed and his smile reached his eyes, warming their gray depths. "Thank you for the tea. Perhaps I'll see you again in the morning. Good-day."

Without waiting for a reply, he rejoined his companions as they took their leave of Faith Russell. Juliana was left to stare after McKenna's retreating figure. Abruptly she turned her efforts to clearing the remnants of their tea and squaring away the kitchen. Every inch of the light station was required to be shipshape and clean, with everything in its appointed place. A surprise inspection was always a risk, and she wanted no demerits to befall Point Lobos because of her.

Faith took in the forceful busyness of her young charge with a shrewd glance and retired to the front parlor where she sat by the window, sewing rolled hems on new handkerchiefs for her husband. James Dutton, as he had every day since he had regained enough energy to sit up, busied himself with Juliana's sketchpad until he tired and lay down to rest.

Pevie, at suppertime, discussed the next day's chores with the keeper, paying compliment as always to Faith's endeavors in the kitchen. For their meal this night she had braised a chicken with fresh carrots, new potatoes, and peas, with peach cobbler and cream for after. It was Bernard's favorite meal, and Juliana noticed how his gaze lingered on Faith. If the light were brighter, she knew his wife's blush would be revealed. She glanced at Pevie. Even though he ate his supper and replied to the keeper's comments, it seemed to her that his mind followed the road to Santa Rena. And where his went, her own was wont to wander.

She lay down her napkin hastily and touched Faith's arm.

"Faith, I'll see if Mr. Dutton is awake and ready for his supper."

James Dutton was wide awake, his head bent over his sketchpad, his concentration so complete he didn't notice her approach. Juliana tapped his shoulder.

The blond head jerked up. James Dutton grinned sheepishly.

"Sorry, Miss Russell. I'm afraid I get carried away sometimes. Please sit with me while I eat. This looks wonderful and smells heavenly!" But, like Pevie, his attention seemed caught elsewhere. He gulped down his evening meal, reaching quickly for his sketchpad once more.

"If you'd just look out the window, Miss Russell, and turn your head a bit. Yes, yes," he said and eagerly took up his pencils. "That's perfect!"

He worked in silence for several minutes as Juliana gradually relaxed and forgot to be self-conscious. Her gaze lengthened, and she watched the waves roll onto land and out to sea again in the bay below. Like a temptress, the sea was always beckoning her to leave her high sanctuary and go boldly out into the world.

Sanctuary. The word echoed in her thoughts, and suddenly she was restless, her concentration broken. She moved abruptly, then remembered where she was and why.

James Dutton smiled cheerfully and waved away her words.

"You mustn't apologize, Miss Russell. If anything, I should do so for monopolizing your time whilst I've been here! Thank you for allowing me to sketch you."

He handed her the sketchbook, and Juliana touched her finger to lips. He'd caught her in a mirror image—the slight smile of self-mockery as she'd held her pose, the weight of her dark hair, the shape of her nose, a face altogether different from those of her adopted parents.

"If you think they'd like it, I shall give the sketch to your parents as a gift for their most welcome care."

Juliana started to correct him, then checked herself. Faith and Bernard were all the family she had. What did it matter if James Dutton believed them to be her natural parents?

The next morning, aloft on a ladder next to Pevie, she dipped her brush into the paint tray and applied it vigorously to the fog signal building. Like he had in old times, Pevie was singing loudly and off-key, making up verses whenever he forgot the words, which was frequently.

"Come all you young sailormen, listen to me, I'll sing you a song of the fish in the sea. Up jumps the lobster with his heavy claws, bites the main boom right off by the jaws! and it's...windy weather boys, stormy weather, boys! When the wind blows we're all together, boys! Blow ye winds westerly, blow ye winds, blow! Jolly sou'wester, boys, steady she goes."

Juliana laughed, the wind catching her laughter and flinging it wide across the morning sunshine.

Pevie paused in mid-song, and Juliana, craning her neck over his shoulder to see what had caught his attention, saw below her the figures of the Duttons and Will McKenna. Sarah, seated in the rear of the buggy, was turned toward her brother and Will as they helped James Dutton onto the seat next to her. Will remained still for a long moment, staring up at the fog signal building as the echo of her laughter died away. He tipped his hat to Faith Russell, who stood on the porch, and climbed into the front seat to take up the reins. James Dutton waved in their direction. Sarah's head inclined toward her brother, then she too twisted toward them and raised her hand in farewell.

Gripping the ladder, Juliana freed one hand and waved back, Pevie following suit. Then Will snapped the reins and the buggy rolled smoothly away from the Point Lobos light station. Pevie watched until the vehicle was out of sight, the visitors well on their way to San Francisco and a life as strange to Point Lobos as if they had come from a foreign country, then picked up his brush and met Juliana's gaze with a rueful smile at the sigh which also escaped her. Juliana attempted to smile back, opened her mouth, and started to sing.

"*Up jumps the squid with his eight arms, he says, shove over, matey, and sound the alarms! And it's....*"

Pevie groaned exaggeratedly.

"For heaven's sake, me beauty!"

He rolled his eyes, raised his voice, and joined her until Lilly added her distressed bellow to the noise, and they subsided with gasps of laughter.

Juliana stopped and pitched the pebbles she'd collected one by one into the surf. Her menses were imminent, and she found herself suffering from the usual combination of uncomfortable bloating, lower back pain, and irritability that generally marked this time for her. Faith Russell, after one look at her sour expression, had banished her to the beach with the admonition to walk off her bad mood—and, hopefully, her aches and pains—before coming back.

Far out to sea a ship was passing the point, heading for more southerly ports. A memory of Will

McKenna flitted through Juliana's thoughts. Three months had passed since the *AlyceGee* had sunk in the bay and she'd stood in the lighthouse talking with him of his travels to more southerly ports.

Tucking up her skirts, she climbed to one of her favorite childhood haunts, a pile of granite boulders that spilled into the water, leaving a flat-topped, dry perch at this time of day. Now the sun-warmed stone eased her discomfort as she hugged her knees and followed the lone ship's passage. For a moment she wished for her watercolors, but she put that thought from her, too, and let the sounds of the ocean fill her mind, lulling her restless mood. She would steal another moment or two of peace here, she promised herself, then she would return to the light station and help Faith with the day's long list of chores. There was milk to be churned, clothes to be pressed, and soon the midday meal to prepare.

A gull screamed and wheeled above her as a shadow fell across the rock. Juliana twisted about as suddenly a rough hand clamped across her mouth and an arm closed about her waist, dragging her to her feet. The sudden upright shift was dizzying, and she fought to clear her sight as a coarse voice hissed in her ear.

"Where is it, missy, where's the little gold key?"

The pressure about her waist tightened in warning.

"Mebbe she's got it on her an' we ought'a take a look 'fore we dump her in the bay," a second, higher voice urged.

Dimly, Juliana heard the voices echoing as if from a far distance. Her head was spinning, her body limp with shock. Like figures from her childhood nightmares, the hands reached into her present to attack her once more, and the terror of that eight-year-old child filled her mind. She must get away! Stop! Stop! They were hurting Nana Angelina! No... no....

Juliana struggled to push the nightmare away. That was a long time ago. A long time. This was real, now, this morning. Her attacker dropped her unresisting body to the rock at his feet as his partner groused.

"Fool! Baggy said we ain't s'posed to kill her 'til we git the key!"

Her attacker shoved back, rocking the second man on his feet. Juliana's panic rose. The ghost of her terrified childhood surged forth. Hands, hands grabbing at her! Must get away! To Nana Angelina! Desperately Juliana rolled away from the voices arguing above her.

"Hey! She ain't dead!"

"Grab her!"

Whimpering, Juliana heaved herself over again as fingers grasped at the folds of her skirt. Then she was falling free. She fought her fear long enough to push out and thrust herself away from the face of the rocks. The momentum of her fall tore her skirts from the grip of her attackers. As she plummeted into the bay, the rushing waves filled her clothing and dragged at her, but the sheer force of her entry into the cold seas drove all thoughts from her and she kicked instinctively to propel her sodden weight to the surface. As her head cleared the water, Juliana sucked in a lungful of air, coughing and gasping and treading water until her blurry vision cleared and she could get her bearings.

The current had carried her around the boulders away from her attackers and now she found herself washed well down the curve of the bay, just south of the light station. Little beach remained here, but she recognized this bit of shore. If she could make it to land at an angle, that narrow strip of sand should mark a tumbled cascade of boulders. Hidden from sight behind those rocks, if she remembered rightly, oh please, should be a steep, rocky path that would bring her around in a loop to the rear of Point Lobos. Juliana cast one last panicked glance down the bay. Nothing stirred; no gulls broke the silent canopy of California blue above her, no figures moved on the shore.

She struck out slowly, hampered by the weight of her soaking skirts, but too frightened to take the time to remove them. Too tired from the shock of the unexpected attack to do more than focus on the struggle to follow one stroke with another and carry herself closer and closer into shore. Luck was with her, for the current helped. After what seemed a drawn-out eternity, her feet touched bottom, and she was suddenly standing waist-deep in the flotsam and jetsam trapped among the rocks at water's edge. The water pulled at her sodden clothing, trying to drag her back into the bay.

Why? And who? Like flies buzzing about her head, the questions confused and frightened her— she gulped back a sob. She half-turned towards the bay. She had to go back. Maybe she could save them. Another sob escaped her. Maybe they hadn't drowned yet. No, she pushed the weight of her hair from her face. No, that was wrong. They were dead and buried in the cemetery a long time ago—those two who had died when she was taken from the sea. Those men. Her thoughts faltered. Home—that's where she needed to go. Home to Bernard and Faith. She'd be safe there. Safe again.

Wearily she pushed her way forward through the water to the shore, dropping to her knees and crawling onto the narrow spit of sand that marked the edge of the bay. Collapsing onto the sand, she tried to will the shivering to stop and strength to return to her aching limbs. At last, she sat up, gathered her skirts as best she could and twisted and wrung as much water from them as she could. She tried to do the same with her hair; water was streaming down her face and neck, but she was so tired, it was all she could do to push the weight of it out of her face. Only then did she rise unsteadily onto her knees and push herself upright. There were the boulders; the trail would be behind them.

Juliana hobbled around the pile of rocks, brush catching at her clothing, pulling at her hair. Reaching the rough trail, she tried to hurry, but slipped on a stone, falling to one knee with a bone-bruising impact. Crying now, she gathered her will once again until she was upright and moving awkwardly in the right direction. There was no sign or sound of the two men who had accosted her, a good thing since all her energy and effort were expended in following the steep, zigzagging trail up the rock cliff to the southern reaches of the Point Lobos light station.

Point Lobos and sanctuary.

The station appeared abandoned as Juliana secured the garden gate behind her and trudged up the path to the keeper's quarters. Removing her waterlogged shoes, she let herself into the kitchen, glad that Faith wasn't there to see her. Hiking up the cold, heavy weight of her skirts, she ran clumsily upstairs. In her room she stripped off her clothing in mounting frustration, as her numbed fingers refused to respond with their customary agility. Toweling herself dry, she pulled on her dressing gown and turned her frenzied attention to the wet tangles of her hair. Hurriedly she worked first a comb then a brush through the thick dark tresses. Twisting and pinning the mass of hair into a loose knot, she dressed as quickly as she could in a fresh combination of shirtwaist, skirt, and stockings.

Gathering up her discarded garments with hands that still shook, she noted with dismay the damp spot on the floor where they lay. She would have to hurry downstairs, hang her wet things up to dry outside, then grab the mop to deal with this before anyone saw her. Before she had to explain. Because she mustn't cry. They told her she mustn't cry. They told her. And now they were dead. A sob escaped her, then another, and she stood, panic flooding her thoughts as she fought for control. She was safe. Bernard and Faith had rescued her. She was safe with Bernard and Faith.

She started downstairs and trod in a wet patch. Horrified, she saw that a trail of puddles marked her panicked flight through the keeper's quarters. She rushed downstairs, but was brought up short by the sound of voices from the kitchen. That dry, unemotional tone could belong to none other than Luther Prendergast, chief inspector for the U.S. Lighthouse Service district that included the Point Lobos light station. A surprise inspection! Today!

With a mounting feeling of dread, Juliana hugged the cold wet bundle to her and walked slowly into the kitchen.

"... the U.S. Lighthouse Service, as you are well aware, Mr. Russell, sets certain standards that must be upheld."

Prendergast, a spare man of average height, turned humorless black eyes upon her as she entered, dismissed her, and turned back to Bernard, who stood impassively before him, Faith and Pevie silent at his side. "These demerits will be entered into your record."

Dismayed, Juliana opened her mouth to protest, but stopped as Bernard's gaze shifted and with a barely perceptible shake of his head cautioned her to hold her peace.

"And I strongly suggest, Mr. Russell, that you maintain a firmer hand upon the members of your household in the future. I give you fair warning that I expect this unfortunate incident will not be repeated." With a nod of grim satisfaction, he nodded at the now drying puddles trailing from the outer door across the kitchen floor, the threat implicit.

Bernard had received a black mark on an otherwise unblemished record, and she, Juliana, had put it there. After he had taken her in and given her love and affection and a home all these long, secure years! The compounded shocks of the day rendered her numb. She stood mute and passive as Luther Prendergast finished his inspection and took his leave. At length she felt gentle hands pulling the damp articles of clothing from her hands, guiding her to a seat.

Tears streamed down her cheeks and with them she found her voice again and raised anguished dark eyes to the keeper.

"Bernard, it's all my fault. I'm sorry. I'm so sorry. You should've let me explain to Mr. Prendergast. It's all my fault!" Her face twisted as her voice broke. "I had to get away. And I got so—so wet swimming back to the path. You know that one, that path down past the end of the station. If I could tell Mr. Prendergast, he'd have to understand. They meant to kill me! He said so! So I had to go in the water; it was the only way!"

"What!"

Juliana paid no attention to the horrified exclamations of her friends as she tried to stop the flow of tears. Then Faith's arms were around her, and Bernard pressed a handkerchief into her hand as Pevie poured a cup of hot, strong coffee and set it before her. When her sobs subsided and she was able to gulp several sips of coffee, Faith released her and Bernard cleared his throat.

"Tell us what happened, Juliana, and then we'll send for Sheriff Walker," he said.

Haltingly, Juliana repeated the sequence of events that had culminated with her disastrous retreat to the light station. At last she stopped. There was something else, some detail that she could not remember.

"A gold key?" Pevie's forehead crinkled as he frowned and interrupted her train of thought. "There must be some mistake. Maybe you misunderstood," he began, but bit off whatever else he meant to say at the sudden look which passed between Faith and her husband.

"It's not a key," Faith said slowly, and Bernard finished for her, "but perhaps it has some significance, perhaps it is a key in some sense to someone?"

Faith patted Juliana's shoulder as she rose. Returning a moment later, she handed Bernard a small leather pouch. Pevie's frown deepened and Juliana stiffened at the sight of the pouch. The keeper shook out a tiny object that caught the light and concentrated it, glowing on Bernard's palm. Faith's arm tightened once more about Juliana's shoulders as the younger woman began to shake all over.

As if her hand moved of its own volition, Juliana watched herself reach out and gingerly turn the piece with a tentative finger until the tiny golden mask peered up at her. No more than an inch across, the eyes mere slits, the simple lines of the mask outlined features foreign to the modern world. The face they represented was watchful, neither malevolent nor overtly cheerful, but waiting as if it held some secret knowledge. Her voice, so low her friends could barely hear, shook.

"Poppa gave it to me because I was his first Juliana. Nana said I could wear it, but I must keep it tucked under my collars."

"Nana?" The soft whisper of a question came from Faith.

"Nana Angelina."

With a swift, convulsive gesture, Juliana pushed Bernard's hand away. "No, no, take it away! I don't want to see it! I don't want to remember!"

"Remember what, Juliana?" Bernard demanded sharply.

She shook her head wildly.

"No. No. Those hands. Those hands reaching for me. And Nana Angelina crumpled on the ground. There's blood on her forehead! No, no, no!" Her hands covering her face, Juliana burrowed against Faith's skirts as she had when tormented by nightmares as a youngster. Faith held her and stroked her hair until the shuddering calmed. When at last she raised her face, Bernard had replaced the mask in the small leather pouch he had stitched for it years ago.

Juliana drew a deep breath.

"Nana Angelina was my grandmother."

"And the hands?" Pevie prompted. Bernard shot his first assistant a look of reproach.

"From my nightmares," Juliana began with a bitter laugh, "or so I thought." Her hands flew up in helpless frustration. "I can't remember very well. All I see are images—broken images. Nana lying on the sand, dead. And hands grabbing me. Just that one image and nothing before and nothing after until you plucked me from the sea, Bernard."

"Except just now you said your papa gave you the charm," Pevie reminded her, earning himself another pained look from the keeper.

"But I don't remember him." Juliana's voice was dulled, flat. "I can't recall anything at all, and now what I can't remember has reached out to hurt you. I'm so sorry, Faith." She turned tear-brimmed eyes to her friends. "I've brought disgrace to the light station, Bernard. How can you ever forgive me?"

"Nonsense." His deep, calm voice was assured. "Whatever lies behind this"—he touched the pouch—"and this attack upon you, it wasn't the fault of an eight-year-old child, and it is not your fault now, Juliana. Luther Prendergast is a man who enjoys finding fault; sooner or later he would have done so, even at Point Lobos."

He smiled. "I want you to try and put this from your mind for the rest of this evening, Juliana. Pevie and I will mount a watch tonight after we secure the station, and tomorrow I'll send him into Santa Rena for the sheriff. All right?"

"Come, Juliana dear," Faith said, coaxing her to her feet. "We'll get you upstairs where you can lie down. You're shivering with cold! I'll bring you some hot soup." She made a moue, then grinned at the younger woman. "In spite of what old Mr. Prendergast says, this station is immaculate. Try not to worry, dear."

Juliana allowed herself to be led to her room. When she was undressed and settled in her bed, Faith returned with a bowl of hot soup as promised. After Juliana had taken enough to satisfy Faith, she was permitted to ease her aching body between the sheets. Convinced she wouldn't be able to rest, she closed her eyes only to avoid upsetting her friend any further. To her surprise she slipped almost immediately into a deep and dreamless sleep, as though her body wanted to shut down her thoughts and provide her mind a respite from the day's shocks.

Awakening much later, Juliana lay quietly, thinking past her panic and fear. The deep silence of a household abed surrounded her. Try as she might, she couldn't force memory to return. Only the one flash, her grandmother fallen, blood pooling on the sand about her, and hands reaching for Juliana. It seemed to her those vague sweet dreams that had come so tantalizingly to her as a child might also have been remnants of other tattered memories. Someone, as improbable as it sounded, wanted her dead today, in her present. Was it only coincidence that some menace had threatened her as a child, killing her grandmother in that act of desperation? If only she could remember!

There must be a connection between that event and the attack upon her today. The gold mask charm she'd been wearing when Bernard pulled her from the sea appeared to be the most likely link. Her fists balled at her sides. The mask was meaningless to her, except in the recurring nightmares that plagued her. Yet now it took on the quality of an overt threat in her waking life—and not only to her, but to those she held most dear, Faith and Bernard Russell and their livelihood at the Point Lobos light station. Juliana curled up tightly on her side. What if another attack was made on her and one of her friends suffered for it? What if damage was done to the station? How could she prevent disaster from striking again when she had no idea where the danger was coming from?

Bernard and Pevie couldn't watch over her twenty-four hours a day. The light station demanded all their time and energy. She couldn't bear to be a burden to those she loved. A cold thought dawned slowly. If she left Point Lobos, then the threat to the station would be removed. And if she could lose herself in a city like San Francisco, perhaps she could save herself as well. If only she could remember who she had once been and what the gold mask charm meant! But she had lived at Point

Lobos for fifteen years, safe and sound, and memory had not returned.

No: she must leave the sanctuary provided by the light station.

Throwing back the quilt, she made her way to the window and opened her curtains. Moonlight flooded the small bedchamber, providing light enough to aid her in packing her valise. Besides her everyday work clothes of skirts and blouses, she owned two good dresses. These she hurriedly added to her valise, then quickly dressed in a serviceable navy blue serge skirt and a plain white shirtwaist. Her duster and her boater could be worn. At the last minute she rolled up the trousers, sweater, and boots that she wore during emergencies and added them to the valise.

At the back of the single shelf in her closet her searching fingers encountered her paints and drawing materials. She didn't know whether she would ever try to use them again, but they were the only possessions she owned that spoke clearly of who she was, who she had grown up to be. From her bedside she added her copy of *Incidents of Travel* to her bag, then hesitated at the small leather pouch that lay there. Discarding the bag, she held the tiny trinket in her hand and saw that Faith or Bernard had replaced it on the chain from which it had once hung suspended about her neck. Fumbling with the clasp, she secured it about her neck again for the first time since she had come to Point Lobos, then quickly thrust the pendant out of sight down the front of her shirtwaist. An odd feeling came over her as she did so: that she was not running away from her unknown past, but into her future.

Drawing paper and ink from her small desk , she scrawled a hasty note to her friends, writing that she would contact them as soon as she felt it safe to do so. She left the note on her pillow and took up her valise. Easing open her door, she listened for a moment then made her way cautiously downstairs. In the morning, Faith would assume Juliana was still sleeping and leave her undisturbed until Pevie and Bernard had their breakfast.

Those few precious minutes would delay the discovery of her flight. Since she intended to ride their only horse into Santa Rena, pursuit would be slowed considerably. She meant to be waiting at the bank when it opened in the morning. Over her protests, Faith and Bernard had insisted on paying her a wage of five dollars a month since she turned eighteen; her bank account balance stood at roughly two hundred and fifty dollars. It was a tidy sum, but one that wouldn't last long if she couldn't find some means of earning her living. She would have to begin spending right away, for her train fare to San Francisco and the livery charges for Pattycake, their Morgan. It wouldn't be fair to make Bernard pay for his horse's keep when she borrowed it without his leave.

Pattycake whickered softly as Juliana fumbled with saddle and bridle. By the watch pinned to her shirtwaist, she knew the time to be nearly two o'clock in the morning, midway through Pevie's first watch. If she led the mare along the grassy edge of the lane, she could keep hidden in the trees long enough to be out of sight of the tower. Pevie was an excellent first assistant; she knew his attention would be focused on the bay.

Her heart beating loudly in the silence of the night, Juliana halted the Morgan and fumbled for the stirrup. With a hard lump in her throat, she fought back tears. If only she could see her friends one more time, to thank Faith and Bernard and Pevie for their love and generosity and the immeasurable gift of their friendship. But she had repaid their kindness with near disaster, and the sooner she was away, the better it would be for them all.

Turning the mare's head to the road, she set off at a determined canter for Santa Rena.

CHAPTER FOUR

Beating vigorously at the rugs in the mid-morning sunshine, Juliana paused as a sneeze escaped her. With one final battering attack upon the last braided rug in the row, she picked up her basket and returned to the kitchen where she exchanged her rod and basket for a bucket of hot, soapy water and a scrub brush.

Libby O'Bryan looked up from her pile of mending as Juliana started to climb the stairs.

"Mind you're careful with Mr. Potter's books."

"Yes, Libby. I'll see they don't get wet."

With the faintest of sighs, her landlady shrugged and bent her bony shoulders over the shirt in her hands, resuming her repairs. Years of pessimism and small defeats colored her sigh as though the worst must be anticipated in any situation, no matter how trivial, and no matter that Juliana had yet to perform her duties in any but a satisfactory manner. Now the thin lips grimaced as if the slight movement of her shrug had brought her pain. Juliana checked her upward stride, but Mrs. O'Bryan's features relaxed as she adjusted the position of the wrapped foot resting on a stool before her.

Juliana continued on her way, recalling as she did her precipitous meeting with her landlady and current employer.

She had stepped down from the train in San Francisco, standing for a moment in near panic at the overwhelming activity going on about her. The day was getting on toward evening, her body restless from the long hours on the train, and her stomach reminding her that she hadn't eaten any lunch. She made her first order of business, then, to find a café where she could sit and peruse the evening edition of the local paper. Over a bowl of bean soup with cornbread, she read advertisements for boardinghouses and found one establishment that sounded promising: *Rosalie Fish's Boardinghouse for Young Ladies.* On Market Street, wherever that might be. She looked up from the paper at her server, a large red-faced girl whose smile and ready greeting had favored nearly every other patron who entered the café by name.

"Ev'ning, Mr. Rawlins. How's the missus?"

Juliana beckoned her, and after taking her customer's order, the young waitress nodded briskly and made her way to Juliana's table.

"I'd like more coffee, please, and, miss, can you tell me where to find this address?"

The girl's eyes narrowed as she read the advertisement, then to Juliana's surprise, shook her head vigorously.

"Oh, no, miss. No, you don't want to be going down there."

Taken aback, Juliana stared at the young woman.

"See, that's a part of town with lots of wild goings-on. No respectable lady's going to venture down there, let alone live there."

Her shrewd brown eyes took in Juliana's well-traveled appearance, the valise tucked under the table, and she continued quickly.

"Let me get Mr. Rawlins' order in, miss, and I'll bring yer coffee. If you want a bit o' advice, I think I can help you out."

True to her word, she returned in a few minutes with fresh coffee and a scrap of paper.

"Now this is my cousin Hazel's address. She keeps a clean boarding house between Valencia and Guerero Avenue in the Mission District. Nothing fancy, but all her girls is nice, upstanding citizens. Clerks and students at the teachers' college and that sort. Her rates is reasonable, too. Just tell her that Ellie sent you."

Her eyes darted around the room as she checked to see whether any of her customers needed her attention.

"See now, you take the Third Street line to Market, then the *Omnibus* to Valencia. Get off at Twenty-First Street. Hazel's place is the fifth house in the row between Valencia and Guerero. See, it's all writ down for yer. Mr. Jenkins, he writes a good hand, he does."

Juliana left her benefactor a generous tip and made her way to the proper streetcar line, clutching Ellie's paper in her hand like a lifeline. After disembarking at Market Street, she stood uncertainly for a moment to get her bearings as the streetcar moved on down the line. Market Street teemed with activity with groups of sailors and miners jostling well-dressed businessmen who scanned the headlines of the *Examiner* as they waited for the cars that would whisk them away to Pacific Heights or the Western Addition. Juliana noted with surprise the number of women among them, some young enough to still be giggly after a day's work at the factory or the shop or the office. Others, the washerwomen with their shoulders sagging in a hopeless, tired droop and their hands roughened and reddened from the day's long hours, waited patiently, saying little. Perhaps their minds were on suppers to be cooked, the waiting mouths to be fed, the work to be done before their own day ended.

No one paid her the slightest attention, and Juliana was glad, her mind too numb to worry about how long it would take her to find work before her savings ran out, and she wouldn't be able to pay the unseen Hazel's reasonable rates.

As she waited, clutching her bag and shifting her weight from one foot to the other, a car clanged and clicked down Market Street and came to a stop. All around her the waiting crowd surged forward, even as the passengers streamed down from the streetcar. Juliana, caught in the press, struggled to hang onto her valise as she was pushed to the rear of the flow.

Someone trod on her skirt as a half dozen foreign sailors whooped past her and pounded after the car. In their good-natured, slightly weaving stampede they parted for a woman who had just fought her way through the crush. But one blond young sailor, his cheeks flushed from high spirits of one sort or another, grinning from ear to ear, whirled the woman about by the arm into the line of his shipmates, one of whom gaily twirled the hapless passenger past him as if they were part of a dance line. The woman, her arms full of packages, whirled around as she was released, grabbed at a slipping package, and lost her footing. She went down heavily on her right side, striking the pavement with her elbow, a weak, astonished mew escaping her.

A moment later, a slender, gray-haired, black-robed priest bent over the woman, who moaned quietly. Juliana set her valise down beside the pair and quickly gathered the victim's scattered packages together as the priest asked the woman's name.

"Now, Mrs. O'Bryan, is it? I'm Father Anselmo from the mission church." He nodded at Juliana, who gripped the frightened woman by the upper arm and helped Father Anselmo draw her to her feet. Mrs. O'Bryan winced and stifled a soft cry as her right foot took her weight, then she straightened.

"Thank you, Father, miss, but I'm—" she broke off involuntarily as she took a step forward and gasped. Father Anselmo took hold of her arm.

"Let us help you to a doctor, Mrs. O'Bryan, who can attend to your injury."

"No, no," she insisted faintly. "Here comes my car. I mustn't miss it." She turned a pale face to Juliana standing beside her, the woman's packages under one arm, her valise in the other. "I'll take those, thank you, miss." And to the priest she said, It's only sore, Father. I'll put it up when I'm home again. Miss?"

Juliana's eyes met those of the priest. "If you can help her onto the car, Father, I'll carry these for her and see her safely home."

"An excellent idea, Miss...." The priest let the pause linger, but Juliana pushed ahead of Mrs. O'Bryan without replying. The ride on the North Beach line cost them five cents each, and as Juliana escorted her heavily limping companion to her home on Lombard Street in the Latin Quarter, she discovered that Mrs. O'Bryan was a widow, that she ran a boardinghouse, and that the woman had no reliable help to assist her until her injured foot could heal. She also had a spare room, and after a sidelong glance at Juliana's valise, Mrs. O'Bryan offered the room in exchange for Juliana's help with chores until she could get back on her feet. After that, Juliana could pay half the rental fee for her room in exchange for some help with chores until she was able to procure steady, fulltime employment.

It was a godsend, Juliana reflected now as she carefully stacked Mr. Potter's treatises on philosophy and moral order on a chair. With the care of four permanent lodgers in her hands, she worked as hard as she'd ever done at the lighthouse. She bit her lip at the thought of Faith and Bernard Russell, but reminded herself fiercely that no one would be troubling them now.

And she might as well have fallen off the face of the earth, for who would ever think to look for her at Mrs. O'Bryan's private rooming house?

The following day, Libby O'Bryan poked her head around the door to the dining room where Juliana was laying the table for the midday meal.

"I'll finish that for you, Juliana. It's a beautiful morning, it is. You be off and enjoy yourself."

"Yes, Libby, thanks. I'm going." Juliana folded the last napkin, swept one last glance over the table, then picked up her wrap and let Libby shoo her out the front door into a day so sunny and cloudless she felt her spirit expanding as she drew in a deep breath. With a wave to her employer, Juliana struck off across the street, stopping only long enough to post a letter to Faith and Bernard.

She'd sent them a letter once she had settled in at the boardinghouse, giving them her address and begging them to forgive her flight, and reassuring them as to her good fortune at finding a home and respectable employment, as well as her continued well-being. They wrote often, updating her on life at the light station and begging her, in return, to remain vigilant.

Her letter deposited, Juliana's thoughts returned to her landlady and employer. Olivia Maria O'Bryan, née Vivaldi, was born in San Francisco to immigrant Italian parents who had lived and worked in San Francisco for fifteen years before returning permanently to the old country. Their daughter, then seventeen years old, had astonished and confounded them by remaining behind, and marrying a sober young Irishman by the name of Paddy O'Bryan, a roofer by trade. It was he who had christened his young bride "Libby," a name she held to still, as if young Olivia belonged to the past. A fall from a Nob Hill mansion under construction had permanently retired Paddy from his trade ten years ago, at which time he and Libby had purchased the house on Lombard Street and opened it as a boardinghouse. Her beloved Paddy had died four years before Juliana's arrival, and Libby had gone on with the business, fading quietly away, or so it seemed to Juliana, with the loss of her husband and partner.

With companionship and help, however, some of the bloom began to return to her cheeks even as her ankle mended. She gradually began to relax, and a tentative friendship had blossomed between the two women. Now, some three months after their fortuitous meeting, Juliana and her landlady were on first-name terms and shared a companionable evening together most nights. The biggest drawback to having one's employer as one's only friend, Juliana reflected ruefully, was that she had no friend with whom she could share her half-day off mid-week, nor her Sundays, when she had the whole day off. Libby and Paddy O'Bryan had always kept the Sabbath for rest, and Libby continued the tradition after she was widowed, often inviting Juliana to join her at Sunday Mass.

Today, however, Juliana was determined to push away her thoughts of loneliness and homesickness and enjoy the day. If it hadn't been for the circumstances that led her from home, she would have been delighted to explore San Francisco.

Her destination this afternoon was North Beach, where she debated for a moment whether to have her lunch at Luchetti's café, then changed her mind in favor of the produce markets filled with fresh fruits and vegetables from the Italian-owned truck farms beyond the Mission District. Newly baked bread with gorgonzola and mild salami, a pear, and rich dark coffee were hers to savor as she found herself an unoccupied bench overlooking Fisherman's Wharf.

Great piers protruded into the bay along the waterfront, where the feluccas of the Italian fishermen were the most colorful of all the boats whose comings and goings captured her attention. All around her the sounds of the Italian language swept over her, and she sat there quietly, letting it roll over her like protective coloring. The first time she had ventured away from the house on Lombard Street, she had been grateful that her looks allowed her to virtually disappear into the crowded streets. Yet it was then that she'd made an astonishing and disconcerting discovery about herself, for it had slowly dawned on her that she could understand a great deal of the Italian language that filled the air around her. And the first time she visited a market, she found herself replying in the same language, without thought, as though she had used it only yesterday.

The experience had prompted strange, nightmarish dreams of which she remembered little, sleeping poorly for nights on end. As she watched the feluccas skimming across the bay, now, it seemed to her that perhaps the time had come to face those nightmares by the light of day. Could she learn something from them that would help her now? Deliberately, she set herself to recall all that she could of her past.

To begin with, the steamer whose wreck had literally tossed her into the arms of Bernard and Faith, had started its voyage from San Francisco. Had she been born in this same Italian neighborhood? Could her parents, laid to rest in Santa Rena—she forced herself reluctantly to acknowledge them—had they walked these very streets? And with that thought came another, one that made her catch her breath and choke on the last bite of bread she'd been chewing. Had she sought shelter, then, in the one part of San Francisco that had surely spawned those who had killed her grandmother?

Coughing and sputtering, she managed to swallow the offending piece of bread just as someone diffidently addressed her.

"Excuse me, miss, may I be of some assistance?"

Involuntarily, Juliana's head jerked up, and she found herself meeting the surprised gaze of James Dutton, paint rag in hand and a decided odor of turpentine wafting from his cuff.

"Miss Russell! Juliana!"

She cleared her throat.

"Mr. Dutton! Good afternoon, how are you?"

A delighted laugh escaped him.

"I'm perfectly well, as you may see for yourself. How marvelous to see you again! Are you visiting friends?" Without waiting for an answer, he swept a hand in the direction of an easel and stool set up some yards to the left of her bench. "I came out early this morning to do some oil studies. Do come see, Miss Russell! I've been toiling away for hours and I do think, well, I *think* it's going well, but a critical eye never hurts!"

Before Juliana could get a word in edgewise, she found herself on her feet following James like a duck on a string. For a long moment she stared at the canvas. A grand, sweeping view of the bay had been roughed in. A flurry of movement swept across the picture, rebounding endlessly from the edge of the canvas, setting all to motion again. She transferred her gaze to the busy scene before them and was aware of her companion holding his breath beside her.

"It's a wonderful premise, Mr. Dutton! You've caught the vitality of the bay with a visible sense of exuberance and—and affection, I'd say."

"You see it, too? Wonderful! Yes, Juliana, I love to come here. There's a vivid quality to life in the Latin Quarter—so many different people and languages! No artificial structure or posturing to the people who live and work here, no social pretense. Nothing." He broke off with another sudden laugh.

"Sorry, I get carried away sometimes. You mustn't mind my chatter."

"No, I see what you mean. But there's also a sense of quietness and calm here as well," she said and tapped a finger at the canvas. She made a convulsive move to pick up a brush, then self-consciously pulled her hand back.

"I say, Juliana, here, I mean, Miss Russell, do you paint? Would you care to have a go—?" Dutton suddenly squatted down and rooted through a leather rucksack. He stood up with a sketchpad and drawing pencils "—with these?"

Greedily, Juliana nodded, the back of her throat constricting tightly as she reached wordlessly for the art materials, a sketchpad and pencils. Her sleep was already plagued by nightmares. If drawing made the situation worse, perhaps her dreams would bring back new visions of her past. It was a risk she must accept. "Thank you, Mr. Dutton, and please, call me Juliana."

His shy smile was enhanced rather than marred by the crimson crease in his cheek as he ducked his head with pleasure.

"And I'm James, Jimmy to my friends, Juliana." His own fingers were hesitating over his selection of brushes. "I think I'll add a few more details in this fore section before...." His sentence trailed off open-ended as he grasped a fistful of brushes with one hand, the other daubing energetically at the depth of the wharf before him.

Juliana settled on her bench, her eyes drawn by a pool of stillness in all the activity, a single overturned dinghy next to a shadowed pile of tarpaulins and netting. Two dark-haired boys, no more than eight or nine, had sought refuge in the shade. There they divided their attention equally between their shared lunch of bread and cheese and a penny magazine. Absorbed in her study, Juliana jumped when a hand closed on her shoulder.

"Sorry to startle you, Juliana, but you didn't hear me calling you." James stood back and his sister nodded in Juliana's direction. "Here's Sarah, come to escort me home. We wondered if you would join us for a cup of coffee first?"

"Yes, please, Miss Russell, do join us." Sarah added her invitation to her brother's, and Juliana, on the verge of refusing, thought of the lonely hours to be spent in her room and caught back her polite refusal. "I'd like that, thank you, Miss Dutton."

James had already packed away his canvas and painting materials, his rucksack casually thrown across a shoulder as he held his sister's arm at the elbow.

"There's a café just across the way."

He started off slowly, his sister in tow. Juliana, gathering up her bag and the borrowed sketchpad, was drawn into a discussion of the city's decision to garrison the federal troops to be sent to fight in the Mexican-American war. All San Francisco seemed to regard the garrisoning as an open fiesta, although Sarah gently chided her brother at this remark as they settled themselves at an outdoor table.

"I think the populace is well aware of the implications of the troops, Jimmy. But, tell us, Miss Russell, what brings you to San Francisco? Are you visiting friends? And how are your parents and Mr. Pevie?"

Sarah Dutton's pale features were diffused by a soft blush at the mention of Pevie's name, Juliana observed with interest, and addressed herself hesitatingly to the inevitable with an inward sigh. She looked up to meet James Dutton's questioning gaze. Sarah Dutton, it was clear, couldn't see the glance they exchanged, but she caught the nuance of that moment's awkward silence, and her hand gripped her brother's.

"The last time I saw him, John Pevie was fine, as were Faith and Bernard Russell."

"What do you mean, Juliana, when you *last* saw them?"

"I left the Point Lobos light station more than three months ago, James, to seek my fortune in the big city."

"Oh, my." There was a soft intake of breath from Sarah.

Juliana rushed on.

"The light station is such an isolated world. I wanted to explore more of the world, perhaps pursue my—my drawing, for which there's never any time at Point Lobos."

She flipped open the sketchbook to her drawing. James immediately took the sketch and held it to the light, his attention diverted from the tale of her departure from Point Lobos. Sarah sat quietly, her face tilted toward her brother as he examined the drawing in silence for several moments. When his eyes met hers, Juliana found that relief flooded her as bright interest—rather than pity or politeness—filled his face. He passed her sketchbook to Sarah, who held her left eye close to the drawing.

"One of your moments of quietness, and rather neatly expressed." James said and smiled, and Sarah relaxed beside him and nodded happily in agreement. "How wonderful to have found a fellow artist, Juliana!"

"You're much too kind; I fear mine is only a small talent."

"I'm sure you do yourself a disservice, Miss Russell… Juliana." Sarah shyly echoed her brother, calling Juliana by her first name. "Tell us, where have you found lodging?"

As Juliana explained her position at Libby O'Bryan's boardinghouse, Sarah blinked, and Juliana feared that her companion lived such a sheltered life that it was hard for her to understand that some young women might need to seek work.

"How fortunate for you, Juliana, to come so quickly to a decent place of employment! I have heard tales in my women's group. Utter tragedy sometimes befalls unfortunate young ladies upon their move to the city."

Startled by Sarah's unexpected understanding and pragmatic acceptance, Juliana blinked in surprise and found herself forced to reevaluate her image of this slight young woman—and liking what she learned.

"Sarah belongs to a bohemian group of young San Francisco suffragettes. They're madly plotting all sorts of socialistic actions, including giving females the vote!"

"Oh, go on, James Dutton! Behave yourself," his sister admonished him with a fierce affection, but he only tossed back his head and laughed.

"As much as it pains Father, I heartily encourage Sarah's activities, Juliana. He would keep her in a glass cage if he could." His sister's face clouded for a moment, and James quickly squeezed her hand and changed the subject.

"Would you care to join me here Sunday afternoon, Juliana? We can paint together and criticize one another's efforts shamelessly and after—"

"And after," Sarah broke in decisively, "you will come and take Sunday afternoon tea with me. Please, say you will!"

Why not? Juliana thought. Surely painting would not bring any more vivid nightmares than had the attack on her at Point Lobos. And if it did, perhaps something would come back to her, some clue to tell her who posed a threat to her well-being and why. Her thoughts brightened—besides, James not only had talent, but he possessed an honest eye of appraisal, and she craved a knowledgeable companion to cast an eye over her work. She would enjoy spending more time with Sarah, whose animated features made her seem less shy and more intelligent, full of humor and curiosity.

"Thank you, both of you. I'd very much like to come to tea."

"Good. That's settled, then." Sarah rose to her feet. "You'd better see me home, Jimmy. Father's ordered dinner early this evening."

Arriving at the wharf early Sunday afternoon, Juliana set up her watercolors and donned one of

Paddy O'Bryan's work shirts, donated by Libby, over her good blue muslin summer dress. She sat with hands clasped loosely in her lap and observed the bay quietly for a few minutes. Being isolated at Point Lobos for all those years, she hadn't been able to attend church very often, and she found now that a period of reflection in moments like this served as a time of grace for her, yielding a sense of communion, a sense of renewed purpose, a sense of peace. It seemed to her that God would not turn his back upon her heart and soul, although Libby seemed determined to draw her back into the folds of the church. Juliana had accompanied her landlady to the small parish church once or twice recently, as she felt more comfortable getting out into the community and less frightened that she would present herself as the target for a second attack.

Taking a deep breath to relax, Juliana took up her pencil and began to sketch the outlines of a still life that would later be washed with color once she had captured the essentials. For the purpose of her initial study, she had purchased a small bunch of asters from a Chinese hawker. These were loosely arranged in a canning jar brought along for the purpose, now half-filled with water. The varied colors and shapes of the blossoms created a pleasing challenge, and she was engrossed in her sketch when James Dutton appeared. Glancing over her shoulder briefly, he grunted with approval as he set up his easel.

"I've a filthy headache today, Juliana, so you mustn't mind if I'm a bit quiet."

"I'm sorry to hear that, James. Should we abandon our painting for another day?"

James' fine hair caught the light as he shook his head.

"Not at all. It's the lingering effects of my seafaring accident. Some fresh air, sunshine, and an interlude of work, and I'll be fit company again, you may be sure."

They worked in silence for a while, each periodically taking a break to stretch, walk about for a few moments, and inspect the other's efforts. Turning to her own study, Juliana reflected wryly: "You make my own efforts seem insubstantial and amateurish, James."

He was working today on another scene of the harbor, this one with the feluccas at rest and their lateen sails furled. Close up, the picture appeared chaotic—all rough edges and bits of bright colors daubed on. But from the distance of a few paces away, the painting came into focus, capturing the brilliant play of light, the crowded boats, the jutting piers, everything caught and held in suspension. The technique was rough admittedly, yet held the promise of brilliance. It spoke of long hours in the studio and hinted of exotic, earthly landscapes. Falteringly, she tried to put her impressions into words for her companion's benefit.

"You see all of that?" James' narrow face glowed with a shy pleasure. He wiped his hands on a painting rag, then rummaged in his knapsack and drew out a jug of sweet cider, two cups, and a handful of ginger cookies. "Mrs. Martin packed enough for the both of us."

The younger man chewed thoughtfully for a moment and gestured at his painting in progress.

"I've been very fortunate to have had the luxury of time—time to study, to travel, to work. But you," he added, his blue eyes sweeping back to her face as he indicated her watercolor with a nod of his chin, "your own work has a delicacy, a sureness—or a confidence perhaps, to leave yourself out of the painting while capturing a moment of time—whether it's two children reading or a bouquet of asters and—."

"I mirror life," Juliana interposed with a self-deprecating shrug, but James Dutton shook his head vigorously and pulled her over to stand before her work.

"No, no, not at all, Juliana. When you drew those children, it seemed that you knew those two moppets intimately, as if you'd borne them. Just like it seems to me now that you've looked so long and carefully at this leaf and this blossom that you've understood their very essence and put it here, on paper, with such clarity that no one could ever mistake this leaf or this blossom for any other."

His words resonated some chord deep within her, and Juliana half-closed her eyes, staring at her study. It was true, when she had the luxury of a few stolen moments, she was drawn into a complete absorption of her subjects, and it was only after a period of silent observation that her hand would go to her brushes and she would begin to paint. Jimmy had just explained that moment to her: it was when her inner eye told her she could put all the particular elements of her subject into a whole, when she understood how all the details defined one blossom, one leaf, one boat, one child, that her knowledge could be communicated to her hand. She smiled happily at her companion.

"Your work and mine," he mused, "so different, not better or worse."

"You're very wise to be so young, Mr. Dutton," she teased him. "You've put your finger on my methods, and now I'm eager to see how that knowledge affects my work."

Seated with her study before her again, Juliana selected a group of yellow asters and schooled herself to concentrate on one slender spray of blossoms. At length her study absorbed her and the sounds and sights of the pier were lost to her. And without thinking about it or willing it to happen, she reached for her brush and dipped it in water, touched it to color and rapidly, deftly began to apply a pale yellow wash to paper. An hour later, tired, but with an underlying satisfaction, she looked up to find her partner packing up his gear.

"Time to be getting back. Sarah's anxious for your company, and I don't want to disappoint her."

The Mason Street cable line took them out of the Latin Quarter to the Jackson Street line, which they rode west to Pacific Heights. As they entered the Pacific Heights neighborhood, the distance traveled seemed far greater to Juliana than that of a few miles, but rather could be measured in the vast differences between the crooked, crowded lively streets of the Latin Quarter and the precise blocks of imposing Italianate, Queen Anne, and Colonial Revival homes that dominated every corner they passed in this part of the city. Smaller Stick-style rowhouses frequently stretched down the middle of blocks between the larger, more ornate corner mansions, but in other instances, those modest structures were being torn down to furnish bigger lots for additional homes of gigantic proportions. Stately trees and other plantings were evidence of rear gardens. Juliana's imagination failed her as she tried to conjure up a similarly lush garden in the postage-stamp rear of Libby's property.

Jimmy tugged at her elbow, pulling her along with him as they disembarked at the corner of Jackson and Webster.

"I hope you don't mind a short walk, Juliana. Home is less than two blocks north, at Webster and Broadway. My father inherited the place from his uncle, James Dutton." He smiled. "I'm named after him, as a matter of fact. Although," he added, "the old man was a terror, even with one side paralyzed and him confined to a wheelchair, or so I've been told."

The young man shuddered, and Juliana looked at him curiously. "Great-Aunt Alyce passed away shortly after we moved here. He died five years ago and left my father the lot." He came to a halt suddenly and gestured at a house set in a wide, tree-shaded lot on the southeast corner of Webster and Broadway.

The Dutton mansion was a fairly restrained Italianate structure, compared with the more flamboyant Queen Anne dwellings situated on the other end of the block. The main body of the house was painted a sedate blue-gray, while the trim was glistening white with the details of the cornices and columns picked out with a sunny shade of yellow. A flight of twelve broad steps, flanked by blooming white spirea bushes, led up to a porch that spanned the width of the house. An arched double doorway with a fan light was flanked by two narrow, similarly arched windows on either side. Above, elaborate cornices topped five more arched windows. A half dozen Corinthian columns, spaced with spindled balustrades, held up the porch roof. Identical potted topiary trees guarded the entryway. The depth of the house could be guessed at by the distant carriage house visible far to the rear of the property.

A chill breeze gusted along the hem of Juliana's skirts, eddied down her collar at the back of her neck, and sent a shiver through her body beneath the lightweight fabric of her summer dress. She shivered again as the sky darkened, gripping her arms across her chest to halt the tremors of her body. Thick black wreaths hung from every heavily curtained window, save where a single thick candle lit each of the parlor windows to the right of the entrance. She twisted away from the gloved hand that reached for hers. No, she did not want to climb those steps into that house of mourning.

"Juliana? Miss Russell? Are you feeling well?"

Juliana raised a slow hand to her cheek, her vision clearing as she focused on James' anxious face. She came suddenly back to reality as she absorbed the bright, unclouded sky, the perfect stillness of the afternoon, and the calm blue-gray house before them. She produced a short, embarrassed cough and forced an edgy smile for her companion.

"Please," she said as she took his elbow, "let's not keep Sarah waiting. I should've eaten more lunch, I daresay. But now we're here, I find I'm a bit nervous."

James patted her hand, quick to reassure her. "The place can be overwhelming, but you're not to worry. Since Mother passed away two years ago, we live very quietly. Tea is generally just myself and Sarah and Henry, too, when he isn't engaged in some sporting affair. You'll see."

Juliana set her face to the house, straightened her shoulders, and they mounted the steps. Even so, she could not keep her fingers from tightening their hold on James' elbow. If he noticed, he gave no sign.

The entry hall had finely polished oak floors with dark, oriental runners positioned down the exact center. Delicate wooden fretwork embellished the inner doorway, curving along the corners and echoing richly in the balustrades of a sweeping staircase that rose to the second floor. Two sets of identical doorways opened to the front rooms on either side of the hall. Potted palms framed the entrance doors. Paneled wainscoting rose halfway up the doorframes, with dark rose paint still adorning the walls above and a pale blush pink topping off the walls and flowing onto the ceiling.

Juliana gulped, trying to slow the beating of her heart. A buzzing noise was building in her ears and she thought she might faint as she walked down that hallway with James. A marble-topped mahogany pedestal table held a large blue and white Oriental vase; opposite the hallway, a second table, mate to the first, held a graceful Boston fern, its fronds brushing the floor. The first set of doors opened beyond, one to either side of the hall. Past them, a second set of curio tables presented the reverse pattern, another blue and white vase, another well cared for potted fern. As if nothing was ever allowed to change here, not even the color of the walls. She took a deep breath and then another. Whatever was the matter with her?

Jimmy indicated the left-hand door as he ushered her down the hall.

"That's the ballroom. Not," he said, shooting her a quick, humorous look, his brows going up, "that we ever have occasion to use it. And there," he nodded at the right-hand door, "the front parlor. Another little-used room these days."

An image of candles and flowers and a long, dark coffin swam before her. The coffin lid was up. The scent of all those masses of flowers wafted into the hall. Juliana tore her gaze from the parlor. What on earth was wrong with her? James seemed not to notice the shiver that ran through her, but waved his hand at the second set of doors at the foot of the staircase. "Also to the ballroom on the left; Great-Uncle James' library on the right."

Juliana, aware that her arms and jaws were rigid, deliberately relaxed her tightened fists. Then they were walking past the stairs, a dining room appearing to their right.

"Here we are," James announced cheerily as he led Juliana into the back parlor with a flourish, "parched and famished for your food and for your sparkling conversation," he teased as Sarah Dutton raised her face to greet them. Juliana's gaze moved beyond her hostess. Involuntarily she stopped short, her companion bumping into her from behind. Seated in a comfortable chair next to Sarah, in a relaxed posture that spoke volumes of his apparent familiarity in this household, sprawled Will McKenna.

"Hallo, Jimmy!" He smiled at Juliana. "Miss Russell."

Henry clapped his brother heartily on the shoulder, propelling them both forward again and breaking the catch of air in Juliana's throat. She greeted Sarah and accepted a seat beside her on the settee. Jimmy took a seat beside his friend, while Henry pulled up a chair to the side of the tea table and began pouring tea and passing plates of delicate sandwiches and sweets.

Sarah accepted her cup and turned to Juliana, while Will, Juliana noticed, kept half his attention on Jimmy's chattering and half on Sarah and her guest. Once again, a faint frown creased his brow as his gaze widened to include her. It was a glance that discomfited her, for she could think of no reason why she could have irritated him, and she could only conclude that his disfavor stemmed from a personal dislike. Perhaps he was not favorably impressed with a woman who must earn her living, especially one who presumed to accept invitations from her social betters.

Juliana's chin went up a fraction at that thought, but she had the uncomfortable feeling that she was misreading the man who lounged so easily and laughed so readily with his hosts. Then his lazy gaze crossed hers again, and this time behind the amiable sweep of those gray eyes she knew she was being watched. Discreetly, but persistently. Why? Forcing herself to relax, she responded to Sarah's questions concerning their morning's progress. Her hostess' interest, at least, was unfeigned, although not entirely without purpose as Juliana noticed to her amusement.

Sarah gently but doggedly guided the conversation to more personal questions, until at last the subtle, heightened shift of color in her fair cheeks and the slight attentiveness of the tilt of her head warned Juliana that Sarah was approaching her ultimate quest.

"Painting on the wharf must make you feel at home, Juliana, with the sea to keep you company as it did in Point Lobos." With barely a pause for a murmuring assent from Juliana, she continued, "I hope your parents and Mr. Pevie are well these days." The merest hint of a question invited her guest to be detailed in her reply.

"I've had letters from Faith and from Pevie just this week, Sarah. Faith reports the weather has been merciful so far this summer, and Bernard expects to have a second assistant keeper join them within the month." As she paused to savor a delicate lemon-flavored pastry, Juliana was startled to note that Will—who had yet to address a single remark to her—had stiffened and was frowning once more. So his disapproval was not for her after all, but for Sarah's continued interest in Pevie!

Far be it from her to be churlish in the sharing of Pevie's letter.

"Pevie writes that he's looking forward to Mr. Patterson's tenure as second assistant keeper. He hopes Bernard will allow him a few days' leave and has expressed the hope of paying me a visit here in San Francisco to reassure Faith and Bernard of my well-being. I'd enjoy showing him the sights of the city, but I'm afraid I'm not very familiar with San

Francisco yet." She let her words trail off with an expression of regret.

Sarah turned eagerly toward her brothers.

"We could so ill repay Mr. Pevie's generosity as to let his visit go unremarked by some token of our gratitude."

"Yes, of course," Henry picked up on his sister's intention. "We'd be happy to arrange a day's sightseeing, Miss Russell, if you'd permit us to entertain you and your friend when he comes to town."

"I'm sure I wouldn't want to impose," Juliana began doubtfully, but James waved a hand airily and cut her off.

"Not at all. John Pevie's a fine fellow. You must let us know at once if he is able to arrange a visit."

And he meant it, Juliana could tell; there was an honesty in his voice and actions. She smiled gratefully at him.

"I will, you may be sure of it. Pevie will be delighted."

Beside Jimmy, Will's brow darkened like a thundercloud as Sarah's dainty hand sought his sleeve, her sweet smile flashing like a ray of sunshine before him.

"You must come, too, Will. We'll have a grand outing. Please say you will?"

The tension drained from the lean figure, his brow smoothed out, and his features softened as he covered Sarah's hand with his own. "As you wish, my dear. I'd be delighted to join the party."

The sight of that dark head bent protectively toward Sarah's pale features stirred a sudden well of melancholy deep within Juliana. She took a hasty gulp of tea and looked away. As she stared unseeing at the walnut mantel with its mirrored pier glass and curio shelves, the conversation eddied about her. Henry recounted to James the acquaintances whom he had seen earlier in the day. Juliana blinked and returned her attention to Sarah, only to find Will McKenna's gray eyes upon her in an open, direct gaze that held a question, offered assistance, hinted at some deeper concern. The hair stood up on Juliana's neck.

He opened his mouth to speak.

CHAPTER FIVE

"Sarah, my darling, is that a new dress? Rose was your mother's favorite color. You should wear it more often."

Startled, Sarah jerked her upper torso toward the wide doorway to the hall, and at the same time reached out blindly to set her teacup down.

"Father!"

Without thought, Juliana leaned forward to select another fruit tartlet from the tray with her right hand, while at the same time rescuing Sarah's cup with her left and gently returning it to its saucer. It was, she recognized fleetingly, the same protective reaction Henry had shown at the lighthouse, to save Sarah from unwanted attention. In doing so, she caught the warm approval of Will's gray eyes on her and was glad he couldn't see the blush marking her cheeks as she turned to acknowledge her introduction to Sarah's father.

Richard Dutton dropped a hand on his daughter's shoulder and brushed her brow with his lips. Here was what Henry would look like in another twenty years. The youthful burliness translated into a compact bulk carried with a dignity of bearing emphasized by clipped sideburns and dark hair graying now to silver. Heavy-lidded eyes registered the presence of his sons, the full lips tightening as he caught the faint whiff of turpentine from James' stained handkerchief. Juliana surreptitiously started to wipe her hands on her napkin and caught herself. Richard nodded at Henry, waving away the proffered teacup, and greeted Will as he took the seat James had abandoned in favor of a low stool near his brother.

Henry took up their conversation where they'd left off.

"No, no, no! Jimmy! Bill Smith lost that race long before the last buoy. Never should have let that Anderson lad on the crew, if you ask me."

Richard's intent gaze fixed upon Juliana.

"So you are the young woman responsible for saving my son's life. Please allow me to convey my gratitude. How fortunate that you have found employment in San Francisco." His sardonic gaze flicked briefly, unmistakably, over the figure of his younger son.

Juliana's glance widened and slowly she returned her cup to its saucer. A chill went through her. Richard's quick eyes noted the tremor; his teeth gleamed as he smiled at her.

"It was my job to assist Mr. Pevie, the first assistant keeper, Mr. Dutton, in the absence of the keeper," she replied, trying not to grit her teeth.

"Ah, I see," came the smooth rejoinder. "You often worked alone with this assistant, did you?"

Juliana returned her cup to its saucer.

"My duty was to assist in the event of an emergency, Mr. Dutton." Then she turned to Sarah, whose attention was caught by a good-natured escalating argument between her brothers, and touched her arm. "I'm afraid I must go now. Thank you for having me to tea, Sarah."

James began to interrupt his brother, but Will forestalled him by rising to his feet as Juliana did so.

"I must be going myself. Please allow me to see you home, Miss Russell."

She opened her mouth to put him off, but thought better of it as James protested that he'd see her home.

"Thank you, Mr. McKenna. You're very kind to offer. I enjoyed our morning, James." She took her leave of Henry and Sarah and their father, her shoulders stiff and her jaw aching with the effort to keep it from clenching. She would not mar Sarah's kindness by letting her anger show.

Juliana allowed Will to hand her into his buggy, staring ahead without seeing. With one malicious glance, Richard Dutton had effectively put an end to any further acquaintance or friendship with his children. She could be certain that no new invitations to tea or other outings would be forthcoming. Beside her, Will maneuvered them skillfully through traffic, all his attention on the streets about them. Only once did he speak, to inquire her address. Miserably Juliana sat beside him, furious with Richard Dutton for his sly insinuations and with herself for ever thinking she could make friends beyond her own station in life. Surely the man could not believe what he had inferred! Disgust filled her at the thought of him. What a vicious mind, so skillfully contained beneath a smooth veneer of politeness!

When they at last reached the house on Lombard Street, Will jumped down and held out his hand to assist Juliana from the buggy.

"Pray don't linger, Mr. McKenna," she told him curtly, "I can see myself to the door. You mustn't be seen with the likes of me!"

Will flinched, his gray eyes hardening, and withdrew his hand.

"Excuse my imposition, Miss Russell," he said, his mocking tone cutting at her composure. Then he relented. "I think you will find that Sarah, James, and Henry are cut from finer cloth than their father," he said. "Their mother saw to that." His mouth tightened in a mirthless grimace. "I'm sorry you think so little of me. Good evening."

With quick grace, he undid the reins of his mare and tipped his hat to Juliana. The breath went out of her as his words struck at her and her eyes blurred with tears. Appalled at her own behavior, she flung herself forward, one hand raised.

"Wait, Will! Please!"

The angry spurt of gravel as the buggy wheeled away from the curbside left her standing alone, her arm upraised. Quickly she let herself into the boardinghouse, tears beading thickly on her lashes. Why had she taken her anger and frustration out on Will McKenna? Shame burned her cheeks, and she wiped away the tears with the back of her hand. Forcing a smile on her face, she joined Libby in the parlor.

"Oh, my dear, you're home. Come sit next to me. Now tell all, all about the house and the family. What sweets were on the tea tray?"

Later, Juliana bathed her face with tepid water from the basin in her room, then sat on the edge of her bed and pulled a brush through her hair with one hand while squinting at her features in the hand glass. Did Richard Dutton really believe she would pursue his son? Why not? Was it so difficult to believe that a man might find her attractive? She had a face, she decided, that needed the levity she'd shared with Pevie. For too long now her features had been drawn into a sober, mistrustful cast. But the rest of her... she had never run to fat, though her waist was not as nipped and tucked as was currently fashionable. Her body curved and swelled in pleasing proportions; then her mouth crooked in a grin, and she made a face at herself in the mirror.

Will's words came back to ease her distress and anger. The Dutton children had not, in fact, seemed to be possessed of the same disposition as their father. The grin faded as the image of strong features and a clear-eyed gaze filled her mind. Oh no, my girl, she warned herself. That one was equally above her station, no matter how she might wish things were different. She lay the mirror aside, not wanting to confront the longing she could see in her face. No matter, she had managed to alienate him with her ill-directed outburst. Throwing off her robe, she blew out the lamp and lay down to sleep.

The golden idol stalked her, its stylized features alive with a fury that sent her away from the sandy promontory onto the stony slash of a trail that led up the vertical face of the sea cliffs before her. The detached part of her, the one who observed the scrambling figures of her dreams, recognized the southern trail at Point Lobos. Then the scene shifted.

As the frantic climber won free of the slope, she faced not the lighthouse and its outbuildings, but only another trail more precipitate than the first, and where this one led, she could not say. Behind her, rising from the cliff below, came her pursuer, the gold head turning unerringly toward her, the eyes glittering as sharp as obsidian. Juliana leapt for the trail before her, for the clasp of a hand that closed firmly about her wrist and pulled her to safety. "Don't look down," a quiet voice cautioned, and in that moment she did so, catching a glimpse of a world so high and wide, the river flowed beneath her as a thin, dark curving line. Mountains all about her pierced the heavens' vault, and a cold assaulted her, so terrifyingly numbing, that she gasped for breath.

Gasping for breath, Juliana awoke with a start, shivering, hugging her pillow in the same way she had clung to the solid rock wall in her dream's vision. She huddled beneath her quilt, fighting off both the fear and the images of her nightmare. It was cold, so cold there in that high place, but if only they could reach the valley, there they would find sanctuary. Warmed now, and drifting back to sleep, she did not wonder at who "they" might be, or why she was so certain that sanctuary was near.

With morning, the dream was forgotten.

Libby didn't ask why no more visits were arranged, or why Juliana assiduously avoided Fisherman's Wharf on her free afternoons. Instead, she gently reminisced about some of her favorite afternoons spent visiting the city sights with Paddy. Juliana used the anecdotes as a guide to her own exploration of the city. The Mission District, with its adobe and tile-roofed mission church, for one, and the Golden Gate Park with its gazebo and Regina waterlilies, a massive yard wide in bloom. Juliana carried her sketchbook with her wherever she went, accumulating a bulging notebook of odd souvenirs of her daytrips. The folds of a woman's intricately cut sleeve on the streetcar ahead of her, the tramcar pulling onto the top of Mt. Tamaulipas, the gingerbread trim of a Queen Anne house in Oakland, the shy grins of a trio of Chinese youngsters on their way to kindergarten.

Yet she grew increasingly loathe to set off on her own, at first restricting her excursions to midday, when crowds of people were certain to be abroad. Even after a month had passed since her tea with Sarah and James, she was reluctant to leave the boardinghouse at all. Edgy and resentful because of her nervousness, she also found herself once more prone to moments of acute homesickness for Point Lobos, for the reassuring presence of Faith and Bernard. Her letters from Faith and the occasional missive from Pevie warmed her; she tried not to think badly of the younger Duttons. They were from another, more socially constricted, world.

Even more frightening was the creeping feeling she was being watched whenever she ventured away from Libby's boardinghouse. As if someone were following her steps to and fro. Try as she might to dismiss her vague fears as unfounded, the prickling feeling would grow between her shoulders until she squirmed with uneasiness and quickly concluded whatever errand had taken her out, fleeing back instead to Lombard Street. If Libby noticed her deepening reluctance to venture out for marketing or pleasure, still she said nothing to her young friend.

Sunday morning was the exception. Libby adjusted her peplum jacket over her high-necked blouse, then donned her hat, picked up her reticule and gloves, and nodded her readiness to Juliana. This time Juliana didn't demur, but followed her landlady obediently to Mass. The morning sky was cloud-free, the day cool and quiet. Together they walked the four blocks to the tiny church of St. Francis, its pews filled with the families of the Latin Quarter. To her relief, Juliana didn't feel the quiver of alarm, the sense of being watched on this occasion. She relaxed as Father Joseph led his parishioners through the liturgy, setting her attention determinedly on his words. Lulled by the peace of her surroundings and the voices of the choir raised in song, she stiffened suddenly as her shoulders twitched.

From somewhere from within the congregation, someone was once more watching her.

Carefully, her neck twisting slowly as if corseted in whalebone, she turned her head to the left. Her gaze moved back to the choir, then as the congregation knelt to pray, she risked a quick glance over her shoulder. Did a head drop too quickly there, where an old man, hair a white ring around a bald pate, bowed his head in prayer? She could not see his face.

As the prayer ended, she watched the elderly gentleman from the corner of her eye. He rose and lent his arm as support to a woman at his side, her figure partially blocked from Juliana's view by her companion, so that she glimpsed only a short, rounded body wrapped in black shawls. Although the man didn't turn in Juliana's direction, she found her thoughts drawn to him throughout the remainder of the service.

He couldn't recognize her. If she had been born in San Francisco—which seemed possible as that had been the departure port for the ship which had carried her to Point Lobos—then she had been only a young child when she sailed. But a thought came to her and excitement jolted through her fear. What if the old man had seen in her some resemblance to someone known to him? A neighbor, a friend, someone he saw in the daily hub of life in the Quarter? With a mounting impatience, she waited for the Mass to end.

At last, her handkerchief twisted into a crumpled knot, the final blessing was given and the pews began to empty. Juliana followed Libby and tried to keep her eye on the elderly couple. Once she was certain she glimpsed the old man's back, but as the congregation fragmented into friends greeting one another, relatives snatching up new babies, neighbors pausing for an exchange of pleasantries, she found her progress slowed and caught at Libby's elbow.

"I'll wait for you outside."

Politely skirting and excusing herself through the lingerers, she blinked in the bright morning sun and surveyed the small knots of people chatting on the steps in front of the church. Disappointment clouded her features, and she bit her lip, looking the groups over more slowly this time; but still there was no tall, lean old gentleman like the one she sought. On the verge of hot, irrational tears, she bit her lip.

And yet what, she asked herself angrily, would she have done if they *had* been standing on the steps? Accosted them and demanded to know why an old man's glance had lingered on her? No; it was a vain hope to read too much into one chance gaze. Juliana moved down the steps to wait for Libby under the shade of an oak, lost in her thoughts. A hand touched her shoulder, and she whirled, white-faced, to find Henry Dutton looming over her, hat in hand.

"Excuse me for startling you, Miss Russell." His brown eyes mirrored his confusion. "But Sarah would like a word, if you...." his voice trailed off as he gestured with his hat toward a waiting buggy from which his sister lifted her hand in a tentative wave.

Sarah's cheeks were crimson, but her smile brightened as Juliana approached, and she leaned forward.

"Hello, Juliana. A gentleman boarder at your home told us that you were at Mass with Mrs. O'Bryan. Father's expecting us for luncheon, but I asked Henry to drive me over. I want to invite you to a meeting of my Wednesday afternoon women's club. We've been working for women's suffrage, but this week is something different. The club is hosting a lecture by...." A clatter of children spilling free of their parents washed around them, and Juliana strained to hear Sarah's words. "...and I think you'd enjoy it. Please say you'll come?"

Juliana, watching Sarah's embarrassed but determined effort, knew that the young woman was almost certainly defying her father in pursuing her friendship with the lighthouse keeper's daughter. Will's judgment had been accurate after all. A rush of pleasure filled her.

"Thank you, Sarah. I have a half-day free on Wednesday. I'd like that very much. Why don't you tell me the address and time, and I'll meet you there?"

Sarah beamed at her, and Henry, quickly patting

his pockets, extracted a slip of paper and a stub of a pencil. "Here, I'll jot it down for you, Miss Russell."

"No, no," Sarah protested quickly, "we can collect you on our way, Juliana. I insist."

"Thank you, Sarah, but I often run errands before my half-day off begins. I'll just catch the nearest streetcar."

Sarah gave in gracefully as Henry handed over his slip of paper.

"We'll look forward to seeing you then, Juliana."

"We must go, Sarah," Henry interrupted his sister quietly. "Father will be waiting."

"Good-bye, Sarah, Henry!"

As Juliana stepped back from the street and scanned the thinning crowd for Libby, it came to her that she had completely missed the subject of the lecture and the name of the speaker. Sarah had said something about women's suffrage. Not a subject much debated at Point Lobos, since women keepers were part of the U.S. Lighthouse Service. She might find herself much enlightened. No matter the topic. It could be about mustard plasters for all she cared. The prospect of a planned engagement bolstered Juliana's flagging spirits. Some of her uneasiness slipped away. Perhaps it had been engendered in part by her loneliness and sense of isolation. Self-imposed?

That thought returned to her later, making her frown as she cleared the supper table. Was she afraid to face her past? Or of reaching out for friendship in the fear that no one could be trusted? Yet the attack at Point Lobos had come after years of safety, of a lifetime growing up in the peaceful isolation that was a lighthouse keeper's lot in life. It was only after that peace had been disturbed by the unexpected storm, when strangers—James Dutton, son of a wealthy San Francisco merchant, and his friend Will McKenna—had been stranded in their midst, that trouble had come hunting her at Point Lobos.

With a small jolt of surprise, Juliana realized how little she knew of Jimmy's friend. All Will's attention and concern had been directed at his friend and at the desperate situation after their rescue. He hadn't spoken of himself at all. More disturbing was the way he watched her, as if he were judging her. Comparing her to Sarah? Did he want something from her? Had he never seen a woman who worked for a living? Or was she simply reading too much into their brief encounters? And then there was Henry and Sarah Dutton, who had come to Point Lobos to take their brother home. Juliana rinsed the last of the supper dishes and dried her hands. Her head ached with going over and over the same facts.

It seemed inescapable that some tie existed between the events surrounding the wreck of the *AlyceGee* and the attack on her. If it were only a coincidence, where did that leave her?

With an unseen, unknown enemy. One who might strike again at any moment. In that case, she could make no defense or preparation for her safety. If somehow Will or the Duttons were responsible, she might be able to discover what that connection was—should her friendship with Sarah be allowed to grow. And if no connection were proved, she would have a friend, and that was a circumstance to be welcomed.

Wednesday came with fog and a light rain that held throughout the morning as Juliana set about her chores at the boardinghouse. Mr. Potter was feeling poorly, his arthritis cramping his fingers so he could hardly take notes for his continuing study of philosophy. After her first few weeks at the boardinghouse, he had approached Juliana about transcribing his notes on such occasions, while he could still make sense of the crabbed writing. Her handwriting was elegant and clear, and Mr. Potter's appreciation was voiced again and again on those days she was able to help him.

"Not at all, Mr. Potter. It's no hardship at all. Mrs. O'Bryan and I run the house fairly smoothly between us. I'll just finish this last page for you, then I'll be off for the afternoon."

Libby decided to combine the daily shopping with a visit to her husband's widowed great-aunt, leaving Juliana ample time to copy Mr. Potter's notes, then dress carefully in a freshly pressed shirtwaist and her best navy serge skirt. She had no idea the number of other ladies who might make up Sarah's group, but guessed they would be like Sarah herself—young women with enough leisure to cultivate interests away from their homes.

She couldn't dress her hair in the most fashionable styles, so she settled for a French braid, securing the end of the braid in a neat coil at the nape of her neck. Try as she might, loose wisps escaped the braid and curled about her face. Adjusting her straw boater, trimmed for the occasion with a bit of navy and red figured ribbon, she gave up the attempt to subdue her hair. She wanted to appear intelligent and sober and interested; a tangle of curls would hardly aid that impression. Collecting her duster and reticule, she checked to see that she had coins enough for her fare there and back, and to purchase a coffee if the occasion should arise after the lecture.

The Larkin Street Women's Group met on the third Wednesday of each month in a private hall on Russian Hill. A shallow dais with a podium faced the entrance. Several orderly rows of folding wooden seats were arrayed before the podium, with broad central and side aisles arranged for easy access to the seats. Most of them were filled, Juliana saw as she paused hesitantly on the threshold and searched the throng for Sarah. A surge of more women filing in behind her thrust Juliana forward into the hall. She caught sight of Sarah's face turned attentively to the young woman at her side, one hand fixed on the empty seat next to her.

Juliana quickly made her way up the aisle, excused herself to the seated members of the club, and whispered a hurried greeting to her hostess. As she did, a young woman stepped up to the podium and rapped smartly upon it for their attention, the gigot sleeves of her walking suit's jacket brushing the podium. The light reflected from her round spectacles, and her thick, fair hair puffed gently above the high starched collar of her bodice. Nodding as the group quieted, she smiled generously at the audience.

"Thank you, ladies—and gentlemen—of the Larkin Street Women's Group." This brought a murmur of laughter and Juliana noticed that a fair number of men, accompanying wives, girlfriends, and sisters, were sprinkled throughout the crowded hall. "My name is Regina Farsley, and as president I am happy to welcome you to a very special lecture. This afternoon we have as our topic The Healing Plants of California, presented to you by an eminent scholar in the field of pharmacology and experimental therapeutics. Ladies and gentlemen, I have the honor of presenting to you Dr. William Jordan McKenna."

Confused, Juliana thought back to that moment outside the church and realized she hadn't actually heard what the program was to be. Suffrage, indeed! Will—'an eminent scholar'? An enthusiastic round of applause resounded in the room. Will rose from the front row and strode to the podium.

"Thank you, Mrs. Farsley, and the members of this society, for inviting me to speak with you today. This is but a fragment of the long history of natural medicine. Think, if you will, upon the first inhabitants of this land, indeed, of our own ancestors in the rude beginnings of European civilization, of the ancient Romans and Greeks and Egyptians. Healers, physicians, mid-wives, primitive shamans—each in his or her own way striving to restore the balance of health to the sick and injured."

He paused. "In this modern world in which we find ourselves, those times may seem to be as remote from us as the ancient healers of the Greeks and Romans. What do we have in common with those ancient healers of yesteryear? We have the same cornucopia of medicinal plants and herbs. And we have the foresight and the energy to seek new cures for old complaints, here in the New World, in the jungles and mountains of South America, in the depths of Asia, in the hinterlands of darkest Africa. And yet, we might travel no further than our own backyards, to the countryside of our own California, to find natural prescriptions for what ails us."

A stir of interested murmurs quickly subsided. Will stood relaxed at the podium, leaning slightly forward in his enthusiasm, his eyes meeting Juliana's for a moment. He might have been speaking just to her.

"Take the desert windflower, or anemone. Did you know that the native inhabitants of California used the flower crushed or fresh to make a poultice for the relief of sores and boils? And doveweed or turkey mullein—it grows all over the state, a silvery annual with yellow flowers. The Pomo Indians take this common weed as a tea, well-strained, for a fever's chills. Now the ocotillo provides both flowers and roots...."

From her seat next to Sarah, Juliana listened with growing interest as Will beguiled and amused his audience with tales of little-known uses of local flora. His face lit up as he punctuated his discussion of local lore with occasional comparisons to more exotic locales, clearly some of those trips he'd mentioned at the lighthouse. His talk was well-received and the lecture ended after an hour with an opportunity for the assembled members and their guests to mingle with the speaker as they partook of refreshments.

Sarah's walking costume accentuated her tiny waist; the starched collar of her white shirtwaist rose above the twin lapels of her charcoal tweed Norfolk jacket to frame the delicate features of her face, flushed now with pleasure. She drew Juliana by the hand to the refreshments table where she made a selection from the sweet cakes arrayed before them, directing Juliana to secure two cups of punch. Juliana, steered toward the dark-haired woman next to whom Sarah had been seated during the lecture, found her gaze meeting a pair of lively gray eyes as Sarah performed the introductions.

"Marthe, may I introduce to you Miss Juliana Russell? Juliana, this is my dear friend, Dr. Marthe McKenna."

"How do you do, Miss Russell? It seems that Sarah and I both owe our brothers' lives to you and the assistant keeper, Mr. Pevie."

Startled, Juliana stared in to a pair of familiar gray eyes. Two Dr. McKennas?

"Thank you, Dr. McKenna. If I performed my duties well, it's because Bernard Russell and John Pevie trained me to high standards."

"I shan't argue the point, Miss Russell." Marthe McKenna's laugh, a deep-throated sound, rang out spontaneously. "My brother was indeed fortunate for your training and your courage."

"Do you share a practice with your brother, Dr. McKenna?" Juliana sought to change the subject. "How is it that you both chose to study medicine?"

Marthe McKenna's fond gaze flickered to her brother and back to Juliana.

"Will's not a practicing physician. He's a medical detective! Oh, he earned his degree at the Medical College of Ohio in Cincinnati, the same as I did and our father before us, and I daresay he could diagnose what ails you if he put his mind to it." Another deep-timbered chuckle escaped her. "But my brother's interest lies in searching out new medicines, new cures for·disease and physical ailments."

"Sometimes I think he prefers the search because it satisfies his wanderlust," Sarah spoke up matter-of-factly, a trifle wistfully.

Juliana looked at her curiously. If Will McKenna's obvious penchant for Sarah Dutton was returned with this fond exasperation, instead of passion, perhaps that might explain his desire to get away.

"But he always comes home sooner or later," Marthe observed dryly, her words so pat upon Juliana's own thoughts that she felt certain that her assumption was correct.

"Like mullein, I'm a perennial, Marthe. You'd have to pull up my roots to be rid of me permanently." Will McKenna dropped an arm about his sister's shoulders. "Hullo, Sarah, Miss Russell. I didn't realize that you were a member of the Larkin Street Women's Group."

"She isn't yet," Sarah told him, and Marthe finished for her, "But we're always recruiting new members to our cause."

"Tell me, Miss Russell," Will McKenna's left brow lifted as he asked lightly, "are you prepared to march for women's suffrage?"

"I'm afraid I'm not very well versed in the ideas behind the movement, Dr. McKenna, but I'm certainly prepared to listen to their arguments."

"Hear, hear!" Marthe's gray eyes twinkled, "we've the beginnings of a convert, Sarah! Let us press our advantage."

"Yes!" Sarah's animated features glowed, and she turned impulsively to Juliana. "Please say you'll come to our next regular meeting, Juliana. I've some pamphlets you may borrow, if you'd like. I can drop them off before the meeting."

"And I...."

Across the enthusiastic planning of Sarah and Marthe, Juliana met Will McKenna's gaze as he stared at her with his brow creased in that frowning concentration she was beginning to know. Did he so dislike her? Or was he afraid that Juliana's continued association with Sarah might well bring Pevie into Sarah's orbit again? Then he shook himself and nodded at her cup.

"May I refresh your punch, Miss Russell?"

"Please."

He guided her to a seat, Sarah and his sister now caught up in an impromptu discussion with their sister members over the latest handbill dispatched by the local Harrods Bay Smoking Club, an all-male bastion given to long-winded diatribes against the suffragettes. As Will made his way to the refreshments table, Regina Farsley waylaid him with a question that was met with whoops of laughter from the group around her. Sarah and Marthe withdrew from the crowd and sat down some distance from Juliana, their heads together. Juliana relaxed in her seat, happy to put her troubles behind her for the moment. Through the laughter and lively discussions heating up around her, words suddenly penetrated her contented mood. She looked up to find Sarah and Marthe still deep in conversation.

"I worry about him, Marthe." Marthe's reply was lost in the noise.

"No, he doesn't remember anything that happened in the months before the accident. His holiday abroad, the sailing, the wreck of the *AlyceGee*."

Juliana noted the reassuring hug Marthe dispensed.

".... often tired, abominable headaches, hasn't even unpacked his crates...."

".... headache powders... time...."

Lest they turn and consider her to be deliberately eavesdropping, Juliana twisted about in her chair just as Will McKenna successfully withdrew from battle and skirted the edge of Regina's group, two cups of punch held high.

Juliana sipped hers gratefully. Her companion gestured at the vivacious knot of discussants.

"As a progressive thinker, Miss Russell, it seems to me that you'd fit right in with the Larkin Street Women's Group."

"Progressive? How did you arrive at that conclusion, Dr. McKenna?"

Will shrugged.

"Oh, your unusual upbringing at the light station—unusual for a woman, that is."

Impatiently, Juliana shook her head.

"I wouldn't identify myself as progressive, Dr. McKenna. Living on a light station often means living in isolation. Everyone must be able to do whatever needs to be done. Man or woman, it makes no difference. Faith and Bernard between them taught me how to manage the inside and outside duties of the light station. It wasn't a choice I had to make, although I must say that women make very competent keepers. Just as," she added smoothly, "I'm sure your sister is a fine doctor."

"Bravo, Miss Russell, I salute you." He suited

action to words and sketched a two-finger salute. "But I'm certain the membership of the Harrod's Bay Smoking Club would heartily disagree. And they would certainly call you a progressive, modern young woman, addressing your parents by their Christian names."

Once again, his tone was light, almost teasing, but his gaze lowered briefly and she thought for a moment that sharp interest flickered in his eyes. She answered quietly, with only a slight hesitation.

"My... parents lie buried in Santa Rena, Dr. McKenna. Faith and Bernard Russell raised me as their own child."

"I'm sorry, Miss Russell, my apologies for intruding into your private affairs."

"Pray don't let it concern you." Juliana set aside her cup. "I enjoyed your talk, Dr. McKenna, but I'm afraid I must be going. If you'll excuse me? I must thank Sarah."

"Let me see you home, Miss Russell," he began, but Juliana demurred.

"Thank you, but...." she began to say just as Sarah's group broke up.

Sarah came to join them, pulling at Will's arm to tug him in the direction of two young women who stood chatting with his sister.

"Mary Ellen Kramer and Dolly Wilson are dying to tell you all about the botanical specimens they collected from the mountains of Greece, Will. You can monopolize Juliana some other time," she added and tossed a quick smile at Juliana.

"That's all right, Sarah, I must say good-night. Thank you for inviting me this evening."

As it turned out, Juliana wasn't the only person

to be leaving, and she walked along to the trolley stop with several other members and their guests who engaged her in a discussion of their own home remedies. Juliana reflected, as she transferred lines and settled down for the ride back to Libby's boardinghouse, that she might seriously entertain Sarah's invitation to join her group. The women had been warm and welcoming.

Hopping off at her stop, she walked along Lombard Street, part of her thoughts noting how late the days were growing, and part turning over the overheard snippets of conversation between Sarah and Marthe McKenna. There was little doubt that Sarah was worried for her younger brother. But Marthe was a doctor, and she hadn't seemed overly upset, so perhaps.... A niggling sound jelled in her mind, and Juliana's back stiffened.

Footsteps on the walk behind her? Resisting the urge to stop and look around, Juliana clutched the throat of her jacket and stepped up her pace. She was barely a block from home. Across the street and ahead of her, an elderly couple strolled slowly toward Valencia. The footsteps behind her matched her pace. Frightened, Juliana half-turned, to see a short, portly man mopping at his brow with a handkerchief while he muttered under his breath and consulted his pocket-watch. He passed her with barely a glance and trotted ahead.

Juliana's stiff shoulders relaxed and she breathed more easily. Of course it had been nothing. She was letting her imagination run away with her. The boardinghouse came into view; she could see the porch-lamp Libby had left on for her, its light just becoming necessary as the evening drew on.

She'd be home momentarily and all would be well.

That was when she was suddenly grabbed and dragged into the alley that lay in darkness. She drew breath to scream and a fist cuffed her right ear. A rough deep voice whispered hoarsely, "None o' that, li'l missy." Her attacker shifted his grasp of her arms so he was holding her by one hand, while the other began to squeeze her throat. Tears sprang to her eyes as she gagged, choking and gasping. She was going to die! In a dark alley, only moments away from light and hope and help!

But not like this, Juliana suddenly thought, not tearful and passive. She kicked back at the man behind her, connecting with his legs and he grunted, dropping her arms without slackening his hold on her neck. With both hands freed, she clawed at the hand that was draining her breath from her.

"Fight the panic! Think!" Bernard's calm voice echoed in her mind. He'd led her through rough seas any number of times. She let go the man's hand and with a quick, backward thrust, gouged at his eyes with her thumbs. Startled, her attacker swore, taking an involuntary step backward as he flung her about with him. A high whistle pierced the air and Juliana's face was suddenly buried in a scratchy homespun sleeve smelling of fish as she was lifted from her feet and thrown on a heap onto the ground. Her unseen assailant ran away down the alley, leaving her blinded and retching on her hands and knees in the dirt.

"Good Lord! Miss Russell! Juliana!"

She could barely hear the voices through the ringing in her ears, and then someone gathered her into their arms. Fingers briskly undid her high collar, and a cloth smelling of lavender wiped the vileness from her mouth and cheeks. The grip on her adjusted, an arm scooping up her legs and skirts, the movement registering in that small portion of her mind that was still fully aware and protected behind the fear, the shock, the bruising violence that echoed about her body and soul.

Other cries reached her in that state of shock. Libby. The boardinghouse. She was safe. Safe. Now tears poured forth, and silent, hard sobs shook her. Why? Why? She had nothing, knew nothing, remembered nothing of her life before she was reborn as Juliana Russell. Who wanted her dead so badly that they should strike again and again? And where could she run this time when she could not put a face to her enemy? Juliana willed the sobs to cease; there would be questions to be answered, authorities to be faced, but she could not stop the sobs which shook her.

Someone was rocking her, murmuring soothing, incoherent sounds against her hair, stroking her head. Then at last, exhausted, the tears ceased. She might have been a child again with loving arms keeping the outside world at bay. Like her special friend. Mama's young admirer, Poppa called him. But he liked her, too. Sometimes he rocked her when she was sick. Like now. Charmed, she let go the struggle, turned her head into his chest, and slept.

CHAPTER SIX

When Juliana awoke, sunshine was streaming into her room. She touched her throat, which felt bruised and aching, and as the events of the night before returned to her she felt depression settling in. Perhaps the attack last night had nothing to do with the attack at Point Lobos—perhaps bad luck simply gathered about her. But she couldn't make herself believe that; it was too much of a coincidence.

A sense of helplessness assailed her, born from the knowledge that whatever danger threatened her had now followed her to the Lombard Street boardinghouse. She could not, must not, expose Libby O'Bryan to harm. Yet it seemed to her in that moment of despair that no matter where she ran, she wasn't going to escape her unknown pursuers. Pushing herself slowly into a sitting position, Juliana rested her elbows on her knees and cupped her chin with both hands, considering one inescapable fact. In each case, the attacks upon her had followed her contacts with the Dutton family— and with William McKenna, came the unwillingly thought. Yet, how could she explore that connection when she could not find a place of safety? As she swung her legs gingerly over the edge of the bed, panic rose up in her mouth. No time, now, to waste in futile speculation that served only to chase her wits away. She must leave the boardinghouse immediately and preserve Libby's well-being if she could not secure her own. Rising with an effort—her body stiff and unresponsive from her bruises—she dressed then hauled her valise from the bottom of the armoire and packed her few belongings once again. Tired from the effort and dispirited, she stood indecisively at the window, fingering the headache powders left for her by the doctor who had come the previous evening, roused her, and then administered one powder. She tucked them into her valise and stood looking out onto Lombard Street below. A soft knock sounded, and Libby peeked in at the door.

"Juliana! Dear, you have a visitor this morning. Do you feel well enough to come down to the parlor?" When Juliana nodded, Libby crossed the room to her and squeezed her shoulders with a self-conscious hug. "It's a Mr. John Pevie. Come from Santa Rena, he says."

"Thank you, Libby. For everything," Juliana managed, her voice a hoarse croak.

Pevie's broad-shouldered form brought tears to her eyes. He took one long step forward, exclaiming with shock at the bruises above her collar she couldn't hide. For a long moment he held her close, strong arms folded about her, the sun slipping through the parlor windows and warming her from without, so that between Pevie and the sun, Juliana's fear melted slightly and she managed a shaky smile. Before either of them could speak, the doorknocker rapped smartly against the front door, and the rustle of Libby's skirts could be heard as she answered it. Pevie dropped his arms and stepped back, drawing Juliana after him toward the faded brocade settee.

"Juliana," he began.

"Juliana," Libby echoed, stepping into the parlor. "I've told them that you're engaged, but they insist on seeing you." She half-turned to the hall as the Dutton siblings spilled into the doorway behind her.

Sarah stepped hesitatingly into the room, squinting as she sought her friend. James was at his sister's skirts, with Henry looming behind him. Will brought up the rear. Will, Juliana had time to notice as she rose, looked pinched around the nostrils. as perhaps, she thought, he found the proceedings distasteful. He sought a place with his back to a window.

Pevie jumped to his feet. Libby looked anxiously at her charge.

"Thank you, Libby," Juliana said. "I'll see them for a few minutes, if you don't mind?" Mrs. O'Bryan excused herself, leaving a moment's silence immediately broken by everyone speaking at once.

"Are you hurt badly?" James came to her and took her hand. "When we heard!"

"You must come home with us, I beg you," Sarah cried.

"Father offers the hospitality of our home for as long as you like," Henry added gruffly.

Only their friend remained silent. Pevie took her other hand and gently urged her to be seated, his voice sharp, cutting through the concerned babble of the Dutton family.

"Was it the same men, Juliana, as the first attack upon you?"

Sarah's breath caught on a near sob and an instant hush settled over the room. Will moved sharply to attention, then Juliana shook her head helplessly, touching her throat as the sudden movement hurt her. Will's hands clenched, but still he said nothing.

"No," she said and coughed, cleared her throat, and continued in a strained whisper. "No. It was one man only, Pevie, tall and strong. More than that, I can't say. I didn't see" here she faltered, remembering that hand encircling her throat, squeezing the life from her "his face."

Pevie, his eyes grim, took in the shocked, silent faces of their companions.

"I see that Juliana hasn't informed you of her true reason for leaving the Point Lobos light station," he said. His questioning glance hesitated on Juliana. She inclined her head carefully, and he retold the story of the attack upon her as she walked the beach at Point Lobos.

"Incredible!" James said softly. "Your parents dead, your past a mystery, and the only clue to it all the necklace you wore when you were rescued from the sea!"

"James," Sarah said, reproving her younger brother, "you seem to overlook Juliana's danger in the drama of her early years." Her brother had the grace to blush.

"As I see it, then," Henry interrupted, "you'd do well to accept Father's offer, Miss Russell. The house is overrun with help. You need never be alone, at least until we get to the bottom of this matter."

"Please, Juliana!" James spoke urgently. "I know you don't like to hear me say it, but you saved my life. We'd be honor-bound to offer our assistance even if you weren't our friend. Please, let us help you?"

Pevie said nothing, but Juliana felt the solid bulwark of him next to her, lending his support.

"It seems I've nowhere left to run," she began, her eyes downcast. She looked up and met Sarah's troubled gaze. "Thank you, I accept." Pevie's hand tightened over hers, and she continued. "My things are packed, if you would help me fetch them, Mr. Pevie? And I'd like to speak with Libby before I leave."

Libby O'Bryan took one look at Juliana's face and gently pulled the younger woman into her arms for a timid embrace.

"You'll be leaving me, then?" As Juliana nodded, she slipped her hands free and caught Juliana's. "It's best, dear. 'Tis certain we can't look after you properly here. The Duttons will see to your safety, I'm sure. But, oh," she exclaimed softly and hugged Juliana, more strongly, "we'll miss you for sure." She straightened. "I'm thinking I just may find another girl to live-in. It's been that good to have another woman in the house. You take special care, now, won't you?"

In her room, Pevie picked up her valise, then set it down. He faced her squarely.

"'Tis true, Juliana, I don't much like you going there. It seems to me everything started after these people came into our lives. You could be walking into a trap."

Standing by the door, Juliana stirred restlessly.

"I know." She lifted helpless eyes to her childhood friend. "I know," she repeated. "It's what I've told myself. But I can't run forever, Pevie. Somehow I've got to find out who wants my life forfeit and why. I can't believe it would be James or Sarah or Henry." She faltered, unable to go on. If not them, then who? Will McKenna? She flinched at the thought, and Pevie came to her, his hands gripping her shoulders.

"Just stick to Sarah, me beauty, like a babe to its mother's skirts. Don't you be finding yourself alone with any of the others until we can sort this out."

"But how?" Juliana met his gaze, saw the fear and frustration boiling within her mirrored in his eyes.

"We'll find a way. We must."

At the buggy, Henry stowed her bag away as Sarah turned to Pevie.

"Mr. Pevie, if you've no other plans for the evening, will you dine with us? Father will be ever so pleased to meet you."

"Yes, do," James joined in, and Juliana's mute plea removed any hesitation he might have felt.

"Thank you, Miss Dutton. Sure and I'd like that very much."

Sarah's color deepened as her younger brother helped her into the buggy. Will's features tightened, and he caught Juliana's eye on him as she was handed in next to him. He turned his attention to the horses. A coldness settled in the pit of Juliana's stomach. Well, she thought crossly, if Will was put out by Pevie's presence, so be it. It was as obvious as the boot on her foot that Sarah was taken with Pevie, and Pevie, she thought, eyeing him as he stood watching them drive away, was a fit rival for any man. She lifted a hand in farewell.

Richard Dutton was nowhere to be seen when Sarah left Juliana in the room across the hall from hers at the back of the second floor. The bedroom had a forlorn air about it, as if little used, and as Juliana glanced about, it struck her as being plainer than the grand furnishings elsewhere in the mansion would have led her to expect. A simple curved iron bedstead, painted white, sat between two windows which overlooked the rear grounds. Next to the bed was a small dressing table with a low wooden stool, also painted white, a simple dark green cushion topping it. The walls were dove-gray, the woodwork white, the floor bare save for the bright splash of colors—deep reds and blues and greens—shining in a small Turkish rug. The same vibrant colors exploded across the patchwork quilt which covered the bed and a silk throw tossed casually across the arm of an over-sized wooden rocker placed to catch the light from a window.

Juliana lowered herself into this, absently stroking the shawl across her knees as she noted the pictures propped atop the mantelshelf, one of them a colored photograph of a thin, youthful woman in a deep emerald gown, seated before a backdrop of burgundy velvet curtains pooling on the floor. A quality of eagerness and a hint of humor lingered about that face with its unruly fair tresses. Other frames held sketches, watercolors, and surely, on the wall above the bed, that was a Lionel Adams still-life, a blue enameled pot turned on its side, spilling yellow pears out onto a rough planked tabletop that also held a lantern, a sheaf of asters in wild, fragile colors, and a small burlap sack, its top fallen open to reveal glistening coffee beans inside.

A sigh escaped her as one toe set the rocker gently to motion. The movement sent a hint of lavender adrift in the room. She was bone-achingly tired and afraid, her shoulders stiff with tension. She rocked some more, tilting her head back and closing her eyes. Softly she sang and found herself obscurely comforted by the melody.

"*Sleep, my love, and peace attend thee,*
All through the night;
Guardian angels God will send thee,
All through the night."

"I always loved that lullaby when I was a child." Sarah's wistful voice startled Juliana's eyes open. "Did your mother sing it to you? I always fell asleep in the middle of the second verse. Oh!" Sarah clapped her hand to her mouth. "Forgive me, Juliana, I didn't think."

"I must've stayed awake for at least that verse," Juliana replied with an attempt at a smile, shrugging. "Don't feel bad, Sarah. It just came to me as I rocked. My mother must have crooned it to me, but I remember nothing. Nothing," she repeated firmly and rose. "Do I have time to freshen up before lunch?"

With only Sarah and Juliana in attendance, luncheon was subdued. Juliana tried to attend to her hostess' attempts at conversation, but her head throbbed and she could summon no energy to respond to Sarah. After the plates were cleared, Sarah lay down her napkin.

"I won't attempt to entertain you, Juliana, and you mustn't feel that I require you to dance attendance upon me. May I suggest that you go straight up to bed? If you'd prefer, I can have Mrs. Martin send up a tray for supper."

Juliana managed a smile, impulsively gripping Sarah's hand.

"Thank you for understanding, Sarah. But could you see that I'm awakened in time to join you for dinner?" She most fervently wished to sleep, and only because she felt an obligation to her friends would she face dinner with their father. Her cheeks flamed anew as she recalled his insinuating remarks.

Juliana might have been meeting Richard Dutton for the first time when she came down for dinner. Sarah's father was coldly outraged at the attack upon her, offered her the hospitality of his home for as long as she cared to stay, and expressed his opinion of the San Francisco police force in no uncertain terms when two officers arrived shortly before dinner to take Juliana's statement.

No, she did not see the man who had accosted her. No, he did not attempt to grab her purse, nor did he say anything more than that quick warning when she attempted to scream. Yes, he meant to kill her. Here she pulled the scarf away from her throat, the bruises chillingly visible. The sergeant who was taking notes clucked sympathetically as he duly recorded the extent of her injuries, his small measure of human concern earning him a sour glance from his superior.

"There were no witnesses, miss, and very little evidence at the scene, save for the dust kicked up when your assailant dropped you. I'm afraid there's not much hope of finding the miscreant by now. Probably a drunken sailor. Try not to go about alone after dark." The officer nodded and pointed a finger at her. "You were lucky, Miss Russell, that Dr. McKenna saw fit to follow you home, else you might not be here today."

Will had followed her home? For what purpose? To drag her into that alley? But surely he wasn't nearly as tall as her attacker? To see that his man did the job properly? As she tried to order her confused thoughts, Richard broke the silence.

"Hmph. Clearly the local constabulary will spend little or no effort on solving your case," he remarked caustically as the door closed behind the officers. "I would like to apologize, Miss Russell, for my behavior at our previous encounter."

Acutely embarrassed, Juliana spoke hurriedly.

"It's forgotten as though it never happened, Mr. Dutton."

"You are too generous, my dear." He had the good manners to look sheepish and at the same time slightly amused by her discomfiture as he pushed his chair back from his desk. "I'm afraid James is all too easily taken in by a pretty face and pretty manners, Miss Russell." He drummed his fingers on the edge of his desk. "There have been several instances in which I've had to discourage, shall I say, several unsuitable young women." He smiled then. "The boy is like his mother, too sweet-natured to see behind a false front of affection. I regret to say that I was guilty of a hasty assumption when you appeared in San Francisco so suddenly upon my son's safe return from Santa Rena."

He stood up.

"I'm appalled by these attacks upon you, and, fortunately, I've more resources to spare than our local police force. Please hear me out, Miss Russell," he continued as Juliana squirmed. "I propose to hire a private detective agency, such as the Pinkertons, to get to the bottom of this affair."

"That's far too generous, Mr. Dutton," Juliana protested. He waved away her concerns.

"I can well afford to be generous, Miss Russell. After all, you gave back to me the life of my youngest child. Pray allow me to help you in any way that I can."

In the end, Juliana forbore arguing and acquiesced with a murmur of gratitude.

"Nonsense. I shall have Henry inquire into the services of an investigator at his earliest convenience tomorrow. Let me caution you to go nowhere alone, Miss Russell. This house is never empty of my staff; you need not fear these premises." He stood. "Now, shall we go in to dinner?"

Richard's good humor continued throughout dinner. Expertly and without the slightest hint of being patronizing, he drew Pevie into the conversation, which ranged from the inevitable discussion of the perils of a keeper's life to current events in San Francisco and California. Juliana could not help but compare this with his attitude toward her. Clearly Pevie was not pursuing his younger son; but had it not occurred to the man that his daughter was grown into a lovely woman, one worth pursuit by any clear-eyed gentleman?

As Juliana spooned up fresh berries and shortcake, she studied the expressions that crossed Richard's face as he conversed with his children and guests. His face bore a mild look of indulgence for Henry's spirited defense of the new port building on the waterfront. Henry thought it a bold edifice well-suited to a modern, cosmopolitan city. James took up the opposite position, more to egg his brother on than to express his real opinion, it seemed to Juliana, and to this their father listened with half an ear, his attention captured by every laugh or comment from Sarah.

No, Juliana thought with sudden insight, in his eyes they are still children, most especially Sarah. Sarah—nearly blind, protected but not coddled by her brothers, both of whom had sense and love enough to recognize and encourage her independence. But her father saw her still as a little girl, his only daughter, fragile and maimed and to be held aloft from the pains and troubles that life could bring. This Juliana understood from the involuntary wince that escaped him as Sarah adjusted her view back and forth from one speaker to the next.

But he is the one who cannot see, Juliana mused as she fought back a yawn, if he did not notice how animated Sarah's features became as she and Pevie planned a day's excursion around the sights of San Francisco.

It was colder now, the cold so fierce it bit deep into her marrow, cooling the very core of her physical being. The hand that pulled her along had long since ceased to feel as if it belonged to a separate being; the one to whom it was attached seemed simply to be an extension of herself. Head down, blinded by the snow, she drew upon the resilience that pushed her past endurance during all those long ago emergencies at the Point Lobos light station, when she had manned the oars with Pevie or Bernard. Chin tucked in, she set one foot in front of the other—her mind held somewhere in abeyance of this soul-chilling world—and followed the tug of the hand that guided her.

The dream chill lingered as Juliana came slowly awake in the pre-dawn darkness. As she curled up beneath her quilts, her movement released a teasing hint of lavender. She closed her eyes, willing warmth and sleep to return. If only... her sleepy mind turned some thought toward the light of consciousness... if only... a sigh escaped her and first one fat tear then another slid down her cheek to wet the pillow. Her mouth trembled once, like a child's hurt, then sleep reclaimed her and the puckered mouth eased, the unbidden thought slipping back into darkness.

"How do you do, Miss Russell?"

The deep voice addressed her as smoothly and politely as Richard Dutton might have done, but it belonged to Samuel T. Jones. His coffee-colored features rose in sharp contrast to the crisply starched white collar at his neck. Six feet tall, he was broad-shouldered and quiet on his feet.

"'T' for Terrible," he informed her with a twinkle far back in his eyes, "because my mam said I was terrible to behold as a child." A great booming laugh invited Juliana to join in. Her mouth twitched and she relaxed. Those quick dark eyes noted the moment of release, and the investigator slid a thin notebook from a pocket of his suit jacket.

"Mr. Dutton, he's already explained the bare facts of your present difficulties, Miss Russell. If you'd be so kind, I'd like you to repeat in detail as much as you can recall of each incident."

At first haltingly, then with more confidence, Juliana did as she was asked. When she reached her arrival at the Dutton's home, she stopped, chilled by the memories, her hand creeping to the collar of her dress. The Pinkerton agent caught that involuntary gesture and snapped his notebook shut.

"Right, miss. My job's questioning, watching, collecting and sorting information. Pinkerton will put some inquiries to hand. We'll keep you informed of my progress in the near future. Anything else happens—anything at all—let us know right away."

Richard nodded, clearly dismissing her as he turned his attention to Mr. Jones. Juliana found herself at loose ends for the remainder of the morning. Sarah had firmly let her know she was not expected to contribute in any fashion to the running of the household. Nor was she required to participate in any tedious round of morning calls. That, Sarah explained, was the province of the idle rich. Sarah filled her time by volunteering two mornings a week at a local kindergarten, and rolling bandages for the Red Cross or delivering luncheon to elderly shut-ins twice a week in the afternoons. Other times she attended to her duties as the presiding female in the Dutton household and with her women's groups.

Since Juliana had to meet with her father and the private investigator, Sarah had arranged to come home for lunch.

In the meantime, Juliana wondered, how was she to fill the hours until then? Browsing in the library, she pulled out a copy of Shakespeare's comedies and retreated to her room where she delved into *Much Ado About Nothing*. She had barely reached the scene of the masked ball, with Beatrice slandering a disguised Benedict, before her eyes grew heavy and the book fluttered to her lap. Really, she admonished herself, anyone would believe she was an invalid if she couldn't keep herself awake midmorning! Perhaps a short nap would refresh her, before Sarah returned. Maybe James would join them for lunch.

No sooner had she closed her eyes than she sat straight up in bed, listening intently. Had that been a faint step outside her door? Nothing stirred, no other sound reached her, and slowly she lay down again. Now her shoulder dug stiffly into the mattress, and she turned over. It was no use; she could not sleep on her left side. Maybe on her back. Groaning in defeat, Juliana swung her feet over the edge of her bed. A headache was coming on; she could feel the first faint pounding along her temples. Where had she put those headache powders the doctor gave her at Libby's? With mounting frustration she pawed among the contents of the dressing table to no avail. Where? She patted the pockets of her dressing robe. Empty, save for a handkerchief. This sense of panic was out of proportion to her need. If she could not find her powders, then perhaps Mrs. Martin could be persuaded to brew a cup of chamomile tea. Dr. McKenna would surely approve. Both doctors McKenna, she thought, a slight smile crossing her lips.

Mrs. Martin, sympathetic, prepared the tea as Juliana waited. Thanking her, Juliana took the fragrant tea and retreated to the library with her book. A quiet interlude might soothe and calm her. She sank into the deep red leather wingchair by the fireplace, her book open on her lap, and savored the aroma and taste of her tea. Back to Benedict, then, wounded by Beatrice's verbal beating and begging the prince to send him hence on any mission. Gradually she was drawn once more into the story, pausing to take more of her tea before it cooled, and at last her headache diminished.

With a start, Juliana came back from the sun-drenched Italian villa of the play and saw that it lacked an hour before luncheon and Sarah's return. She would beg a second cup of tea from the kitchen to take upstairs as she dressed for lunch. She had reached a decision even as her conscious thought was engrossed with Dogsberry and his band of half-witted constables. Idleness was not suited to her nature. There must be some gainful employment to fill her hours, some worthwhile cause in need of her energy and talents. Sarah would understand and plead her case to Richard Dutton. Juliana could not hide forever.

She stopped, her gaze focusing sharply in the here and now. She took a quick breath of air, her grasp tightening on the china cup she held. A portrait faced her, hung between two sets of bookshelves that had hidden it from view. This was the face of a Dutton, no mistaking the stern features, the air of authority, the high cheekbones and blue eyes. The man was within a few years the age of Richard Dutton, but it was not he. Even from his portrait, this man commanded one's attention. He seemed to look her over from head to toe, comparing her to some unyielding standard, judging her in the same instant, and finding her wanting. A sneer might have curved those full lips.

"No! No!" Her breath came out in a rush of denial as she flinched away from the portrait, flinging up her hands to ward off that harsh gaze.

Teacup and saucer crashed to the carpet, unheeded. Juliana picked up her skirts and fled to her room. Safe in the rocking chair, she pulled the silk throw about her and rocked, murmuring over and over as tears coursed down her cheeks.

"I am Juliana. I am Juliana," she repeated over and over until her words pierced her fear and hurt and she stopped rocking in confusion. "I am... Juliana," she repeated, uncertainly. "Juliana," she whispered to herself, "Juliana Russell."

Sarah didn't press Juliana for conversation during luncheon, for James joined them after all. He too was quiet and reflective, barely responding when his sister addressed him. Halfway through the soup, he stood suddenly and excused himself, pleading a headache.

Juliana watched as Sarah bit her lip anxiously. Her friend turned impulsively to her as they heard the front door open and close.

"Juliana, would you like to accompany me to visit Marthe this afternoon? We'll find her at the clinic like as not, but with any luck she'll have a moment to spare us."

So it was that Juliana found herself being driven with Sarah to a double Queen Anne house on Webster Street. Timothy—stable boy, groom, and driver—handed Sarah down, before offering a hand to Juliana. Tidy flowerbeds graced the small plots of lawn to either side of the walk which ran up to a shared porch upon which two bay windows and entry doors mirrored one another. The two sides of the house differed in one significant detail. The right side had a graceful squared tower that spanned two stories with the third open to the elements beneath its roof. The tower lent the house a certain touch of whimsy that appealed to Juliana. Sarah knocked on the left-hand door. It opened after a moment to a pert young woman with striking wheat-blonde hair escaping her cap. Her wide mouth curved into a delighted smile as she clasped Sarah's hand and drew her inside.

"Good afternoon, Miss Sarah!"

"Good afternoon, Annabelle."

"Dr. Marthe is taking a breather, Miss Sarah. You've come at just the right time. Let me take your wraps," she said and nodded as Sarah shed hers. "Go on through." She nodded again briskly, still beaming.

Juliana followed Sarah down the hallway with its benches—it was Dr. McKenna's waiting room—through to a door at the rear of the hall. Knocking as she opened it, Sarah called out.

"It's just Sarah, dear. And I've Juliana with me."

The door gave onto a sitting room where sunlight played through lace curtains. The light fell across a polished wooden floor, an upright piano, stacks of papers, and books piled high upon a low table, striking a sofa where Marthe McKenna half-reclined. She opened one eye.

"I'd jump up and hug you, Sarah my dear, but I'm exhausted. Hello, Miss Russell!" She laughed, straightened her spine and moved a pillow. "Please join me."

Sarah looked at her friend with sympathy and concern.

"Not Mrs. Labeaux?" Sarah asked.

Marthe's gray eyes crinkled at the corners and her curls bobbed as she nodded, sighing hugely.

"And her brood," she added dryly.

"All of them?" Sarah accepted a cup of tea from Annabelle.

"No. Only the six youngest," Marthe explained. "Each one whining for a treat and walloping the next smallest one when their mother wasn't looking!" She laughed. Her shrewd eyes took in Juliana's pallor, although she said nothing. Her glance took in Sarah, who was fidgeting with her saucer and cup. "He's still having headaches, isn't he?"

Sarah let out a sigh of relief, her mobile features tinged with worry and guilt.

"I hate to add to your burdens, Marthe, but Jimmy came home with another vile headache this afternoon. Do you think you should see him again?"

Marthe rose and gestured to Sarah.

"Step into the office a moment, dear. Let me check my notes, then perhaps we'll try a stronger prescription for young Jimmy. If you will excuse us, Miss Russell?"

Juliana set aside her half-finished cup of tea and pressed her fingertips to the base of her skull, kneading her neck muscles. Her own headache was beginning again. Maybe she should ask Dr. McKenna for a stronger sedative herself. Through the partially opened door, she could hear Sarah's troubled voice and Marthe's murmured replies. Restlessly, she wandered to the window, where the drapes were pulled back to let the day's light brighten Marthe's sitting room.

The view overlooked the rear of the lot on which the house stood. A tall hedge along a fence to the left gave plenty of privacy, while to the right and rear of the lot, a small stable served the same purpose.

Between this and the rear addition lay an orderly kitchen garden with vines trellised up the stable wall and fruit trees neatly espaliered along the fence which edged the property line between stable and house along the far side of the garden.

The other half of the lot was given over to herb and flower gardens with room only for a sundial in the midst of the former and a bench in the center of the latter. Juliana identified roses and daisies and surely those were lilies, but many other flowers blossomed in profusion. The total effect was of a lovingly tended riot of color and smells. Juliana thought of the ordered gardens at the Dutton estate, their stiff homogeneity cold compared to this inviting informality.

Turning away from the sight, Juliana drifted idly to the table with its stacks of books. No light reading here; these were all massively thick tomes stacked one upon another. Picking one up, Juliana was startled to see foliage sticking out from the book.

Marthe's light laugh resounded from the door.

"I see you've discovered my brother's treasures, Miss Russell. He isn't content to have his own rooms strewn with all manner of flattened flora; he needs must clutter my space as well!"

Picking up a book at random, the doctor carefully opened its pages to reveal a delicate pressed flower with buds, leaves, and stem intact.

"Treasures?" Juliana asked.

"He brings them back from his travels," Sarah told her, and Marthe nodded and continued.

"They're specimens to be tested eventually for curative properties, but until they've been accurately drawn and labeled, they over-run every available inch of space."

"Drawn?" Juliana began to feel half-witted, repeating the word as a glimmer of hope opened before her.

"Yes. If a plant shows promise, it must be fully identified and recorded for future research."

"And who," Juliana ventured, "does the drawings? James?"

"Oh no," Sarah said and laughed. "To be fair, he's done a few over the years, but Will wouldn't let him do more."

"My brother doesn't want to interrupt Jimmy's work," his sister explained. "So Will hires local artists when he can find someone with an eye for detail who's reliable. His last artist moved back east a year ago, and no one has proved suitable since. Hence," she added with an expansive wave, "the clutter."

Sarah's face grew still as she took in the stacks of books, then she swung around and gripped her friend by the arm.

"Marthe, I've the answer to your need. Juliana! She's a marvelous artist. Her watercolors are superb!

"Really? How perfect! Juliana, what do you say?"

Juliana gulped, unable to speak. Before her lay hours of work, work that needed exactly her skills, work that needed to be done, work to keep her mind from the dark atmosphere that pervaded her waking hours at the Duttons'.

Marthe looked at Sarah's eager expression, the mute appeal and hunger in Juliana's eyes, and nodded decisively. Opening a window, she leaned over the sill to pluck a geranium from a flowerbox.

"Here, take this home and make a study of it. When you've finished, we'll show it to Will and see if he approves."

"Thank you, Marthe." Juliana clasped the doctor's hands in hers. "In the morning, when the light is best, I'll begin."

"You can use Jimmy's studio. I'm sure he won't mind." Sarah hugged her friend, brushing her lips across Marthe's cheek. "Thank you for everything, dear."

With a borrowed smock over her shirtwaist, Juliana sat at a work table in Jimmy's studio, her paints to one side. First she would sketch the geranium as it lay before her, blossoms and leaves together. Then she would do a close-up of the flower. As she planned, she was already putting pencil to paper. Only after she was satisfied with the pencil sketches would she reach for her watercolors. Caught up in that easy flow of intense concentration, Juliana didn't note the passage of time or the increasing stiffness in her back until at last she lay down her brush and looked with weary satisfaction at her collection of pencil and watercolor studies of the red geranium. Surely the good doctor would find the samples ample demonstration of the seriousness of her intent. Carefully, Juliana refrained from identifying to herself which doctor whose praise she sought.

A hand reached over her shoulder to pick up a sketch.

"Lovely!" James leaned a hip against the work

table. "Sarah told me you've been volunteered to help Will. You don't mind?"

As she shook her head, he absently dipped a brush in the water container to clean it; his gaze sweeping the large room. Two work tables and an easel stood grouped near tall windows. Stools were clustered about these, while a series of cabinets flanked a wall, holding neatly mustered supplies. Racks held frames and an untidy group of canvases were stacked with their backs to the room. Juliana hadn't explored these, feeling that James might think her presence in his studio intrusive enough without her prying.

"I love this room," he said softly. "My Aunt Katherine was an artist. This was her private studio when she was younger, before she married." One hand gestured at the well-lighted space with its sturdy, practical furnishings. "Sometimes, I feel as if she's still here, working alongside me, although lately...." His blue eyes turned to Juliana, a slight flush along his cheekbones. "I don't mind you working up here, Juliana. I enjoyed painting with you by the bay.

"Please," he rushed on as she opened her mouth to reply, "please, I'm not trying to embarrass you, Juliana. It's just that Father doesn't seem to approve of my friends, nor of... me," he added lamely, then shrugged. "I liked working with you."

Juliana smiled and rose.

"And I with you, James. If Dr. McKenna agrees, perhaps I can do some of the work here if he'll allow me to bring his precious specimens home." She gathered her sketches together. "You don't work with your Aunt Katherine? Doesn't she paint any longer?"

"No!" The vehemence of his reply startled Juliana. "No!" He winced.

Juliana made a movement toward him as he rubbed his head.

"Another headache. I'm afraid I'll get no work done today. Will you excuse me, Juliana?"

She followed him from the room. Her initial spurt of energy deserted her. Time enough in the morning to share her sketches with Sarah. A light supper in her room and to bed early, then, to rest up for what the morrow might bring.

CHAPTER SEVEN

For one curious moment, Juliana thought she saw pleasure flare in those cool gray eyes as Will silently held her sketches one by one up to the light in Marthe's sitting room. After she presented Juliana's work to her brother, Marthe had gone out seeing patients. Juliana hadn't known Will would be in, and she kept her hands deliberately relaxed in her lap as she awaited his response.

In the silence, she could hear Sarah talking from the hallway.

"Mrs. Harris, why don't you come by the kindergarten one morning and see for yourself the head start it will give your Albert and Ernest with their schooling? Imagine having a little time to yourself mornings...."

After what seemed an interminable wait, the Dr. McKenna of immediate concern to Juliana turned his attention to her, his eyes alight with satisfaction.

"These are wonderful!" He handed the sketches back to her reluctantly. "You can start any time. I've a workroom in the tower you may use if you wish. I pay a flat rate per piece, twenty-five cents each, but I do provide supplies. I'm particular about the quality of paper and paints used for my studies. Is this agreeable?"

Work to do—and pay for it as well?

"Agreed." She put out a hand to cement their deal. Will shook it gravely. "I'll begin this morning, if that's convenient?"

"It is beyond my wildest hopes."

He turned away from her as the clinic door

opened and Marthe came in, though he was still speaking. "Tell me, did you take up painting to capture the wild coast at Point Lobos?"

"No," she said absently, her attention distracted by the sketches and the promise they represented. "I used to play with colors all the time as a child."

"So you have the job?" Marthe asked, looking with sharp interest from one face to the other. "How wonderful! Please, Juliana," she begged dramatically, waving her hands at the room before her, "feel free to begin with any of these massive tomes. With any luck, my sitting room will be cleared of Will's treasures before he collects another batch!"

Her words were graced with good humor, and she gave her brother a dazzling smile. "I'm teasing, Juliana. Don't let Will rush your work in any fashion."

She linked her arm with Juliana's.

"I've a smock you may borrow, whenever you want to begin."

Juliana nodded, but her eyes were on Will's as her own words echoed in her mind: *I used to play with colors all the time as a child* .... She hadn't picked up watercolors at Point Lobos until she was fourteen and restless, without any companions her own age to keep her company. She didn't remember playing with paints, but the statement rang true somewhere deep inside her, and she knew it was some memory from her life before Point Lobos.

She forced her attention back to Marthe and found Will's gray eyes fixed upon her, a question glinting in their depths.

"I'll begin at the Dutton's, if I may? James has

offered to share his studio with me."

"How wonderful! Is he painting then?" Marthe asked, and Juliana could only shake her head. Quick disappointment and concern flooded Marthe's face.

Juliana said, "I only know that there's a stack of canvases in the studio."

Marthe turned to her brother. "He's not himself, Will, and it worries me."

He hugged her.

"Give it time," he said reassuringly. "Nature must finish the healing process."

Every day after that, Juliana breakfasted early to take advantage of the first strong morning light, and she set to her task with a will. Those moments in the studio became her refuge from the oppressive weight that seemed to have permanently settled over her since her arrival at the house at Webster and Broadway Street.

Each new specimen absorbed her, drew her into a forested vision that soothed her fears and comforted her. She soon fell into a routine. At midmorning she would take a break, a habit encouraged by James, who'd begun to join her regularly. At first he stayed only while she had her tea or coffee, often bringing her tray himself; but later, after the first week, he pulled a stool up to a window, then spent time rummaging in a cupboard. He never mentioned the unfinished canvases. Juliana had quickly looked them over in light of Marthe's comments and found not one completed, not even the one of the bay. He never, to her knowledge, went out to paint anymore. Where and how he spent his days were unknown.

"You don't mind if I join you for a while, do you, Juliana?" He frowned. "Haven't seen my sketchbook, have you? I'm sure it wasn't filled." He shrugged at his absentmindedness and pulled a fresh one from a drawer, chose a charcoal pencil and art eraser, then positioned himself at the stool where he could overlook the view of the side yard, the street below, and Juliana. Sometimes as they worked together she'd feel his eyes on her and knew he was adding another sketch of her to his growing collection. She didn't mind, for his headaches came less and less to bother him on those days he joined her; even Sarah remarked upon how much better her younger brother looked.

Luncheons were usually taken with Sarah or sometimes James, while at times Sarah arranged for Juliana to meet her for lunch, often in the Latin Quarter, and once at the regal Palace Hotel. After such outings, they often attended a meeting of one or the other of Sarah's clubs. Once a week, on Thursdays, Juliana would make her way to the clinic to deliver her most recent batch of drawings for Will's appraisal.

He was always at home on those days, escorting her to his study in the tower where he scrutinized each drawing as though greeting old friends. A particular drawing might elicit a grunt, a chuckle, or a sigh. After the first such display, he looked up to catch the uncertainty on her face. Did he not approve?

"Juliana! I'm sorry I laughed. Rest assured, I'm not mocking your splendid efforts." A grin lit up his features as he tapped the sketch in his hands. "You should've seen me trying to reach this specimen. It's a creeper, you see. The blossoms were opening high up on the tree trunk. I made several false starts, and at last was making progress up the trunk toward my elusive prize. When I reached out to pluck a specimen, the 'vine' I was clinging to uncoiled and I found myself falling backwards with a very startled snake in my grasp! Fortunately," he added with exaggerated relief, "*not* poisonous! It slithered away as soon as we hit the ground." He tapped the drawing and grinned again. "But I won my prize!" Juliana laughed.

On one such occasion, Annabelle greeted her at the door.

"Dr. Will is assisting Dr. Marthe in the clinic, Miss Russell. He said you may leave the sketches or wait, if you'd like?"

"I'll wait, please." These afternoons were her one certain respite from the Dutton house, the doctors' home always welcoming, like a refuge. Yesterday had been especially upsetting, but she had no one with whom to discuss the incident. She was certain that she'd caught a glimpse of Samuel T. Jones in the morning from the studio window as she'd taken her break, alone for once. But by the time she ran downstairs, there was no sign of the Pinkerton detective. Henry, whom she found in the library, assured her that his father was at the office and no one had come calling. Henry did not explain his own presence in the house at such an hour, and Juliana did not think it her place to ask. Had there been news? Why not let her hear Mr. Jones' report? Why would Henry lie?

She noticed as she paced Dr. Marthe's sitting room that her clothes were beginning to hang loosely upon her frame. Her appetite had abandoned her, and it was only for Sarah's and James' sakes that she made any effort at all to eat at mealtimes. Both Faith and Pevie wrote to her weekly, Faith filling her letters with details of life on the station to take her mind from her troubles, while Pevie grew increasingly impatient with the lack of progress in her case. He was, he told her, coming to San Francisco to relieve the Angel Station lighthouse keeper for the few days it would take the keeper to attend the funeral of an aunt in southern Oregon. Pevie went on to write that at the insistence of Bernard, he was extending his stay by two days in order to see her and carry back reassurances to the station master and Faith that Juliana was well-cared for.

Richard Dutton had been distracted at supper last night, retiring directly after their meal to his study with the terse command that he not be disturbed. Unwilling to intrude upon her host, in spite of her certainty that Mr. Jones had been around to the house, Juliana had bidden Sarah a good-night and retired upstairs. Standing before her door, she'd hesitated, then made her way to James' studio.

Critically, she studied each sketch she'd prepared for delivery to Will McKenna the next morning. A soft step sounded behind her, and Sarah moved into the lamplight.

"Is everything all right, Juliana? I saw the light," she explained, joining Juliana at the work table and staring down at the paintings spread there.

"No, nothing's wrong, Sarah. I wanted to look these over once more."

As Sarah gazed around the room, a small smile tugged at the corners of her mouth.

"Jimmy's always retreated here to paint. Ever since we were children and would come to visit our grandparents. I used to sit by the window and keep him company."

"James told me that your Aunt Katharine was an artist, that this was her studio when she—"

Sarah's face blanched, and Juliana quickly said, "Sarah! I'm sorry!" She took a step toward her friend. "Are you okay?"

"No! Yes," Sarah forced herself to speak calmly, cast a wan smile at Juliana, and sank down upon a stool. "How silly of me! It's the shock of hearing her name." She met Juliana's puzzled gaze.

"While Great-Uncle James Dutton was alive, Aunt Katharine's name was never spoken in this house."

She sighed. "We still don't speak of her. Once when I was very little, Henry asked Great-Aunt Lucy Dutton when Aunt Katharine was coming home. Great-Uncle James overheard him and threatened to cane poor Henry on the spot. You see, Aunt Katharine and Uncle Leland doted on us; Father was their only cousin and they adored Mama. We called them aunt and uncle. I was only four years old when Uncle Leland took sick and died and Aunt Katharine died not long after."

"How sad," Juliana remarked. "They had no children?"

"What?" Sarah looked startled. "Oh no, Juliana, of course, I didn't explain. Uncle Leland and Aunt Katharine were brother and sister. Uncle Leland was a composer and Aunt Katharine was a painter." She stood up and moved to a window before turning back to the room and Juliana. "Great-Uncle James, according to Mama, was angry with both his children because they wouldn't bow to his wishes. Uncle Leland was a serious composer and had a small inheritance from a maternal uncle. He refused to join his father in a business career. And Aunt Katharine rebelled as well—she was passionate about her art and chose to live her life as she saw fit." She sighed.

"Poor Great-Uncle James, he couldn't find it in himself to accept them as they were," she spoke gently, and Juliana wondered whether Sarah saw the same willful refusal in her own father. "Then Uncle Leland died from pneumonia, and Aunt Katharine soon after. Great-Uncle James had a stroke within a month of her death and never fully recovered. It was arranged that my parents should live here to help with the business and to care for Great-Uncle James and Great-Aunt Lucy."

She was silent, and Juliana took advantage of the moment to remark.

"Your great-uncle must have been terribly bitter, to not have forgiven his daughter even after her death."

Sarah shook her head sadly.

"I don't wish to speak ill of the dead, but Great-Uncle James was a proud, unforgiving man. Aunt Katharine defied him, first because she was serious about her painting, and second...." Color flooded Sarah's cheeks and she whispered, "because she lived a bohemian lifestyle and was the mistress of some unsuitable gentleman."

"I see," Juliana said, and cast an appraising eye

around the studio. This room had been Katharine Dutton's workspace. The woman had planned this methodical, workmanlike room. Clean, well-organized, and stripped to the bare essentials—everything about it spoke of the determination to work at her art. And she wondered at the 'unsuitable gentleman'—had he been chosen simply to defy her disapproving father? If the man had encouraged her artistic endeavors, perhaps he had suited Katherine in spite of society and her father's expectations.

Clearly, the young woman had been as strong-willed in her short life as she had needed to be to be true to herself. Although the old man had banished her name, he hadn't been able to eradicate her spirit. It still shone in this place she had made her own. Juliana felt a sudden, powerful longing to have known this woman with whom she felt a kindred spirit. Tears welled up in her eyes and she blinked them away before Sarah might notice.

"Come," Juliana said, placing her hand on Sarah's arm, "it's late. Let's go down."

At her bedroom door, she paused. "Sarah?"

"Hmm?"

"Was this Katharine's room?"

Sarah turned from her own door.

"Why, yes. Yes, it was. Good-night."

Closing her door behind her, Juliana turned up the light and surveyed the room. The old man might have hated his daughter's choices, but it was clear that he'd left her room just the way she'd last seen it. For remembrance? Or because even in death he could not let her go? The thought made her feel sick to her stomach. Tomorrow, if only for a little while, she could leave this house behind.

When he came out of his sister's surgery and spread her work out in his study, Will McKenna gave no more than a cursory look at Juliana's fresh group of sketches, reaching instead for his hat and her elbow.

"The day is filled with sunshine for a change, Juliana. I need to get away from my studies, and that strong-minded sister of mine has cajoled me into paying a home visit to two of her favorite patients. I'm taking you along."

He swept her from the study and down the stairs to Marthe's surgery before Juliana could utter a protest. Not, she thought as she caught her breath, that she wanted to return to the Dutton household. The old man's spiteful image seemed to dominate the house, and Sarah was occupied with committee meetings. Juliana would find the hours long enough stretching before her once Will's errand was ended.

Marthe tucked a packet into her brother's pocket and kissed him swiftly on the cheek.

"Give my love to them both and tell them I'll come see them one afternoon soon."

Setting off for the trolley-car stop, Will adjusted his loping stride to Juliana's pace and whistled cheerfully. Hands in his pockets, his gaze took in the streets around them, the horse traffic, the passersby—anything and anyone except Juliana, all the way to the stop. Suddenly tongue-tied, she stood and waited quietly beside him, feeling her shoulders begin to lose their stiffness as the sunshine worked its magic. When their trolley came, Will gripped her elbow once more and propelled her onto the car before him, ushering her to a seat near the rear of the car. Content to let him guide her, she relaxed even more so and felt a small smile beginning to form at the corners of her mouth.

When they left the line and started walking again, Juliana glanced curiously at her companion. Will's bright whistle had faded away as the trolley took them into the Latin Quarter. From her stay at Libby O'Bryan's boardinghouse, she recognized some of the landmarks about them and soon saw in the distance St. Francis, the small church where she had joined Libby at Mass. As she turned to look at the man at her side, Juliana found him watching her and surprised uncertainty in that gaze. At once he smiled and nodded as he wheeled in at the gate of a small cottage.

"Here we go, then."

Juliana stared speechlessly at the elderly man who opened the door to them, feeling shock hit her as she recognized him. Will and the old man embraced heartily and exchanged kisses on each cheek.

"Papa Nunzio, this is Miss Juliana Russell, the young artist who drew the sketches I showed you last week." He turned to present Juliana. The old man's face held the same sense of sorrow and dignity she had glimpsed at Mass at St. Francis.

"Juliana, this is Mr. Nunzio Giuliano, a dear friend."

As she stammered a flustered greeting, old Mr. Giuliano smiled gravely at her.

"Please, you are well, *signorina*?" His voice was welcoming, and he indicated a door to the right of the tiny vestibule in which they stood. "Please, you come in, yes?. Come in, be seated."

He raised his voice and directed a stream of rapid Italian at the rear of the house. A rich laugh answered him.

Juliana seated herself uneasily on a stiff-backed chair. The old man's eyes never left her face, and she pressed her hands together, striving to still the trembling that seemed to transfer itself from her hands to her left knee until her leg was quivering. It was much too warm in the tiny cottage. Sweat beaded on her upper lip and one hand went to her collar.

Mr. Giuliano's gaze was diverted from her as Will drew the packet from his pocket and extended it to his friend.

"Marthe sends her love to you both and also this, ah..." He broke off as a diminutive figure bustled into the room with a large tray. Her husband took it from her, and she hugged Will, laughing and scolding him all at once. He laughed and responded.

"Yes, I'm heartless for not visiting more often, but I've brought you a visitor, *cara mia*." He stepped aside to present her to Juliana.

The small, white-haired figure beamed in her direction, then the smile began to falter. Juliana went suddenly still in her chair. The gentle brown eyes, the soft round cheeks crinkled with fourscore years, the scar puckered above her right eye. All the blood drained from her face and without a sound, Juliana pitched straight forward onto the floor.

"Nana Angelina, look, look, I'm a starfish! I've got five arms. Starfish! Starfish!" the child chanted, twirling around and around on the warm sand.

"Bambina, you must stop before you make

yourself sick. Stop, stop, no more whirling today. Enough starfish. Basta. Be my little girl again, si?"

The child ran into her grandmother's arms for a fierce hug.

"I love you, Nana Angelina. Will you tell me a story if we sit over there?"

No, no, no! Don't go over there! Don't go! Juliana screamed helplessly, soundlessly in her mind as the sun glanced off the restless sea, the waves rushing onto the beach and rolling back again as the small round grandmother and her granddaughter picked their way along the sand to a sheltered tumble of boulders. Even as Nana Angelina settled herself comfortably, two figures rose up from behind the rocks, one roughly pushing the old woman from her perch and one seizing the screaming child.

"*Nana Angelina! No, no!*" Through the screams, Juliana could hear other voices, urgently speaking, but the sense of their words could not penetrate her terror.

"She's in shock. Bring blankets, Nana. Papa Nunzio, send Alberto for my sister. Hurry!"

The filthy hands clapped a vile rag over her nose and mouth. A strong, penetrating odor overcame her, and the bright afternoon sunshine, the feel of the wind against her bare legs, the beach, her grandmother lying unmoving on the beach all faded away.

When she came to, she was lying on a narrow bed that swayed back and forth. Without moving, she barely opened her eyes and saw a thin, dark woman sitting on the bunk next to her own. A boat, then. The woman looked up, suddenly, as if aware *of the eyes of the child upon her, and moved quickly to her side as she closed her eyes tightly.*

The woman leaned over her, smelling of stale beer and old fish. She whispered harshly in her ear.

"Listen to me, little girl. We have killed your grandmother, the fat old one, and we have killed your mother and your father, too. If you say a word to anyone, we will kill you. Understand?"

The child lay still, unresponsive and felt the woman's shrug as she straightened up.

"Bah! You are our little girl now, until we say otherwise. We will kill you if you do not obey us."

The small body shuddered against its will, and the eyes tightened as tears spilled upon her cheeks. Laughing, the woman lowered herself to her bunk.

The rocking of the boat was gone, Juliana realized muzzily. They must have put in to port somewhere. She moved restlessly, trying to clear sleep from her mind, and at once, a cool hand was pressed to her forehead. She recoiled in fear and jerked her eyes open.

A young woman leaned over her, her gray eyes sharp with concern and sympathy. Slowly the fear faded, and Juliana turned her head from Marthe to the small room where she lay on a wooden bed that creaked as she moved. Lace curtains fluttered at an open window that let light and air into the room. A crucifix hung above a heavy chest of drawers. Except for a woman's sewing rocker, the room was otherwise bare.

"How are you, Juliana?"

A sound reached them from somewhere else in the house, and Juliana flinched. "My head hurts and my throat is dry. May I have some water?"

After drinking thirstily, she sat up shakily, Marthe plumping her pillows behind her back.

"Juliana, my dear, my foolish brother is beside himself with worry. May he come in for a moment?"

At her hesitant nod, Marthe stepped into the room beyond, opening the door again to admit Will.

"Little monkey." He stooped to sit on the edge of the bed and take her hand carefully in his. "You gave us quite a scare. Are you recovered enough to tell us what happened?"

Juliana's eyes squeezed together as tears ran down her cheeks like the long-ago child she had been, but this time two strong arms enfolded her and rocked her gently, whispering, "Shh, little monkey, shh. You're safe with me."

When her sobs ceased, she lay back against her pillows and stared at the door.

"I thought she was dead. Nana Angelina. *She* said Nana was dead. *They* weren't my parents. I said they weren't, but no one believed me. I... I wished they would die. And then, then the storm came up. It was horrible. Water was everywhere. And wind. You couldn't see anything. We made it on deck, then the ship cracked. Like a toy boat."

She shuddered at the memory. "They did die. In the storm. I... I thought I killed them. It was the last thought I had before I woke up again with Faith and Bernard. That I killed those two. And I could never go to visit their graves. How could I, when I was a murderer?"

Her face crumpled again, and she balled her fists, sitting in bed stiffly, crying silently, like a small child, the pent-up guilt and fear and despair released at last. Will reached his arms to her, as he had done to that little girl long ago. Wordlessly he held her, gazing down at the dark cloud of hair, rocking her and stroking her head until he felt her body relax as her sobs ceased and her breathing became less ragged and more even, slipping into sleep.

This time when she awoke, morning sunshine flooded the tiny bedroom. Dressing quietly, she stepped into the parlor. Sounds and smells guided her footsteps to the kitchen at the back of the house. Her mouth suddenly dry, her feelings shy, she took a quick step back toward the haven of the empty parlor, her fingers nervously pinching her handkerchief. It was too late to retreat to her room. Her grandmother turned from the stove at the sound of her footsteps and bustled over to the table with a pan of browned biscuits.

"Sit, sit, Katerina," she encouraged Juliana. "Breakfast is hot. Eat! Eat!" She raised her voice at the back door.

"Nunzio, eh? Breakfast!" Shrugging, she came to the table, but could not sit still. One small plump hand strayed toward Juliana, then she restrained herself and instead poured a cup of coffee, finishing it off with rich milk and sipping absently as she watched her granddaughter eat.

"Katerina...." Juliana repeated wonderingly to herself. "Maria Katerina Giuliano," she said aloud and looked up to see tears streaming down her grandmother's face. Juliana pressed palms to her eyes, but the sobs broke past her hands, and she felt her grandmother's arms come about her. Blindly she embraced her, crying brokenly over and over.

"Nana Angelina, they said you were dead. They said you were dead."

When the sobs choked into a hiccough, a handkerchief was pressed into her hand, and Juliana released her grandmother to find Papa Nunzio regarding them both, his own eyes damp.

"Papa Nunzio," she tried to smile, looking beyond him where Will McKenna had just appeared. "Poppa said I was his first Giuliano," she started to say, then her voice caught and she pressed her fist to her heart and fought to hold back another sob.

"After... after the storm, I couldn't remember anything—except that. Poppa called me his first Giuliano. When Faith and Bernard asked my name, Giuliano was all I could say."

"And they misunderstood, calling you Juliana," Will put in softly, passing her a steaming mug of coffee

"Yes. So I became Juliana Russell. Katerina Giuliano." Her head ached as though split apart, whirling her thoughts like a kaleidoscope of broken pieces. How they might settle, into which pattern, she couldn't guess. Juliana Russell. Katerina Giuliano. *Who was she?* Her swift, panic-stricken gaze swept past her grandmother to Papa Nunzio. His features softened as he watched her struggle. She saw no bewilderment or confusion in that steady regard, just a calm acceptance and a quiet joy. She cast her eyes down at her twisting fingers, ashamed that such joy did not fill her.

"In time, granddaughter, you will make peace with yourself." Her grandfather's soft words brought a grateful flush to her cheeks, and she smiled timidly at him and took a deep breath to steady herself.

"How did you guess?" She directed her first question at Will.

He in turn looked at Nana Angelina, who rose and returned momentarily with a small portrait. Juliana found herself staring at herself, aged five years.

Will touched the portrait.

"Nana was ill earlier this year with a long bout of influenza. I helped Papa Nunzio and Marthe nurse her. During the long hours of those nights, I often stared at that portrait. When we were thrown together during the storm and its aftermath at Point Lobos, you seemed so familiar. It wasn't until last week, when I came by to drop off Nana's medicine, that I remembered the portrait. I'm sorry, Juliana, that I didn't confide in you. I wasn't absolutely certain. I'm afraid I didn't think what a shock this could be for you after all these years."

Juliana swallowed hard, looking from one grandparent to the other.

"All these years, I was so close to you and never knew. I came to the Point Lobos light station during a terrible storm. The ship that I was on was driven aground and sank. The two people who kidnapped me—and left Nana Angelina for dead—they told me my parents were dead and that Nana Angelina was dead, too. And they said that they would kill me, if I made any trouble for them."

Her grandmother clucked under her breath and her grandfather's brows drew close together.

"They drowned in the storm, but I don't know who they were. Or why they seized me," she finished helplessly. All those years when she would not remember, could not bear to remember her beloved

Nana struck down, her parents dead. She shook her head. If those two had lied about her grandmother?

"My…" almost she could not ask it, did not want to hear her worst fears confirmed. "My parents?"

Papa Nunzio shook his head gravely.

"They were alive when you were taken, granddaughter, although it nearly killed them when they could not find you."

"Katerina was like a wild thing." Nana Angelina's eyes darkened as she remembered. "She blamed her papa. That one—" she blessed herself, "he told her she should come home to him, and he would use his fortune to search for the little one.

"But Katerina refused him once again and would not leave Renato." Nana's mouth trembled, and her husband squeezed her hand. His eyes sought Juliana's.

"Renato met your mama on the wharf one day, granddaughter. We did not know what to make of this fine lady—Miss Katherine Dutton—who won our Renato's heart."

"Renato," Will put in quietly, "was not one to have his head turned easily, for all that he was a handsome fellow."

"Katerina knew her mind," Papa Nunzio continued. "That, we could tell soon enough. She was an artist, a painter. When she and Renato were married, and she had her husband and her painting, and later, her little Katerina, she was a happy woman."

"Except for her papa. That one," her grandmother said, again blessing herself, "he couldn't bear to have his daughter married to our son. Nor would he acknowledge his own grandchild."

Juliana listened in a daze, a sudden memory springing to mind.

"He lied! Grandfather Dutton lied!" She looked around the table at her father's parents and at Will. "His family thinks Mama was Poppa's mistress. Sarah told me that Grandfather never forgave her for leaving and that she died not long after my Uncle Leland passed away."

Her gaze turned inward as she remembered.

"We went to that house," she said, her voice barely a whisper. "All the windows were draped in black, I remember. Poppa didn't go, but Mama and I took the trolley and I held Mama's hand. I didn't want to go into that house. Grandmama Dutton gave me a peppermint, then we went into the big room where Uncle Leland lay. Mama cried, and so did I.

She dampened her lips. "Then *he* was there. Grandfather Dutton. He took Mama into another room to talk with her. Grandmama Dutton held me on her lap and stroked my hair until I stopped crying. Then the door to the other room opened and Mama came out. Grandfather Dutton followed her and raised his cane as if to strike her! But Grandmama stopped him, and Mama hugged her hard and took me, and we left." Her gaze focused on the present.

"He hated Mama as much as he loved her. And he hated me. I saw it in his eyes when he looked at me."

"And Katerina was married to our Renato," Nana Angelina was indignant. "You have sat in the very church where the *papa*—the priest—blessed their union."

Papa Nunzio cleared his throat.

"Katerina's papa sent his nephew, Richard Dutton, later, to tell Renato that he had received a ransom note," he said. "His agents traced it, found a witness who had seen such a child in the company of a man and woman who boarded a ship that sank in a storm. No survivors were reported." He took a deep breath.

"When Katerina heard her child was dead, she was like a woman of stone—she could not sleep, she did not eat, she did not cry or speak. At last Renato decided to take her away, home to Italy."

"Thanks to the Blessed Virgin, she recovered," Nana Angelina said and clasped her granddaughter's hands. "Your parents live, little one, and you have two younger brothers and a sister, all born in Italy."

Juliana recoiled, pushing away from the table. It was too much. Too much to take in all at once. Separated all these years from her family, not knowing who she was, not even able to remember her parents except in dream images she thought were false, wishful thinking, and all the while, they were there, mother and father and unknown siblings on the other side of the world. She held herself tightly as if she might shatter with the news.

A pair of arms came around her from behind. Will. His father, the first Dr. McKenna, had attended the Duttons—and had not abandoned Katherine after her marriage. Will, she recalled, frequently accompanied his father to the cottage in the Latin Quarter. The boy had made time for a little girl, tending her scraped knees and even rocking her to sleep. She bit her hand to stop the tears, but it did no good. Sobs shook her again and Will turned her about in his arms and held her until she could speak.

She straightened in her chair and dabbed at her eyes, looking past him to her grandparents.

"All those years at Point Lobos, I loved my adoptive parents, Faith and Bernard Russell—the lighthouse keeper and his wife. But inside me was a hard core of loneliness and fear and anger. I knew those two buried in Santa Rena weren't my parents, and all those years I thought my real parents were dead. I felt abandoned."

She looked around her in wonder. "But they went away to Italy and had another family."

CHAPTER EIGHT

Stricken, her grandmother reached out to Juliana, then let her arms fall.

"I'm sorry," Juliana whispered. "It's too much—too much to take in. I need time to think—but where...." she stopped in confusion, then went on, her words tripping over each other. "The Duttons—that means Richard Dutton is Mama's cousin, and Sarah and James and Henry and I are cousins as well!" She pushed away from the table and backed away a step.

"I can't work it out at all. Someone kidnapped me as a child—and expected Grandfather Dutton to pay a ransom. But the two of them died for their effort. So who is it who threatens me today?" She backed another step away. "I don't know who to trust. The attacks began after that storm washed the Duttons back into my life..." and you, Will McKenna, she thought but didn't say. "How could they have known who I am? *I* didn't know!" Will's gray eyes reflected a wariness as he reached a hand to her, slowly, as if not to frighten her further, but half his attention seemed directed elsewhere.

"Juliana, why don't you let me take you home? You can rest and decide your next step."

"I think," she said as she looked at her grandparents, "I need to be by myself. And then, then we can think what to do." Juliana's stomach turned over.

"Granddaughter, you must let us tell Renato and Katherine that you live." At her hesitant nod, Papa Nunzio took her hand. "Be careful, granddaughter.

Trust Will to see you home safely."

Nana Angelina hugged her. "Now that we have found you, Katerina, please let us have a chance to know the woman you have become."

Will appeared with her wrap and put it around her. They went outside together and he helped her into the cab he'd called, telling the driver, "Webster and Broadway." Then he said to Juliana, "I must see to Papa Nunzio and Nana Angelina. This has been as great a shock to them as to you. I'll come 'round this evening to the Duttons'." He stepped back and waved the cab forward before she could respond.

Sarah must have been watching from the parlor window, for she flew across the porch to embrace her friend, searching her face inquiringly.

"Juliana! Will told us you were taken ill! How are you? *Where* is he? Trust him to make himself scarce at a time like this."

Juliana gently disengaged herself.

"I'm fine, Sarah. Just tired. I'd like to rest before dinner, okay?"

"I'll call you for dinner," Sarah told her. "Papa will be home this evening and so will my brothers. We've all been anxious for you."

Juliana held her peace until the evening meal was finished and coffee was served in the parlor. Sarah had drawn her friend to sit beside her on the sofa. James pulled a rocker close and Henry stood with his back to the fire.

Richard Dutton took a chair across from his daughter. Aside from a cursory inquiry as to Juliana's health, he had spent the evening discussing the work of a noted German eye doctor currently lecturing in New York.

"I've made arrangements for us to travel to New York, Sarah. Just the two of us. We'll stay with your mama's cousins, and I'm sure you'll want to visit the dressmaker's and the milliner's. And one evening, if you'd like, we might attend one of *Herr Dr.* Mueller's lectures. What do you say?"

Sarah's shoulders drooped, then she straightened and clutched Juliana's hand.

"Thank you, Papa, but I couldn't leave Juliana when she's been ill."

"Nonsense." Richard Dutton's dark eyes dismissed Juliana. "Henry and James will look after her admirably. Now, I thought we'd leave in two days' time—that will give you time to pack. In fact," he paused, his shrewd glance taking in his daughter's mute resistance, "why don't we persuade Miss Russell to accompany you? I have some business associates to see and you can go sightseeing or shopping."

Sarah's face lit up. "Papa! That would be wonderful. What do you say, Juliana?"

Juliana took a deep breath and steeled herself.

"I've had some news, Mr. Dutton, Sarah, I think you should hear," she said. Haltingly, she told them of meeting the Nunzios and the return of her memory. Before she could say more beyond that she was the daughter of Katherine Dutton, Sarah jumped up.

"Why, this is wonderful news!" A wide smile wreathed her features. "Cousin Juliana!"

Henry Dutton said nothing, staring from Juliana to his father, color drained from his face. James leaned back in the rocker and began to laugh, a high-pitched sound that unnerved Juliana.

Richard Dutton rocketed to his feet, overturning his chair.

"James," he thundered, "stop that dreadful racket immediately!" He stabbed a finger at Juliana, his features and neck suffused with blood and the veins bulging above his starched collar.

"By God! I expected something of the sort from the beginning, Miss Russell. Your tale of attacks upon yourself came too pat upon your acquaintance with my son. Mr. Jones has found evidence of your accomplices!" His face reddened further and he took a step toward her. "Yes, Miss Russell! But worst of all is that you should attempt to take advantage of the tragedies visited upon this family for your own gain! Katherine Dutton lies buried in the family plot next to her brother Leland, and her daughter lies with her."

"No. No." Juliana's protest was too faint to interrupt her mother's cousin.

"I am appalled that you would so abuse the friendship and hospitality offered in gratitude. Your behavior is vile, intolerable!"

As Sarah cringed beside her, Richard Dutton advanced on Juliana.

"Out of my love and concern for my children, I hesitate to create a scandal by calling in the police. Be gone from this house by morning! Rest assured, if you spread these monstrous rumors or contact my daughter or my sons again, I will see that you spend the rest of your life in prison. Now go! Get out of my sight!"

Juliana opened her mouth to defend herself, then thought better of it. Richard Dutton's eyes were glittering with rage; the least attempt to defy him might provoke him to violence. She eased herself past him and walked from the room, her back straight and her head held high. She had as much right to be in this house as he—more so, as she was the first grandchild of James Lincoln Dutton. Upstairs packing her bag, she looked around the quiet, graceful room that had been her mother's and felt her heart constrict. Her mother had rocked her once; she could remember her scent and the feel of her warm breath on Juliana's hair as she sang.

Juliana undressed and lay down on the bed, waiting for morning. If Will McKenna came, no one called her.

And no one appeared as she left the Dutton house and made for the trolley line the next day. Hesitating, she didn't take the trolley to the train station, but rather one that took her past the church where the Duttons worshipped. There she alighted and found the Dutton mausoleum. Inside the stone grille, carved stone plaques marked the final resting-place of each generation. She shivered as she found her grandfather's marker and, below him, that of Uncle Leland. To the right... Juliana gasped and the stone grille wavered as she hung on and shook her head to clear her gaze as she read *Katherine Murphy Dutton* and, below it, a smaller plaque bearing only the engraving, *Maria Katerina, daughter of Katherine Dutton*.

On the train to Point Lobos, she placed her bag on the seat beside her, discouraging fellow passengers. She had wired Faith and Bernard that she was coming home, then had waited for hours in the train station for the next available seat on a southbound train. Home! The word set up anxious reverberations in her mind, but she clamped the door shut on them. Home—she was going home to the Point Lobos light station. Home to Bernard and Faith and Pevie.

Sunlight streamed in at the kitchen door and warmed the steps where Juliana sat, churn in hand. The rhythmic splashing of the plunger and the smell of warm cream comforted her. From inside, the small noises of a lid tapping a pot and the creak of the oven door told her Faith was preparing the evening meal. She could see Pevie chopping wood to stock the kitchen and the fog signal building. Somewhere out of sight, Bernard whistled as he always did when concentrating on a task.

Pevie and Bernard were taking care for one of them to be always near her, even if it meant she had to take her mending basket up to the light tower or out to the pasture. She had been home for three weeks, time enough to sort through her memories and reassure herself they were real. She hadn't imagined Papa Nunzio or Nana Angelina, nor the scar her grandmother bore on her forehead.

Juliana paused and lifted the lid from the stoneware crock. Inside, the rich yellow butter was clumping together. Not long now. They would have fresh butter and fresh bread—she sniffed the air as Faith took newly baked loaves from the oven for lunch tomorrow when her grandparents arrived for their first visit to the Point Lobos light station. They would stay in the second keeper's quarters, for Stewart Patterson had not brought his young family to Point Lobos after all. The new baby, born too early, kept them rooted close to their kinfolk.

Everything was as ready as they could make it. She and Pevie would drive into Santa Rena to meet their train.

At midmorning the next day, Juliana steadied the mare and waved to Papa Nunzio as Pevie assisted Nana Angelina from the train. Behind her, a third figure handed down cases to her grandfather. Will McKenna! Juliana hugged her grandmother and let Papa Nunzio help them both into the buggy. After Will strapped their cases onto the back, he squeezed onto the seat beside Juliana as she introduced Pevie to her grandparents. Nana Angelina dimpled as Pevie's blue eyes twinkled at her. Faith and Nana Angelina took to one another like old friends. Before lunch, Bernard and Pevie offered to give Papa Nunzio a tour of the light station. Nana Angelina demurred, electing to visit with Faith and Juliana. Sensing the two women might do better without her presence, Juliana took herself out for some air and sunshine, only to find Will in front of her, hands in his pockets, staring out over the bay where the *AlyceGee* had gone down. He turned at her approach, his expression shadowed.

"How are the Duttons?" she asked. "Sarah and James and Henry?"

"Richard took Sarah to New York. Henry seems to live permanently at his club, and Jimmy?" He hunched his shoulders. "Jimmy is prone to vile headaches when he isn't running around with that Russian Hill mob wining and dining at all hours."

"I'm sorry to hear that." She took a breath. "You've heard Richard Dutton's accusations? Tell me, Will," she urged, his first name slipping out, "who is it that's buried in the Dutton family plot behind the markers for Katherine and her daughter?"

Will took her hand in his, warm fingers covering her cold ones.

"It sounds like something the old man would have done, out of spite for Katherine's refusal to come home," he said. "And you—well, they must have thought you died in the storm. You don't doubt your identity, do you, little monkey?" He lifted her chin with his other hand, his mouth tightening at the sight of her tear-filled eyes. "Juliana, *cara.*"

"Juliana!"

As Pevie came up the path to join them, Juliana twisted away from Will with embarrassment. Pevie's blue eyes noted the strain on her face.

"Faith sent me to tell you luncheon is ready."

Juliana nodded and fell into step beside him. Pevie's arm came around her shoulders for a quick hug. Behind them, Juliana could hear the crunch of gravel as Will followed.

Gathered with the others in the parlor after supper, Juliana sighed as she stared about the room, remembering when it had been James Dutton's sickroom.

"I sat often at the window," she mused aloud to Pevie and Will, "when James was recuperating. He sketched me while I worked. What does Marthe say about his headaches, Dr. McKenna? Do you think he'll paint again if the headaches stop?"

"Jimmy drew while he was here?" Will repeated.

"Yes, often. He took the sketchbook with him when he left."

"The headaches began when he returned home? Perhaps he was moved too soon, I'm thinking,"

Pevie suggested.

"Yes," Will agreed, his tone abstracted. "And he stopped working after he returned home. I asked Sarah—he hasn't even unpacked his crates yet to show them the canvases he sent back from his trip." Will stopped, lips pursed, then he shrugged. "I don't suppose you saw them, Juliana, when you were working in the studio?"

"No, no, I didn't. No crates were stored in the studio, not unless they were put away in the cupboards. I remember James telling me about shipping his paintings home—but you were with him, Dr. McKenna. You joined him on the *AlyceGee*. Didn't he show you his work?"

Will shook his head.

"Only the ones from the most recent leg of his trip. The others he sent directly to San Francisco." He shook his head as if to clear his thoughts, then added lightly. "Once Jimmy's headaches are gone, I feel certain he will paint again."

"Juliana, dear," Faith said, "Bernard and Mr. Giuliano have been discussing these disastrous attacks upon you. Will you show your grandparents the necklace you wore when Bernard rescued you from the sea?"

"Of course." Pulling the trinket from her bodice, Juliana slipped it from her neck and held it out to her grandfather. Papa Nunzio stared at the tiny image for a long moment, then handed it to his wife.

"The story behind this little souvenir begins in the old country, with my papa, Vittorio Nunzio, and my mama," he said. "Where we lived, in Italy, most of the land is held by wealthy families and little enough is left for poor people. There were those in my village who went to North America, especially to the United States—to New York and San Francisco. Others went farther, to South America."

In that moment, the room felt airless to Juliana, as if everyone held their breath, letting the old man's story unfold. "My uncles had done so, always sending money home, and each one planning to come home one day. My older brother Renato was such a one, also. He made his way to South America. He hoped to earn enough money so he could come home and buy land for the family."

He handed the trinket back to Juliana. "Renato came home again after several years. He talked with Papa long into the night. He had brought a little money, not much, although he was very excited, full of laughter. He told Papa he was returning to South America to live. He urged Papa and Mama to come with him. Papa was furious! Papa to go to South America? He argued with Renato all night." The old man shook his head and paused. "The next day Renato went to visit Mama's cousin Angelo who lived down the valley. He was killed in an accident on his way home."

Papa Nunzio blessed himself. "It was a terrible time. Papa would not hear talk of any of his other children leaving, but when I was old enough, I too wanted more than anything to help my family buy land. Against my papa's wishes, I came to America to my uncle. I sent money home to Papa, but after I met my Angelina," the old man's gaze softened as it lingered on his wife "we started our own family and never went back."

Nana Angelina held her husband's hand and addressed her hosts.

"It hurt my Nunzio that his papa should be angry with him, and when our Renato—we named him for his uncle, you see—was old enough, we sent him to his grandpapa Vittorio in Italy for a year or two that he should know his family. Who could help but love our Renato?" she asked with a smile. "Papa Vittorio loved the boy and sent him home again with this exact necklace you wear, Katerina, a souvenir from his Uncle Renato's years in South America."

Juliana held the tiny charm to the light and fastened its chain about her neck again.

"I see." Bernard let out a breath. "So simple, then."

Pevie looked disappointed.

"Then we still don't know why anyone would want to attack Juliana. Certainly not for a trinket from someone's travels—over thirty years ago. 'Tis crazy to think so!"

"This is so, yes," Papa Nunzio nodded. He turned to Juliana. "Granddaughter, perhaps this will lift your spirits. Your Nana and I, we have a gift for you." Papa Nunzio pulled a carefully creased sheet of paper from his pocket and handed it to Juliana. Gingerly she unfolded it.

Arrive San Francisco one month's time. Stop. Letter to follow. Stop. All our love to our first Giuliano. Stop. Renato and Katherine.

"They will be here in two weeks' time, Katerina," Nana Angelina said gently, clapping her hands to her heart as she searched her granddaughter's expression.

"Two weeks?" Juliana echoed.

"Yes." It was Will who answered. "I'll be staying with Marthe. Katherine and Renato can stay in my home for as long as they like."

"Granddaughter," Papa Nunzio addressed her, "you shall decide for yourself if you want to return to the city or have your parents come here to see you." His dark eyes gleamed. "We will make your room ready if you choose to come to San Francisco."

"Thank you, Papa Nunzio." Juliana's voice faltered. Two weeks' time! Faith's hand gripped hers. The thought frightened her. They were strangers to one another. Her parents had other children, two brothers and a sister who could well resent the intrusion of a grown woman into their family. "I have to think what's best to do."

"Of course, Katerina. Come, Nunzio, let us say good night." Nana Angelina touched her cheek to her granddaughter's. "Good night, Katerina *mia*."

"There's no need for you to drive to Santa Rena, Dr. McKenna," Bernard said. "We made up an extra room in the second keeper's quarters. Just in case," he added, "it should be needed."

"Thank you." Will accepted with a nod. "Then I think I will follow Papa Nunzio and retire. Good evening, Mrs. Russell, Juliana."

"I hope you know, my dear," Faith said, turning to Juliana after their guests had retired, "that Bernard and I welcome your parents here at the lighthouse. But we will abide by your decision."

Juliana hugged her and stood up.

"I don't know what to think or do. I can't seem to take it all in somehow."

"Then I suggest you sleep on it, Juliana," Bernard advised. "And now, Mr. Pevie," he reminded him, "the first watch tonight is yours."

"Aye, sir! Juliana," Pevie said, his blue eyes

sober, "sleep well."

At one o'clock in the morning, Juliana threw back her quilts and reached for her wrapper. Sleep wouldn't come, only a strange mixture of longing and apprehension. What if her family didn't like her? Katherine and Renato would be looking for their little girl. That child was gone forever. What would they think of the woman she had become? Slipping downstairs, Juliana pumped herself a glass of cold water, and let herself out on the porch where the cool night air sent shivers up her spine. The windows of the second keeper's quarters were dark, but beyond the shadowed railings of the porch, the reflection of a full moon glinted from the bay below, splashing long shadows across the station grounds and throwing the Point Lobos outbuildings into sharp relief. Pulling her wrapper closer, Juliana leaned against the porch railing and let the sights and sounds of the sea lull her mind. At last, conscious of her cold feet, she turned to go in and discovered Will McKenna watching her from the doorway of the second keeper's quarters.

"I'm, I'm sorry if I—if I disturbed you," she whispered, the chill and something more causing her to stumble over her words.

Will joined her.

"I couldn't sleep" He stepped closer to her. "What brought *you* out this late?"

"I couldn't sleep, either."

"You're shivering, little monkey." Will closed the gap between them, pulling her into his arms. The warmth of him enveloped her, the faint aroma of his aftershave mingling with the clean scent of his shirt. He drew her with him to a rocker, where he settled them both. Juliana relaxed against him. How many times had he held her just like this when she was small?

"More than I can count," his breath tickled her hair and she realized she had spoken aloud. "It felt natural to take care of you."

She lifted her head.

"And now, Will? What does it feel like now?"

He bent his head to her whisper and her mouth met his dreamily, as if the moonlight had woven a warm enchantment about the dark porch and, in that moment, she cast aside her fears and doubts and responded with all her heart to his gentle kiss.

When they pulled apart Juliana was suddenly self-conscious, aware she was in her nightdress on a dark porch in the arms of a gentleman. She ducked her head as though Will could see the bright spots of color burning on her cheeks.

Will lifted her chin and met her eyes.

"Are you warm enough now?" She nodded. "Then I think we should go in, *cara*." His voice caressed her as he set her on her feet, then he pulled her into his embrace and kissed her again, this time setting fire to her lips, her knees trembling before he let her go. "That's how I feel, Juliana."

The wind keened between boulders, whistling its icy breath through the least crack and crevice. Juliana huddled in the shelter of a boulder, pulling the rough blanket about her head like a hood and tucking her chin against her knees as she tried to expose the smallest possible part of her body to the high, thin air that sucked all the warmth from her lungs. She shifted slightly at the pressure from the arm about her and shivered as the wind wormed its way between them until a second blanket was drawn across the first and blocked the wind.

She woke to a sullen sky and a chill breeze, her spirit heavy with dreams she couldn't remember. Juliana sneezed and closed the window. Had she been drawn into the warmth of Will McKenna's arms last night, or was that only the lingering image from another dream? Her fingers touched her lips gingerly; no dream, that second kiss! Her cheeks warmed anew.

When she made her way downstairs, her grandmother and Papa Nunzio were sitting in the parlor with Faith, waiting to make their good-byes. Pevie's voice could be heard outside, and a quick glance showed him with Will, stowing the luggage in the buggy. The two men stood engrossed in their talk as Juliana stepped into the parlor to hug her grandparents.

"I've decided to remain at Point Lobos," she told them. "Bernard and Faith can't readily leave the light station, and I don't want to worry them by traveling alone to San Francisco. My... parents may come here or to Santa Rena, if they prefer."

"We will see to it, granddaughter, and advise you of their desire as soon as possible. You are in good hands here; we will think of you every moment."

Nana Angelina's eyes filled with tears and she hugged her granddaughter fiercely. "Our prayers are with you always, Katerina."

Will McKenna held the reins as Pevie assisted Juliana's grandparents into the buggy. She stood in the shadows, her shoulders slumping, then stiffened as Will turned his head at the last moment and stared directly at her, an unreadable intensity searching her face even in the darkness where she cowered, then he giddyapped to the livery mare and the buggy rolled down the drive.

For two weeks Juliana was alternately excited and nervous. Night after night she ached for sleep to come, and once slipped downstairs to the porch. But this time no Will McKenna came to warm her, and she retreated, chilled, to her room. And, increasingly, under the excitement and nervousness, fear built until it was all she could do not to wire Papa Nunzio and tell him to keep her parents far away from San Francisco and Point Lobos. Katherine and Renato had lived unmolested in Italy, secure enough to raise a family. Would coming home expose that family to the same danger which threatened her?

Sitting on a quilt spread over the warm sand, Juliana reached up to adjust her umbrella, then turned her sketchpad to Faith. A small dun-colored tuft of grass, a razor clam, the hint of sand. Faith murmured appreciatively and passed a glass of lemonade to Bernard. They had brought a picnic to the beach this Sunday afternoon, leaving Pevie in charge of the light station. The sun eased the stiffness of her back, the wind teased the creases from her forehead, and the sea lulled the worries that beset her waking hours. Bernard tapped his pipe and her reverie was broken. She smiled at her adopted father.

"That's more like it." Bernard's answering smile warmed his eyes. "You need to know, we've never regretted taking you into our home and our hearts, Juliana—never a moment, nor thought we'd have been happier if the good Lord had seen fit for us to have a child of our own.

"You've graced our lives these many years. We've been blessed."

Juliana's mouth quivered and she dabbed at her eyes with the back of her hand.

"I couldn't have been luckier," she managed to say, "than to find myself at Point Lobos. Your love and care sustains me even now."

"Wipe your face, dear, you've a streak of charcoal like a patch on your left brow," Faith noted placidly as she gathered their picnic dishes. Bernard grinned broadly and handed Juliana his handkerchief.

"Pevie could charm salt from seawater," Juliana remarked with a touch of asperity as she watched him come through the garden with Lucy Katerina. The young girl's eyes never left his face and her laughter rang clearly through the open window.

"That'll do for now, Juliana. The cobbler is baking and there's plenty of time before supper," Faith said. ". Give her time, dear. She's so much like you at her age, it breaks my heart to see her."

"Ah, there you be, Mrs. Russell," Pevie's saucy smile and wink brought an answering grin to Faith's face. "Miss Lucy has a present for you."

Lucy thrust a small bouquet of marigolds and bachelor's buttons at her hostess with a nervous smile.

"Thank you, Lucy." Faith lay the flowers on the sink drainboard. "Shall we put them in water?"

Juliana joined Pevie.

"Give her time, I'm thinking, Juliana." Uncannily, he echoed Faith. "America is new and strange to her, and Lucy's in awe of you, me beauty."

Juliana sighed. "I suppose my brothers are in the tower with Bernard?"

Pevie nodded.

"For sure they are. And your father's walking on the far stretch of beach—Lucy K. and I saw him from the cliff edge. I promised your sister a game of checkers and I see she's ready for me." He offered the young girl his arm and she giggled, so like Juliana that even Pevie looked taken aback.

She turned shyly to Juliana.

"I will see you at dinner, my Julie?"

"Yes, Lucy K.," her sister said and smiled warmly. "I'll save you a seat next to me."

"Go along, Juliana," Faith urged as she set Lucy's flowers on the table. "Go along with you. All's well for now."

Wandering out to the front porch, Juliana saw her mother had set up her easel on the edge of the cliff overlooking the beach and the Portuguese village. Katherine Dutton Giuliano's blonde hair was graying and her face was lined with fine wrinkles at the eyes and neck, but it had been easy to see the beauty that had captured her father as a young man. As Juliana watched, her mother worked in complete absorption, staring for long moments out over the bay before dipping her brush and laying it to canvas one careful unhurried stroke after another. Bernard had placed a small bench there for her comfort.

Juliana set off for the fog signal building; with all the excitement of her family's arrival, the station's routine must not be allowed to slip. Bernard could ill afford another demerit on her behalf. Slipping inside the shed, she paused while her eyes adjusted to the dimness, remembering the night she'd tolled the fog signal bell while Pevie and Will struggled with the machinery. How could she wish that night had not happened? Yet all her troubles had begun that night. No. Juliana took in the full firebox, the neatly stowed tarpaulin over the bell. Everything in its place, everything ready. No. Her thoughts forced their way out. The danger to her had its roots in the past, when she was snatched from Nana Angelina. Whatever evil had prompted that action, the rest followed as night the day.

Sighing, she closed up the shed and on impulse circled around the path to where her mother sat staring out to sea. Katherine's fierce concentration softened at the hesitant footfall behind her and she lay down her brush.

"I didn't mean to interrupt your work, Mother." The formal term came stiffly from her, but she could not help her awkwardness.

Katherine's blue eyes crinkled as she made room for her daughter on the bench.

"I've reached a stopping point." Her gaze returned to the beach. "I confess I've been watching your father play in the surf."

Juliana followed her mother's gaze and saw Renato on the beach below, shoes and stockings in hand, his trouser legs rolled up mid-calf as he walked along in the rolling surf. His wife smiled and spoke softly to her daughter.

"I was painting every day on Fisherman's Wharf, and your father was working in the

Giuliano's fruit and vegetable stall. They had gardens then outside of the city and brought in freshly picked produce every morning."

Her laughter rang out.

"He passed a remark, one lunchtime, on one of my paintings, and I found Renato was a well-read young man, not afraid to express his thoughts or his opinion—and with the gift of laughter. After that, we often ate a quick lunch together.

"Then one day my painting was going really well, I lost track of time, of where I was. I painted until my arms ached." Her voice softened. "And then Renato was there. He'd brought bread and cheese to share and the biggest peach I've ever seen in my life. We shared it between us and licked the juice from our fingers. We both knew, then." She raised a hand to caress Juliana's cheek.

"Renato saved my life when you disappeared, *cara*. I'm afraid I was of little use or comfort to him in his own time of need, but he tended me and led me back to life. We were blessed with your brothers Nunzio Leland and Massimo, and many years later, Lucy Katerina—your namesake." She turned to meet her daughter's eyes. "You never left our hearts or thoughts, Katerina. And watching Lucy grow up has been both a joy and a painful reminder of what we thought we'd lost."

Juliana bowed her head and clasped her hands beneath her heart to hold back the ache.

"All those years," she whispered, "when I couldn't remember your faces—yours and Poppa's. All those years when I knew something was wrong." Arms came up around Juliana as Katherine pressed her daughter's head to her shoulder. Juliana's arms went around her mother and they held each other tightly.

"Shh," her mother soothed her, freeing one hand to stroke her daughter's brow.

After a time, Juliana raised her head and disengaged herself with a tremulous smile.

"Dear Katerina." Her mother let her go reluctantly. "Let us go in. The light's failing. Perhaps we might paint together one day? I so enjoyed painting with your cousin James when he visited us in Italy."

CHAPTER NINE

"My cousin?" Juliana echoed in confusion. "James Dutton? James visited you in Italy?"

"Why, yes," Katherine answered. "It was six months or more ago, I daresay." She looked suddenly sad.

"Father never forgave me for marrying Renato," she said. "I can well believe he let the family think I was dead when Renato took me home to Italy. But I can scarcely understand why we never received a word from James since his visit, nor why any word of welcome ever came from Cousin Richard."

"Grandfather let the family think you were dead, Mother," Juliana said, puzzled. "So how was it James came to you in Italy?"

"Because, Daughter," a deep slow voice answered her as Renato joined his wife and Juliana, "young James learned that my dear Katerina was alive through his friend, Will McKenna."

He smiled at her. "Will's father, the *dottore*, took care of Mama and Papa. He knew Katerina was alive and living in Italy. But Will's father died in an accident and his own daughter took up his practice, and with it the care of my parents. Too young to remember Katerina, Marthe never realized she was actually a Dutton and her friends' aunt."

He slipped an arm around his wife's waist and hugged her briefly, then continued. "Will hadn't taken up the practice of medicine, of course. Instead, he traveled the world in search of new plants that might yield medicines. It was only after a long illness, when he helped his sister with her patients, that he came to meet Mama and Papa again."

"Imagine his surprise," Katherine remarked dryly, "to find out I wasn't dead after all! As you know, Will and Jimmy are great friends. Will brought him to Mama Angelina and Papa Nunzio. They told him his Aunt Katherine was alive and well. Once he knew that we were in Italy, he came to visit us to find out why his own family was ignorant of our existence."

"Lucy K.!" Juliana's eyes widened. "Lucy Katerina! When Pevie and I rescued James the night of the storm, I nursed him in the kitchen. When he was awake enough to take some broth, he called me Lucy! Even then he saw the resemblance!"

"But after that?" Renato asked

"He's had terrible headaches," Juliana explained. "He doesn't remember the accident, nor the weeks before. He's never spoken of his European trip." Suddenly cold, Juliana stood and drew her shawl more closely about her shoulders.

"Still," Renato persisted, "he sketched our Lucy many times—to capture her on paper, so he could paint her later, this is what he said to tease her. She couldn't sit still long enough for a portrait. Surely his sketches would have jogged his memory?"

There didn't seem to be an answer to that, and Katherine started gathering up her paints. "Come, Renato, dear. Katerina is getting chilled. Let us go in," she said.

Juliana, ahead of her parents on the path, answered her father's question.

"James' artwork was crated and shipped home, but none of it is in his studio," she said. "He hasn't seen his sketches since he left Italy."

They reached the station house, where Lucy's laughter floated out to meet them.

"I win again, Mr. Pevie! You wish to play another game?"

Juliana hung back as her father joined Pevie and Lucy in the parlor and Katherine went into the adjacent keeper's quarters to put away the canvas and paints. Her heart felt hollow, as if the blood were rushing in from far away. Someone else had seen James' sketches of Lucy and of her. Someone who recognized the child and, in her, the woman grown. And had reacted immediately—by making attempts on her life.

Who could have seen and understood? James' old friend and sailing companion—who, more than anyone else, already knew Katherine lived and was likely to have seen the resemblance to a daughter thought lost? But what would Will McKenna gain by her death? What of Richard Dutton? He'd certainly made clear his feelings toward her. Or Henry? She refused to believe Sarah could be involved. Or that James had faked his pain. To what end? Therein lay the key to the puzzle. Why was it crucial that she die? What did they stand to gain? And how, her thoughts coiled and twisted, did the graven image she wore fit into the mystery?

"My Julie," Lucy called from the parlor, "I have beaten Mr. Pevie three games in a row. He is very sad. Please come!"

After dinner, Renato raised his wine glass to those seated at the dining table.

"To Faith and Bernard Russell, for the love and care you have given to Katerina, the daughter we thought lost and now share with open hearts."

Juliana blinked rapidly and Lucy squeezed her arm. Massimo and Nunzio raised their glasses to Faith and Bernard, and Massimo winked at his older sister.

Pevie tipped his glass, then nodded at the sisters.

"We'll trade you Juliana for Lucy K."

The young girl blushed and giggled, while her brothers pretended to consider. Faith laughed.

"They're a matched set to my eyes," Bernard spoke quietly. "I don't think we'll break them up so easily." He turned to Renato. "Will you return to San Francisco then?"

Katherine put her hand on her husband's arm. Renato considered.

"We want to spend some time with Papa and Mama. My sons are eager to see more of the city. I think, if there is work to be had, we would like to make our home in San Francisco again."

Juliana's breath came out softly. It was what she had hoped, that her family would stay. They would have time, now, to work their way back to where they belonged as a family. As if the future opened before her eyes, Juliana saw Massimo and Nunzio married, setting up housekeeping, fathers to their own boisterous broods. And Lucy, carrying her books to school.

Young Nunzio's dark eyes flickered from one sister to the other. "You will come, Katerina, please, to visit us in San Francisco?"

Renato answered firmly for his elder daughter.

"As soon as it is safe for her to do so."

Massimo nudged his brother.

"We will take care of her, Papa!" he protested, thumping his chest with his fist. "Nunzio and I!"

His mother silenced him with a look.

"I'll thank you not to go looking for trouble, Massimo." A crooked frown line etched the corner of her mouth. "Please, let us speak of other matters." She raised half-pleading eyes to Renato, who drew her hand between his own.

"Tell me, Mr. Russell," he engaged his host's attention, "how many lighthouses are strung along this coast?"

Later, Juliana set her tray upon the table, careful to be quiet. The household was asleep at one o'clock in the morning, except for Pevie up in the tower. She'd spent the first hours of his watch with him, reading. Rinsing their coffee cups at the sink, she turned at the sound of footsteps in the hall, then her mother stepped into the kitchen. Katherine's robe was pulled tightly together, her long braid thick over one shoulder. In the shadowed light, the gray was hidden and the years slipped away from her. She might have been Juliana's older sister, until she stepped into the light. Worry lines creased her cheeks and forehead and fine gray hairs escaped her braid.

"What is it, Mother? Are you ill?" Juliana put out a hand, then realized her mother's wide eyes were unseeing as she stepped forward. A low whimpering escaped her. Confused, Juliana reached out to take her arm when a second set of quiet footsteps reached her and Renato followed his wife into the kitchen. Gently he took her arm; Katherine turned at the touch into his arms which he folded about her, murmuring softly as he stroked her head.

Above her trembling form, his eyes met Juliana's, their dark pools deepened by sadness and concern. He spoke softly, a sigh in his words.

"I thought my Katherine would be free of these nights, now that you are found, my daughter."

"Why? What's wrong?" Juliana followed her father's lead and pitched her own voice low.

"She's searching for her lost child, Katerina. She's searching for *you*. I hoped now you were found, she might be able to sleep again. But," he added, summoning a small smile that didn't hide the sadness in his face, "it's been a long time since she last walked in her sleep. Perhaps with time."

Katherine stopped trembling and leaned against his chest.

"Come, *cara*," he whispered to her, "let us return to our rooms."

Juliana followed more slowly, her thoughts weighing her steps. Her father was too kind to tell her the obvious, that her mother's fears still hovered beneath the surface of her relief at having found her daughter, only to realize the child was still threatened.

Would her mother—would any of them—ever find peace?

The sea waves boomed as they broke along the beach below the Point Lobos lighthouse. Juliana paused for a moment, shifting her weight on the ladder. Faith, inside, wiped at a window with window wax, while Juliana, outside, did the same. With her parents and brothers and Lucy gone, the lighthouse was far too quiet. A formless, nameless fear was swallowing the silence and she threw herself into the upkeep of the complex. Behind her she heard the steady whack, whack of the axe as Pevie chopped wood. Climbing the ladder to reach the window next to the porch, she caught his reflection mirrored in the window, saw the yawn he stifled as he pulled the axe free of the block. He and Bernard couldn't continue to guard her day and night. The extra hours were exacting a heavy toll. It would take only one mishap, one slight detail overlooked, to have the lighthouse inspector dismiss Bernard.

And Pevie. Her friend had lost the sparkle in his blue eyes. He never mentioned San Francisco or the Duttons, but that told her what lay on his mind: Sarah Dutton's silence. Juliana polished the wax from the last pane of glass and stepped down from the ladder as Pevie came up the path. She slipped her arm through his in wordless encouragement, and he gave her a shadow of his grin as they rounded the corner of the porch and stopped short at the sight of the bay mare from the livery stable blowing as Will McKenna dismounted.

Juliana's cheeks burned as she recalled their last shared moment, but if Will was remembering the same thing, the memory seemed unpleasant, because he was frowning as he tied up the mare.

"Will!" Pevie strode forward to offer a hearty handshake, unruffled by the unexpected appearance of the doctor. "What brings you to Point Lobos? 'Tis not bad news, I hope?"

Will's dark eyes flashed at Juliana behind Pevie's shoulder, then he nodded.

"Of a sort."

"Please come in." Juliana found her voice and

gestured in front of her, conscious of her work clothes, rumpled and hot from the day's exertions. "Faith and Bernard will want to hear, and there's coffee, with supper soon to follow."

Once Will was seated at the kitchen table like one of the family, Faith poured the coffee and handed him a cup. Bernard finished washing his hands at the sink and joined them.

"Katherine and Renato have been to see Richard Dutton," Will began.

Beside Juliana, Pevie shifted in his chair.

"It was a strained occasion by Sarah's account, but cordial enough," Will picked up his tale. "Richard Dutton, once he got over his initial shock, forthrightly explained to Katherine the terms of her father's will—she had been disinherited for her marriage to Renato and the estate had been left to him for his care of his aunt and uncle."

He stopped. Juliana's face flushed. Trust Richard Dutton to assume her mother had come back for the money. She forced her attention back to Will's account.

"Katherine acknowledged this and said it was what she'd expected," he was saying. "She only came to pay her respects to the family and to request the plaques her father had placed in the Dutton family plot be removed." He paused. "Because both she and her daughter were alive."

"Richard Dutton accepted her claim of Juliana as her daughter?" Bernard inquired.

Will nodded.

"He deeply regretted his previous outburst, but hoped they understood how unlikely it had seemed that events would take such a turn." For the first time since entering the house, Will looked directly at Juliana. "Richard Dutton extends an apology and an invitation for you to come to San Francisco any time you wish. And Sarah emphatically seconded the invitation."

"You didn't come all this way," Faith said, "to tell us something easily conveyed by post. What brings you to Point Lobos, Dr. McKenna?"

For the moment he seemed at a loss for words, then he drew himself together.

"Henry Dutton, Dr. Frederico Peña and I are business partners. We're flush again with funds, so I'm leaving for an extended exploration of the Mexican Highlands. Perhaps I'll get lucky and bring back many new specimens for your drawing pleasure, Miss Russell. I'm sorry; I meant to say Miss Giuliano." He turned to Bernard, his expression worried. "More importantly, young Jimmy's gone missing. He was last seen carousing near the waterfront a week ago. No one has seen or heard from him since." His glance swept them. "I thought there was a chance he might have turned up here? No? If he should, Sarah and Henry will be most grateful to hear of it."

"Why would he disappear without a word? I don't understand," Juliana said and paused. "How long—" her voice caught in mid-word and she cleared her throat. "How long do you plan to be away, Dr. McKenna?"

"For quite some time—at least a year, if our funds hold out. I've forwarded my gear to El Paso in Texas. I'll enter Mexico from there. Henry will set up credit for me in northern Mexico, and then," he added, "I'll make camp with the local villagers and hire a guide for collecting forays into the mountains."

"I see." Juliana did indeed see. An irrational anger seized her. He took no more thought of her than he did his sister, left to run her burgeoning practice alone while her brother traipsed about in dangerous lands to acquire even more of his precious botanical specimens. Did he really think she'd be sitting here a year from now, patiently waiting to draw his specimens? Juliana unclenched her fingers in her lap and took a deep breath. What a fool she was!

"Well then, Thank you for bringing the news of James. If he should be in touch, we'll get word to Sarah as soon as possible." She turned away quickly, following the others into the keeper's quarters. Inside, she pulled at Pevie's arm to hold him back.

"I'm going up to the top of the tower. Tell Faith not to worry about my supper, I'll take something up with me." And before he could reply, she was away. Nor did she come down until Pevie ventured up to relieve her in the middle hours of that long night. Hours in which she tried not to admit, even to herself, why it mattered that Will McKenna would be gone from her life.

Long before daybreak, she heard the soft snuffle of a horse below her window and Bernard's low voice. Will McKenna was away from Point Lobos before Juliana even came downstairs.

For two weeks she carried a dull throb just below her left breast, an ache that couldn't be massaged away and one she would not grant release by shedding tears. Will McKenna—Dr. McKenna, she corrected herself, was a kind man. He had been kind to her because she helped rescue him and his friend from almost certain death. He had no more feelings than gratitude toward her. But she wanted to believe that he felt the same sense of connection and longing that beset her. She wanted to feel his arms about her, feel the beating of his heart against her. But he was gone.

She bent to her chores with a vengeance and fiercely polished every bit of glass or metal at the light station, scrubbing floors and washing walls, even turning out the bedding in the unoccupied quarters. A week later, Mr. Prendergast turned up, unannounced as usual. Point Lobos passed his inspection without a single demerit.

After supper, Bernard pointed his pipe stem in her direction.

"You deserve most of the credit, Juliana, for today's good marks. I daresay Mr. Prendergast will let us be for the remainder of this year. Thank you, my dear."

Pevie winked at her as Faith served the rest of the apple pie (from which she'd cut the first generous slice fresh from the oven for the inspector).

"I'd say Faith's apple pie was the deciding factor, for sure" he declared.

"Here, here!" Juliana agreed, and ate her pie. And for just that moment, the shadow of Will's absence lifted and a sense of peace returned.

Later, in the darkness of her room, she turned her face into her pillow and muffled her sobs, soaking her pillows long before relaxing into sleep.

The next morning Juliana was kneeling in one of Faith's front flowerbeds, pulling weeds and deadheading faded roses, when she heard the sound of hooves on the track. Coming hastily to her feet, she ran to meet Pevie as he dismounted.

"'Tis a telegram. The stationmaster saw me at the hardware store and sent this on to you."

Juliana clutched her collar and reached for the telegram.

"James?" Was it news of James? Surely good news, if he'd been found. Or news of Will? Her mind supplied the pictures.Will hurt in an accident traveling south or attacked by brigands or wild animals in the mountainous highlands of Mexico. She stood there frozen—a telegram could only be bad news of some kind.

Pevie tethered the mare and took her arm. "Let's go inside." He called out to Faith and Bernard. Faith responded from the kitchen where she sat shelling peas as Bernard, seated at the table, attended to the light station accounts.

"Juliana has a telegram." Pevie pulled out a chair for her, Then she tore open the paper. Her head swam with shock.

"No! Oh, no!" She couldn't read the message aloud, but pushed it violently away from her toward Bernard. Faith and Pevie read over his shoulder. *Cara daughter Katerina. Stop. There has been an accident involving Lucy. Stop. Come at once. Stop. Bring the trinket. Stop. Papa and Mama Giuliano.*

There was a moment of shocked silence and then Bernard, practical as always, spoke. "You must not travel alone." Juliana was already starting to rise. "Mr. Pevie, will you see Juliana safely to San Francisco?"

"Thank you, Bernard." Juliana flung her arms

around her adopted father, and he hugged her to him. "The last train goes this evening. You've just time to catch it."

"I'll make you a sandwich while you wash up and change, Juliana," Faith added.

"Don't let her out of your sight, Mr. Pevie," Bernard instructed as he let Juliana go, "until you've delivered her safely to Mr. Giuliano. And please wire us with news as soon as you are able!"

Pevie and Juliana spoke little on the train ride north, for all their speculation couldn't tell them what had happened to Lucy, or why. Juliana worried about the strange request to bring the tiny gold charm. Even as she had the thought, her fingers felt the reassuring form of the trinket beneath the throat of her shirtwaist.

Another thought surfaced sometime in the faceless gray hours that marked the coming of the predawn sky: at least Will McKenna couldn't be involved. He was somewhere in the northern Mexican highlands, unaware of any troubles besetting them.

But what of James Dutton? Where was he? Did his disappearance have anything to do with Lucy? Try as she might, Juliana could not convince herself that her sister's danger was a random occurrence. Lucy's plight was linked with her own. Twice now, nameless assailants had tried to kill her, and in spite of the protection of her father, young Lucy had been vulnerable. Fear paralyzed her. She couldn't think what to do, who to turn to for help. The threat was growing and she felt helpless to stop it.

Katherine Giuliano's features might have been

carved from marble. Not a trace of color graced her brow and her cold cheek repelled the warmth of Juliana's kiss. Lucy sat at her mother's side, the two women gripping each other's hands; she let go only to kiss her sister quickly. Renato held Juliana tightly as if to reassure himself that this daughter was yet unharmed. Massimo and Nunzio clung to their older sister, but she had little comfort to offer them. Her grandmother seemed shrunken and frail, and Papa Nunzio held himself gingerly as though it hurt to move.

As they huddled together in Will's parlor, Marthe came through from her side of the dwelling. Pevie took the coffee tray from her and set it within reach of all, but no one moved to take a cup. Marthe went to stand beside Nunzio as Renato cleared his throat. After an anxious glance at his wife, he spoke.

"When we returned from Point Lobos, Katerina, we settled into Will's rooms. Katherine and I started to look for a place of our own. Your brother Massimo found work on the wharves, and Nunzio and Lucy were here, with Dr. McKenna."

Marthe's face looked pinched and tears filled her eyes.

"It's my fault. I never thought," she interrupted, nearly choking on the words. "I never dreamed anyone would come into the house in broad daylight."

Nunzio struggled not to cry, his face contorting. Marthe's arm went around him and they held each other for support.

"It is not your fault, Dr. Marthe," Papa Nunzio spoke brusquely and his son added, "Nor yours, Nunzio."

"Papa, I should not have left her!" Her brother's voice was hoarse.

"Hush, Nunzio," his father ordered gently. "Your brother and Lucy were in the kitchen, Juliana. Lucy was giving a little girl something to eat while Dr. Marthe examined the mother. Nunzio carried some supplies through to the surgery while Annabelle sorted out the patients waiting for the doctor. They heard the baby wailing in the kitchen and found Lucy on the floor and the back door open."

"Someone held a chloroformed cloth to her face," Marthe interjected quietly. "She was unhurt save for the lock of hair they took."

Lucy spoke up, her voice subdued.

"I did not hear the door open, you understand, my Julie? I was feeding the baby and she was very happy and laughing with me. Then someone grabbed me from behind and thrust a foul cloth against my nose and mouth before I could draw breath to scream. I woke up on the floor and my head hurt for a little while." Her mother flinched at her side, and she finished in a rush. "But the baby was unhurt."

Renato reached into his pocket with a slowness that ate at Juliana's composure. "Nunzio found this pinned to the baby's bodice." He held a folded note out to her.

Pevie leaned over her shoulder as they read the missive together.

This time a lock of hair. Next time, who knows? Have the woman from the lighthouse bring the golden idol. Wait for further instructions.

Too much in shock to speak, Juliana pulled the chain from around her neck and dropped both the trinket and the note into her father's outstretched palm.

"For sure, they must be watching the house." Pevie's eyes narrowed. "Bernard would have my hide if anything happened to you, Juliana. I'll wire him tonight. I'll not be returning to Point Lobos just yet, I'm thinking."

"Of course you are welcome to stay. There is room here for you," Papa Nunzio assured him.

"We have to wait," Renato said, grimacing, "until we are contacted by the person responsible for this—this threat." He crumpled the note as he spoke. Massimo and Nunzio exchanged a glance, but neither spoke. "And now, let us feed Katerina and Mr. Pevie, then find our beds for what is left of this night." He tugged at his wife's arm. "Come, Katherine. You must eat something with Katerina or she will worry."

At this her mother stirred and clasped Juliana's arm.

"Come along, dear. Renato fusses so." She rose, faltered, clung to both her daughters for a moment, fighting back tears.

"Shh, Mother," Juliana comforted her. "I'm here with you now. We can get through whatever happens together."

Marthe persuaded Katherine to take a mild sedative after supper; Katherine took it only under protest and when certain both her daughters were under the watchful eyes of their menfolk.

"I wish Will were here." Marthe caught Juliana's look and shrugged, running a hand through her hair so her curls stood on end. "I haven't heard from him since Texas, the beast. Oh, I know better than to worry. I didn't realize until he left again how much I've grown used to his presence here." Me, too, Juliana thought. Being here in his home made her heart ache. Where was he? Was he safe? Would he ever come back? Marthe reached out to touch Juliana's arm.

"Come round to the lab with me tomorrow, will you? Rico—that's Frederico Peña, Will and Henry's partner—is working too hard, and with the surgery closed a half-day on Wednesdays, I'm taking him lunch. It'll do you good to get out. Say you will! We'll take a cab there and back."

Juliana hugged the young doctor impulsively.

"Why don't we invite Pevie along, so my parents don't worry?"

"Of course, thank you. I'll leave you now, I've got some charts to review before tomorrow."

Pausing in front of her parents' bedroom, Juliana knocked softly. Renato opened the door in shirt and trousers and jalousies. A single lamp burned low by the bed where her mother lay sleeping.

"Marthe sent you some brandy, Father. Please take it," she entreated, holding the glass out to him. "It will help you sleep."

"Yes, Katerina." Her father hesitated, then motioned her into the bedroom. He sat in a rocker pulled close to the bed. Juliana seated herself on a footstool at his knee.

His next words surprised her.

"Daughter," he said, his dark eyes holding her own, "I have been thinking that it must be hard on you to be now Juliana, now Katerina. Katerina was my little girl." His hand reached out to stroke her hair. "But you are a young woman. Would it be better if we—your mother and I—your family—if we put Katerina away and called you Juliana, as your other family and your friends do?"

Juliana reached up to clasp her father's hand. "Thank you, Poppa. But, no. I'm not hiding from my past any longer. I am still Katerina Giuliano and I am also Juliana Russell. And I will answer to whichever name it suits you to call me."

Her father sipped his brandy and a quiet smile lit his dark features.

"You are my first Giuliano," he told her, his deep voice roughened by the brandy and fatigue. He leaned his head back and closed his eyes, still holding her hand. Juliana sat quietly, listening to the rise and fall of her mother's breath, her eyes wandering about the room.

Will McKenna's bedroom.

A faded quilt with a Dresden plate pattern covered her mother in the spool bed. Next to the bed, a dark green paisley tablecloth swathed a table, its surface overflowing with stacked books and notebooks. A mirror above a three-drawer dresser at the other side of the bed reflected back the door to the hallway.

A photograph of an older couple and one of Marthe in her graduation robes were posed on one end of the dresser. An oak armoire rested between two windows across from the bed, while, she turned her head slightly, a fireplace was centered in the wall behind her. A curved mantel clock ticked away the minutes, an ebony box resting between it and a dark red ceramic pot—primitive, molded into the features of some ancient, strong-willed warrior or nobleman.

A painting hung above the mantel. Pulling her hand gently from her father's grasp, Juliana tiptoed carefully to the fireplace and studied it. A brown, Rockingham-glazed pitcher was at the heart of the still-life. Filled with black-eyed Susans, the pitcher sat on top of a fringed, cabbage-rose scarf along with an open letter spilling from an envelope and a set of garden shears atop a pair of work gloves. A neatly lettered signature was painted unobtrusively in the shadows beneath the windowsill: *Lionel Adams*. The painting touched a chord deep inside her. It spoke of simple comforts, like a promise that Will, for all his adventuring, would always come home. Juliana stepped around the bed, careful not to disturb her mother, and reached to turn down Will's reading lamp, looking at the photographs as she did. Marthe looked so young in her graduation finery, like a child playing at being a grown-up. From the style of clothing, Juliana guessed the other photograph must be Marthe and Will's parents, Dr. William McKenna and his wife, Elise.

She reached again for the lamp, then with an indrawn breath plucked a small sketch from a corner of the dresser mirror. One of James' sketches. Of her. Just her head and shoulders, as she must have looked sitting before him in the parlor during his convalescence at the light station. Juliana tucked the scrap of paper back into the mirror's frame, her fingers trembling as she smoothed its edges neatly into place.

A quick glance at her mother's sleeping form and she relaxed, slightly shame-faced at the eagerness with which she had believed that Will might... She couldn't finish the thought. Her mother or father must have tucked that sketch into place.

Returning to her father, Juliana leaned over and kissed him on the cheek. Renato stirred.

"Poppa," she said, shaking his shoulder gently, "Poppa, go to bed now, okay?"

Marthe asked the hansom cab driver to return in an hour and a half, and allowed Pevie to carry the picnic hamper as she led the way down an alley and produced a key to a nondescript door in the warehouse before them.

"Rico often works here alone, especially when Will's away on one of his trips," she explained, unlocking the door and swinging it open before calling out, "Rico? It's Marthe. I've brought lunch."

Juliana stepped just inside the building and let her eyes adjust to the light, Pevie pulling the door closed as Marthe locked them in. The warehouse had been converted to use as a botanical lab. Shelves stood along both long walls, holding presses of botanical specimens. A series of tall tables was lined up down the center of the room directly beneath a row of skylights. Three desks were grouped at the far end of the space, opposite which two cupboards flanked a small door.

Rico was just locking up a cupboard and smiled broadly in welcome.

"*Hola*, Marthe. How do you do?" He wiped a hand and offered it to each of his guests, indicating the table nearest the desks to Pevie. His eyes widened at the introductions.

"So you are the beautiful Juliana? The one who draws the life back into Will's treasures? Please, sit." He pulled up stools to the table. "Excuse me, I will just wash my hands."

When he re-emerged his lab coat had been shed, his hair neatly combed, and he had donned jacket and tie. Rico pulled out a stool for Marthe and Juliana as Pevie unpacked the lunch and sliced their bread.

"'Tis an impressive laboratory you have here, Dr. Peña," he remarked, waving the knife at the arrays of test tubes and vials and mortars.

"Please call me Rico," the young man said and grinned. "Would you believe we started out with one table in a corner of my grandmother's shed? Henry and Will have made all this possible. And Marthe," he added, looking up quickly at the doctor sitting across from him. "Marthe transcribes my notes when I get behind and keeps my science rigorous."

"It's the least I can do, Rico." Marthe turned to her friends. "He'd live in here and never sleep if someone didn't look after him." She smiled with fond exasperation. "Will and Henry are just as single-minded. Would you like more wine, Juliana? Rico?"

Her hand was remarkably steady, Juliana noticed, studiously ignoring the slight flush on the doctor's cheeks as she poured more wine. Pevie asked about the specimens on the shelves and Marthe, laughing, explained how her brother had lugged each precious plant home from destinations near and far. "You recall his lecture, Juliana!"

Juliana listened with half an ear and couldn't help but notice how Rico watched Marthe as she spoke. He ate appreciatively, laughed at the stories of Will's misadventures, and never once let his gaze stray far from Marthe's animated features.

Finally Marthe said, "I must get back to my surgery, Rico. Will you keep the leftovers from lunch? Annabelle's feelings will be hurt if we bring any crumbs back." She indicated the plate of cold chicken, bread, and fruit that remained, along with a half-bottle of wine.

"We mustn't disappoint Annabelle," Rico said, flashing her a smile, then added, "I'll help you clear, Marthe." As Pevie moved to help them, Juliana tugged at his sleeve and pulled him away.

"Let me show you some of my sketches, Pevie."

She kept him glancing through the sketches, their backs to the doctors, until she heard Marthe's step behind her.

"No, don't bother to see us out, Rico. I know the way." Marthe smiled at him. Rico ran his hand through his hair, crumpling his carefully combed curls as she added, "Go back to your research and don't forget to eat your supper."

"Yes, Dr. Marthe." He grinned and they took their leave.

All the way back to the Queen Anne on Webster, Pevie kept up a running commentary with Juliana on the sights of San Francisco. Marthe sat quietly and nodded and smiled, but her eyes and thoughts were clearly far away from her companions.

The small garden at the rear of the McKennas' Queen Anne glistened with droplets of moisture from the fog. Juliana stood quietly at the window of Will's rear parlor and listened with half an ear to the sound of Nunzio reading to Lucy from *The Canterbury Tales*. As if in response to his namesake, he possessed his mother's family's fair hair and coloring. But he had his father's steady temperament and was nearly as tall as his older brother.

Too restless to work at her watercolor sketches, which Marthe had implored her to continue, Juliana stood indecisively at the window. Try as she might, she could not keep busy enough to keep worry at bay, nor the dull ache that seemed permanently settled about her heart.

A movement in the garden caught her attention. Katherine, shawl wrapped tightly about her, was carrying a shallow, rolled basket along the path. She stopped, her worry evident in the drooping line of her shoulders, and as she did, Renato appeared from the depths of the garden. Katherine swung about to face him. Juliana watched her father approach, saw him offer a bouquet of full pink roses to his wife. He filled her basket with the roses, but kept back one half-opened flower he tucked behind her ear. Katherine's hand covered his at that touch, and Renato took her hand in his and kissed her open palm. They moved together into an embrace, and Juliana jumped as if stung, feeling like a voyeur, feeling the ache in her heart intensify.

She fled the parlor, checking herself outside the door to the room she shared with Lucy, then kept going up one more level. Marthe had cleared a work table for her in Will's study. No one would disturb her there.

But instead of taking a seat by her watercolors, Juliana found herself drawn to Will's desk. She slipped behind it to sit in his chair. The wood was worn smooth, the oak the color of honey, warming her. She drew up her knees and wrapped her long skirts about her legs, resting her chin on her knees.

The love her parents felt for one another had clearly run deep and true all these years, as strong now as it had been when they first courted and married.

Huddled in Will's chair, Juliana wished forlornly that she might have what her parents had. Both sets of parents, she amended that thought. Katherine and Renato. Faith and Bernard.

Will had kissed her. Juliana bit her lip at the memory of how her body had responded to his touch. But despite that kiss, he hadn't pretended to want more; he had, in fact, left her, as though that moment had meant nothing to him.

Juliana shook her head to clear it and sat up. Why could Will McKenna not be more like John Pevie? Now, if Pevie kissed a girl, he'd leave her with no doubt as to his intentions. Perhaps, the unwilling thought tightened her throat, Will *had* made his feelings clear. One kiss in the darkness, then he was gone. How much clearer could he have been? After all, he hadn't even come back to Point Lobos to say good-bye to her. His concern had been for his friend, James Dutton.

And that, Juliana sighed, was another part of the ache she felt. Where was James? Sarah and Henry must be mad with worry and fear. She moved to her work table and listlessly picked up a sketch. A soft knock sounded at the door, then it opened and Nunzio stuck his head into the room, his dark eyes grave.

"Katerina, Papa says to please come downstairs." He gulped. "Our instructions have arrived."

CHAPTER TEN

"Well. Biagio Marazzi."

The man who stood insolently just within the parlor door inclined his head briefly at Renato's recognition. "Cousin," he replied smoothly, making no move to introduce the sullen young man beside him.

Biagio Marazzi was of an age with Renato, but stood a head shorter. Stocky, with dark jowls and thick brows above black eyes, he wore a suit that fit well but had clearly seen better days. His companion was slightly shorter and young enough to be his son. Broad through the chest, with powerful arms and shoulders, his hair curled forward on his brow above dark eyes that constantly darted about the room. None of the room's warmth appeared to touch those eyes, and Juliana shuddered.

Massimo reached for her hand and held it tightly.

As Renato said nothing more, the silence stretched for a long moment before Marazzi reached into his coat. Pevie was standing behind the settee on which Lucy and Nunzio sat, flanking their mother. From across the room, Juliana saw him stiffen at Marazzi's gesture.

Nana Angelina sat in a rocker near the fireplace, Papa Nunzio hovering beside her as if to warm his thin frame. Juliana's heart ached at the lines etched deeply into his face. Marazzi pulled his hand free and Juliana gasped, her hand at her throat. Dangling from his fingers was a gold chain holding a golden figurine that might have been the model for the tiny gold mask she carried.

Marazzi's teeth gleamed at her gesture.

"Ah, you do understand," he purred with satisfaction. "You will tell me now the location of the treasure." He paused and waved a hand in the direction of Renato's family. "I promise you your family will come to no harm."

The room erupted with noise. Massimo surged to his feet in protest and Nunzio and Lucy exclaimed in unison, "Treasure?" Pevie's angry voice boomed, "Now, see here!" while Katherine Dutton Giuliano said nothing but clasped her youngest son and daughter closer to her. Juliana pulled Massimo back down beside her.

"Silence!" Renato's voice cut through the confused babble.

"Give me the gold piece, young woman." Marazzi's cold gaze raked Juliana. Fumbling in her pocket for the pouch, her hand closed convulsively around it. How dare this man demand her father's gift to her? He'd placed the chain about her neck himself. Her gaze moved to Lucy and her mother. Slowly she drew the pouch from her pocket and held it out. Marazzi's silent companion stepped forward to snatch it from her, then dumped the pouch's contents into Marazzi's outstretched hand.

The older man quickly held the golden mask up to the light, then turned it about to examine the obverse side, frustration evident in his expression.

"Bah!" Angrily he jabbed a finger in Juliana's direction. "I say again, tell me the location of the treasure."

Renato stepped between his daughter and Marazzi. "She knows nothing, because there is nothing to tell. There is no treasure—only what you're holding in your hand. Take it if that is what you came for, *signor*."

Marazzi's companion bristled and jerked his head up at Renato's tone, but the older man lay a hand on his arm and he subsided. Marazzi indicated the small gold figurine in his palm and spoke to Renato.

"Cousin, let me tell you the story of this treasure. For I will have it in the end. And do not think"—his gaze raked Massimo and Pevie contemptuously—"that we can be frightened off like children." He let his gaze linger on Lucy.

Juliana fought down her fear and rising anger, focusing on the men in front of her.

"It was necessary to get your attention, Cousin," Marazzi said and made a mock-bow in Renato's direction, "in order to ensure your full cooperation. This—" he indicated the figurine "—was handed down to me by my sainted papa."

Unexpectedly, Papa Nunzio spat into the fireplace. "Bah!" he declared coldly. "Bruno Marazzi was an ill-tempered brute of a man who mistreated my sister, your sainted mother." He blessed himself.

A muscle worked in Marazzi's jaw and his eyes grew harder. "When times are rough, old man, one takes advantage of opportunities as they come along. It is true," he said, rubbing his jaw, "that Uncle Renato Vittorio did not willingly part with this trinket. And most unfortunate that he was killed when his horse bolted, before he could be persuaded to share the secret of his treasure." Marazzi's teeth gleamed again in a wolfish grin as Papa Nunzio turned pale and sagged. Pevie caught him before his knees buckled and helped him to the settee. Katherine reached across Lucy to grasp his hand as Marazzi continued, "But treasure there is, have no doubt about it. My papa overheard him tell old Vittorio Giuliano that he had left a treasure well-guarded in South America."

"Even if what you say is true," Renato responded curtly, "we know nothing. The trinket my daughter wears was given to me by *Nonno* Vittorio in remembrance of my namesake. Nothing more. He spoke no word of treasure." Renato gestured impatiently at his family. "Had I a treasure, would I not lavish it upon my family?"

Marazzi's eyes narrowed and he shook his head. "Not if you didn't want it to be common knowledge, cousin. Uncle Renato told old Vittorio, and he passed that knowledge to you just as he passed on this golden mask." He threw the mask angrily at Juliana's feet, and his companion shifted restlessly beside him. Marazzi touched the younger man's arm. "I agree, Stefano, enough talk. A ship is leaving for South America in three weeks' time, cousin. My partner has reserved passage for you. You will come yourself—or send someone in your stead—to travel with us to Ecuador. Once there, you will have one month to deliver the treasure into our hands."

He made no reference to the alternative, nor did his gaze need to shift to Lucy and Nunzio wide-eyed beside their mother. Marazzi flicked a card at Renato. "The ship's name and her sailing date. Have someone there."

Stefano stepped aside, then followed Biagio Marazzi silently from the parlor.

Papa Nunzio's frail voice barely carried to the floor where Juliana now knelt at his knee.

"My sister Elena was the only girl in a family of three sons—me, Massimo, and Renato Vittorio. Bruno Marazzi courted her in hopes of a handsome dowry. When another young suitor sought to court her, Marazzi abducted Elena and carried her away for two days and three nights."

His voice deepened with old pain and he lifted his lined face to his family. "What could Papa do? My sister was disgraced unless she married that brute who took her. Bruno Marazzi expected a generous dowry, more than Papa had to give. And he never," the old man bit off each word, "*ever* let Elena forget it. Biagio," he added bitterly, "was her second child. The firstborn, Georgio, fruit of Bruno's abduction, was stillborn one night when he beat my sister in a drunken rage."

Nana Angelina put an arm around her husband and lay her head against his shoulder.

Renato spoke quietly into the taut silence.

"Aunt Elena had two more children after Biagio, a daughter named Lucia and another son, Stefano. She died giving birth to Stefano. Cousin Biagio was ten years old at the time, Lucia six. Bruno nursed a grudge against *Nonni* Vittorio and his family and taught his sons to hate as well."

Katherine stirred against Lucy.

"Is it possible, Renato, that your uncle left a treasure in Ecuador? Your cousin seems convinced."

For answer, Renato looked to his father. The old man shrugged.

"My brother Renato Vittorio was excited when he came home. He insisted that Papa and Mama should return to Ecuador with him. He was going back to stay. Then he died."

He glanced around the room. "Myself? No, I never believed my brother left a treasure behind in South America. We had so little in Italy, you understand? So little land from which to make a living. Renato Vittorio was a good man. Had he possessed some great treasure, he would have shared his riches with our papa and mama."

"And 'tis certain Bruno Marazzi believed otherwise." Pevie said. "Just so does his fool of a son."

Juliana gripped the foreign talisman and swallowed the bile rising in her throat. She coughed, swallowed again, and drew a shaking breath. "Papa," she whispered, "Papa."

She cleared her throat and spoke louder.

"The answer to this puzzle must be found in Ecuador. I'll go there, Papa. As your firstborn Giuliano, I've carried Renato Vittorio's gift all these years." She raised a hand to quell the horrified protestations that rose about her. "You would've remained safely in Italy if I hadn't come back into your lives." Juliana turned to her mother, pleading. "Don't you see, Mother, I must do this! I must do whatever I can to protect you." She was careful not to add what she was thinking, that she had her own money and would go whether they agreed or not.

"Daughter," Katherine's voice faltered, "I cannot bear to lose you again."

"Then I will see that she comes home again, Mama."

Startled, Juliana met her brother Massimo's fierce gaze.

"Enough!" Renato ordered brusquely. "You will both stay with your mother. It is my place to undertake this journey."

Unexpectedly, Katherine Giuliano shook her head and rose to take her husband's arm. "No, Renato, dearest." She gestured to his parents. "We need your support and protection here with us. Katerina must do this for herself. And Massimo— our son is grown into a man, Renato. He will look after his sister."

Renato took in the large, frightened eyes of Lucy Katerina, the uneasiness of Nunzio, and the huddled embrace of his parents, and bowed his head.

"My son," Papa Nunzio's voice quavered, "the police cannot protect us from Biagio Marazzi's threat. Even if they would take action against him, the threat would live on. Perhaps," he said, looking at Katherine and raising his eyebrow, "*Nuora* Katerina, if you were to take the children with you, perhaps your cousin Mr. Dutton would offer you his protection?"

"No!" Renato's voice nearly drowned out his wife's equally vehement refusal.

"Then I see no other clear course," his father finished, troubled.

A silence followed. Finally Pevie cleared his throat.

"With your permission, Mr. Giuliano, I'll go with Juliana and Massimo on this journey," he said. "No, wait, listen to me." He raised a hand and turned down one finger. "First, Juliana will be in the company of her brother, so I'm thinking my presence won't compromise her reputation." He turned down a second finger. "I can't allow Faith and Bernard to worry. Third, another pair of eyes and ears will come in handy, for sure, and I speak both Spanish and some Portuguese."

Renato regarded Pevie gravely.

"Your job, Mr. Pevie? Surely you cannot simply leave your work for such a long period of time?"

Pevie shook his head.

"Ordinarily, no, 'tis true. But Bernard's getting a second assistant keeper. I know the young man well. Stewart Patterson has a solid record with the service. He's highly capable." He smiled briefly at Juliana. "The baby thrives and the family is ready to come to Point Lobos. I'll apply for a hardship leave—Bernard will gladly support it."

Juliana let out her breath. In truth, she had no great desire to argue with Pevie. It was a great relief to know that she and Massimo would not be setting off alone.

The horse wheeled as it always did, the rider faceless beneath the mask. "Who are you?" Juliana cried out, "Friend or foe? Take it, then!" In desperation, she yanked at the chain about her neck, but the dark stallion reared and hands pulled her from the horse's path.

Juliana awakened tired and keyed up from her nightmare. She and Pevie met Marthe McKenna for an early breakfast to fill her in on the night's activities.

Marthe fingered the gold mask silently, then her face lit up.

"Rico! Juliana, Dr. Peña has a friend, Edwin Markham. He's a research assistant at the anthropology museum in Berkeley. Perhaps Edwin could tell us something about this piece." She sounded enthusiastic.

"Henry Dutton had a telephone installed at the laboratory. Shall I call Rico?"

Moments later, she replaced the telephone's mouthpiece with a satisfied smile. "We're to meet Rico and Edwin at the museum at the close of business this afternoon."

"Aye, splendid," Pevie looked up from his plate of bacon and eggs. "The sooner the better."

Beneath Marthe's hand, the instrument rang.

"Dr. McKenna's surgery," Marthe said, then frowned. "Yes, Sarah." Juliana felt Pevie stiffen to attention beside her. "Yes. Six o'clock at Luna's. We'll look for you there."

Puzzled, Marthe replace the receiver once more, her gray eyes troubled.

"Juliana, Sarah Dutton begs us to please meet her for dinner this evening. She sounded distraught. I took the liberty of accepting for you both."

Pevie nodded. "Where—?"

"Luna's is a modest Italian restaurant in North Beach. We can meet her easily after we see Rico and Edwin at the museum." Marthe shook her head and checked the watch pinned to her bodice. "Sarah rang off as soon as I agreed. She didn't say why, I'm afraid. Now I need to open my surgery. See you at four o'clock?"

Juliana took Pevie's arm and steered him toward Will's side of the house.

"Where's your brother this morning?" he asked, masking his uneasiness.

"Massimo returned to work." She smiled at

Pevie's look of surprise. "He told Papa that he'll need his job when we return."

Pevie smiled involuntarily, and Juliana stopped him in the hall.

"Pevie, tell me," she began and her friend eyed her warily, "why are you determined to come with us?"

He shrugged and let out a deep breath.

"For all the reasons I listed, to be sure, me beauty. But—" he touched Juliana's arm lightly to forestall her next question "—there is this. Did Biagio Marazzi strike you as a man of much means?"

"No," Juliana said and nodded slowly. "His suit was shabby."

"And it costs a packet of money to reserve cabins for a trip to Ecuador, I'm thinking."

Juliana's eyes widened.

"The partner!"

"Yes, indeed." Pevie's voice hardened, but he lowered it so it didn't carry beyond Juliana. "Seems to me the logical choice of a partner must be someone who made the connection between you and the Giuliano family."

"No!" The sharp whisper escaped Juliana. "Not Will!"

Pevie's eyebrows rose, but he replied evenly.

"He knew both families. As did James Dutton," he added. Juliana bit her lip. After all, hadn't she had the same doubts? Pevie continued, "Or, through one or both of them, any of the other Duttons." His voice deepened. "Don't you see, I must know, for Sarah's sake."

Frederico Peña was waiting when Marthe shepherded Juliana and Pevie ahead of her into the museum. A guard waved Rico through a door at the back of the exhibit hall into a warren of offices, workshops, and storage rooms. At any other time, the exhibits would have enthralled Juliana, but today her impatience was such that everything passed in a blur as she followed Marthe and Rico.

Rico led them deep into the labyrinth of winding corridors until he halted, knocked, and opened a door, calling out as he entered.

"Edwin? I've brought my friends."

Edwin Markham's long serious face lit at the sight of his friend. He was taller than Pevie, with pale blond hair receding from a high forehead. As he stood, he unhooked his spectacles, revealing clear blue eyes that summed them all up in a quick glance.

"Please, come in." He waved a long-fingered hand at a table with several chairs pulled up to it. "I gather there's some urgency?" He nodded briskly as he took in their faces. "Then perhaps you'll show me?"

He took the small golden mask from Juliana and studied it with pursed lips. "Ah, indeed." Selecting a key on a ring he took from the pocket of his jacket, he unlocked a cupboard on the far wall of the room and pulled out several deep drawers before he picked out two trays and pushed them on a cart back to the table.

Lifting the covers from the trays, Edwin placed one of them in front of Juliana. She gasped. In workmanship and style, her golden mask had clearly been produced by the same artisans. A larger mask gleamed in its bed of wrappings, while the hammered discs of necklaces caught the light as well. Inlaid earrings with braided gold dangles and gold beading nestled next to exquisite golden figurines—some of people, some of animals and birds—most of which were no larger than her mask.

Edwin gently touched Juliana's trinket.

"Might I ask where you found this?" he inquired.

Juliana told the story of how the piece had come into the family. Edwin unconsciously fingered his spectacles as she spoke.

"These items," he said, gesturing at the material spread out on the trays in front of them, "are from Las Tolitas, the site of an ancient culture on an island along the north coast of Ecuador." He paused and pointed at Juliana's mask. "These artifacts are but a small sample of the gold work produced at the site."

"So," Rico ventured, "Miss Russell's artifact probably came from the same culture?"

Edwin Markham nodded with a wry smile.

"I'd say so, yes, and there's the rub. Your ancestor," he addressed Juliana, "might have stumbled upon an undisturbed cache of gold and salvaged it himself, or he could have simply purchased this piece in any marketplace."

Marthe shook her head. "I think we can rule out the second possibility, Dr. Markham. Would Renato Giuliano have spent money to purchase such a trinket? His sole purpose in going abroad was to earn money to enable his family to buy land in Italy."

"Then perhaps," Edwin's eyes twinkled, "Mr. Giuliano left a cache of archaeological treasure stashed away in Ecuador." The twinkle vanished. "Such a treasure would be worth any cost to a great many people. It's unlikely to have remained hidden away all this time."

He rose and went to a map cabinet, returning with a map which he spread out on the table next to the trays of artifacts.

"Here you see the coast? These are the known sites of the Las Tolitas culture. If you know where Mr. Giuliano traveled, you could see if his travels took him anywhere near these areas."

Juliana eyed the map, a small flame of hope leaping inside her. It might be unlikely that a treasure had gone undiscovered, but now they had a starting point in their quest.

"Thank you, Dr. Markham," Juliana said and rose, "for your time today."

"It's been a pleasure." He stood, the smile back in his eyes. "And if you should ever decide to part with your trinket, the museum would be glad to make you an offer."

Juliana thought of the trouble the golden mask had already caused. Had Biagio Marazzi's sly reference to the death of Renato Vittorio meant that Bruno Marazzi had murdered her father's uncle? Her abduction as a child and near-drowning at the lighthouse—had not the gold mask and its promise of a treasure led to enough disaster?

"I may take you up on that offer, Dr. Markham," she replied somberly, "but not today."

Outside the museum, Marthe lay a hand on Rico's arm.

"Please join us for supper at Luña's, Rico. We shan't keep you late."

Rico's color heightened slightly, and he smiled warmly at the doctor.

"Thank you, I'm pleased to do so, if your friends do not object?"

Pevie and Juliana hastened to add their pleas to Marthe's.

"Good," Pevie said, "that's settled. Let's go." Juliana knew it was only his good manners that kept him from rushing to see Sarah and learn the purpose behind her disturbing call to Marthe McKenna.

Although the dinner hour was early, Luña's dining room was half-filled. Red-checked cloths covered tables where knots of students from nearby university communities hovered over empty platters and steaming cups of good coffee, arguing good-naturedly amid much laughter. Quieter family groups gathered three generations together around several tables pulled close.

In a corner of the room, Henry Dutton rose from his seat next to his sister to draw their attention.

As her party was seated, Juliana saw Rico shoot a questioning glance at Henry, who shook his head in a quick, negative gesture. Rico seated Marthe, then pulled out a chair next to the doctor.

Sarah Dutton's eyes were bright and twin spots of red heightened her cheekbones. Her dress of pale blue moiré cotton accentuated her doll-like perfection, but her hair looked like she'd run her fingers through it, then hastily smoothed it down before pinning on her confection of a hat. Her hands were clamped about her coffee cup, although her drink appeared untouched.

An unobtrusive waiter efficiently collected their

orders, returning immediately with more coffee before departing just as quickly.

"Marthe," Sarah Dutton began, her quiet, even tone clearly a strain for the young woman, her hands never relaxing their tight grip on her cup as she spoke, "have you heard from Will recently?"

At the name, Juliana's heart thumped uncomfortably, and she was acutely reminded of the long and intimate friendship Sarah and Will enjoyed. She stole a glance at Pevie and saw the frown he swiftly masked.

Marthe shook her head with an exasperated laugh. "My wayward brother has yet to write, Sarah. One would think that he would hasten to assure his only sister of his well-being, but, alas, he has not." The doctor gestured at Rico. "I'd wager Rico has been inundated with packages, all containing fantastical new botanical specimens!"

All eyes upon him, Rico flushed, then flashed Marthe a quick grin.

"Every package from Will is a treasure trove of medicinal possibilities! Ah," he said, deflecting their attention to a trio of waiters bearing down on their table, "this looks delicious!"

As conversation lapsed into polite exchanges about the savory dishes before them, Juliana nodded as necessary and eyed Frederico. How adroitly he had evaded Marthe's unspoken question. He had not, she reflected, actually admitted to receiving any packages from his absent partner.

Her glance rested briefly on Henry. His features, usually jovial and open, seemed to share his sister's strain, although his conversation with Pevie was light.

"Sailing is my first love. Not much time for it the last few years, you know. Learning the ropes in the family business." He laughed then, a genuine hearty sound. "A far cry from my youth. Wanted to be a tugboat captain."

Pevie nodded with unexpected enthusiasm, his blue eyes twinkling.

"I'm thinking the tugboat is the most under-appreciated vessel in a harbor, Mr. Dutton."

"Turn on a dime with those double side paddles, and steam along forever on a single load of coal." Henry sighed. "Used to watch them for hours when I was a youngster. Now, well..." he shrugged and turned to Sarah. "Will you have the flan for dessert, Sarah? No? Then I shall abstain, also." He regretfully watched the dessert cart pass their table. Sarah laid her napkin beside her plate; she had eaten little.

"Marthe, Juliana," her voice trembled and she stopped as Henry pressed her hand in support. "It's Jimmy," she continued, her voice low. "He came home late last night." Her eyes filled with tears at the chorus of relief that swept the table, but at the grim look on her face, the murmurs subsided.

"Jimmy slipped into my room after the house was quiet. Henry was at his club. Father and I had a light supper, then Father went out to meet some friends. Even Cook had gone for the evening. I was in my room, half-asleep. I'd been reading."

She took a deep breath. "Jimmy slipped in. He was dressed in shabby clothing and clearly hadn't shaved in days. He assured me he was fine and then begged money from me." Her voice faltered. "I didn't have much cash to give him. He asked for jewelry, then, anything that could be readily pawned or sold."

A bewildered silence met her words.

"Jimmy said he had to go away for a while. I pleaded with him to tell me if he was in some kind of trouble. Perhaps he had unpaid gambling debts, or"—she blushed—"trouble with a woman. He brushed my questions aside and staggered against the chair." Another deep breath. "He hadn't eaten, and I hurried to bring him food from the kitchen. As he ate, I urged him to stay, to confide his troubles in Henry. When he refused, I begged him to see you, Marthe. I can't tell you the pain I saw in his face." She turned hopefully to Marthe. "Did he come?"

"I'm sorry, my dear," Marthe took Sarah's hand in hers. "Jimmy hasn't been to see me, nor have I heard from him."

Sarah's shoulders slumped in disappointment. Henry put an arm about her.

Pevie looked to Henry.

"And your brother didn't explain his behavior?"

Sarah met his troubled gaze, and when her voice came, the whisper chilled Juliana to the marrow.

"Jimmy only said he had some terrible debt to repay."

"Sarah telephoned me at my club," Henry told them quietly, "when she went to fetch food from the kitchen. But Jimmy was gone long before I could get home. I've engaged an inquiry agent to check the train stations and the docks, but the agent has had no luck finding Jimmy or his trail. He's simply disappeared once again."

The image of Samuel T. Jones flashed through Juliana's thoughts as her mind whirled in confusion.

Will gone off suddenly, and now James. His beloved yacht lay at the bottom of the Point Lobos Bay. Where had he gone? What terrible debt could he be referring to? She had an image of James bent over a canvas, his fingers deft and certain, his face alight with the sureness of his gift. She couldn't believe he had harmed anyone.

Was it possible that his trouble was connected to her? To the mystery of her childhood abduction? To the mystery of the golden mask she carried? Had his predicament come about solely because she'd pulled him from the wreckage of his yacht that night at Point Lobos? She closed her eyes as pain stabbed at her. Did she spread misery wherever she went? Suddenly, she wished she could run away again— run back to Point Lobos and sanctuary. Hide away in her tower and pretend she was just the lighthouse keeper's adopted daughter. She became aware that Marthe was speaking and opened her eyes.

"Sarah, Henry," Marthe said gently, her voice holding concern, her pale face a measure of doubt, "it was my professional opinion that James was well on the road to recovery from the injuries he'd suffered when the *Alycegee* capsized. Whatever worry besets him now, I don't believe it's physical in nature."

"Thank you, Marthe," Sarah murmured. Henry nodded, but his normally affable features were guarded.

"You mustn't blame yourself, Marthe. No expense will be spared to find my brother and help him in any way that I may."

In the ensuing quiet, Juliana was surprised to see that Luña's had filled nearly to capacity while they were dining; she had been too focused on the conversation to really notice. A waiter approached Henry, who rose abruptly.

"A message for me... some business matter, no doubt. If you will excuse me?"

Pevie and Rico took the opportunity of Henry's absence to wrangle over the evening's tab. In the end, they agreed to split it.

When Henry returned, Juliana noted that his face was flushed.

"A business matter, as I suspected," he told his sister, "but of some urgency." He turned to Pevie. "Might I prevail upon you and my cousin to see my sister home, Mr. Pevie?" He warded off Sarah's protest with a hand. "I know a cab would take you home, dear Sarah. Just once, indulge my brotherly concern?" In spite of the lightness of his tone, Juliana detected real anxiety.

Sarah didn't argue.

"Do you go ahead, Henry. Our friends will see me home."

In the end, they shared a hansom cab with Marthe, and Rico bid them good evening outside the restaurant. As the cab halted at the intersection of Webster and Broadway, Sarah turned impulsively to her companions.

"I've not been very good company this evening. Let me make it up to you. Please join me for an after-dinner sherry? We've some fresh pears and a wonderful gorgonzola with walnuts."

Before them, the Dutton house loomed dark and uninviting. Pevie and Marthe, Juliana sensed, were waiting for her to decide.

"Thank you, Sarah. That sounds lovely, although

I'm afraid I can't stay for long."

Demurring at the brandy Sarah produced for Pevie, Juliana and Marthe accepted a small glass of sherry and watched as Pevie's smile coaxed the color back into Sarah's pale cheeks. Marthe met Juliana's gaze over the rim of her glass and nodded. For a few moments, they could let go their worries, enjoy the pleasure of their company, the elegant drink, the simple dessert of fresh fruit and good cheese. Breathing deeply, Juliana relaxed.

"Sarah?!" The imperious call shattered the calm of the room. "Sarah?!" Richard Dutton burst into the parlor. A quick glance dismissed the company as of no importance, all his energy focused on his daughter.

"Splendid news, Sarah! *Herr Dr.* Mueller believes he can help you. Surgery is scheduled next week. We leave in the morning for New York."

Sarah's face blanched. Her hand shook as she set down her sherry glass.

"No."

Richard went on as if he had not heard. Such was his excitement, Juliana doubted that he had.

"I rang earlier, but you were out, darling. I've instructed your maid to see to your trunks, Sarah. The *Herr Doctor* expects you will need several weeks to recuperate and—"

Sarah jerked to her feet.

"No, Father! I am not going to New York with you."

"Of course you are." Richard took a confident step forward. "I know I've sprung this upon you, my dear, with little notice." His voice modulated with concern. "And you're tired and worn out with worry for that thoughtless brother of yours, but—."

Sarah interrupted her father for a second time, still in that cold, whiplash tone.

"I am not going to New York, Father. Look at me," she challenged him. "I'm nearly blind, Father. This is who I am, your blind daughter! My whole life, I have endured every medical treatment you could find. No more!" She took a deep breath. "I am at peace with who I am. I'm sorry if you are not."

Richard's face was red with shock and mounting fury, but he mastered his emotions with an effort that made Juliana wince.

"You're tired and overwrought, Sarah. I'm sorry to have pressed you. We'll discuss this in the morning." With that, he withdrew from the parlor as quickly as he'd come.

Sarah turned to her guests.

"You will forgive me, I am sure, if I end our evening now?"

For answer, Marthe hugged her friend hard. "Come to me if you need," she offered stoutly.

Pevie clasped her hand in his.

"If I can be of any service to you, Miss Dutton, please ask."

Sarah's cheeks flushed with pleasure and her chin rose a little higher.

"Thank you, Mr. Pevie. You have shown yourself to be a true friend."

CHAPTER ELEVEN

Pevie *was* a true friend, Juliana reflected, watching him as he stood tall at the rail of their steamship, gazing westward, back toward San Francisco. He'd left Sarah Dutton there so he could accompany Juliana and her brother Massimo on the wildest goose chase ever.

They'd boarded the *Ariadne* five days earlier, and so far, she had not yet caught sight of Biagio Marazzi or his burly young companion, Stefano. Nor had she seen anyone else she knew. The *Ariadne* carried a complement of one hundred and ten passengers and crew. Since passengers were assigned to one of three separate seatings for meals, it was possible that Marazzi was aboard. If so, he had thus far avoided all contact with Juliana's party.

On the first night they steamed past the Point Lobos lighthouse, and the sight of the steadfast light had brought a thick lump to Juliana's throat. Massimo had kept her company until the light was out of sight. It was then that she truly felt the enormity of their task. About her neck the golden mask sat uneasily, their only clue to Renato Vittorio's travels in a foreign land. They had no name, no town even, to point them in the proper direction. Renato Vittorio had sent small sums of money home to his parents, his letters bearing exotic postage stamps but little news. His parents couldn't read, and the letters were read to them by the village priest. None had survived past old Vittorio's death.

The *Ariadne* would steam into the port of

Guayaquil on the coast of Ecuador on the twelfth of July, Juliana knew. Guayaquil was the largest city in Ecuador and the portal through which scores of immigrants passed. She and Pevie and Massimo pored over their map nightly, as if they could force a clue from its ink.

Guayaquil lay at the mouth of the Guayas River, which flowed down to the ocean from the Western Range of the Andes. One traveled northeast through the valley of the Guayas to reach the highland city of Quito, Ecuador's capitol. They would steam past the port of Esmeraldas on the north coast, the place where, as Edwin Markham's maps revealed, the ancient culture of Las Tolitas was centered.

But Esmeraldas itself was cut off from the rest of the country and was surrounded by cacao plantations worked by Negro slaves. How had Renato Vittorio happened upon a previously undiscovered cache of gold from a Las Tolitas site? It seemed highly unlikely, Juliana thought unhappily, given the steady stream of people coming and going through the Costa region.

She turned away from the sight of the ocean churning about them to find Massimo nowhere in sight. She sighed as Pevie joined her. He might have read her mind.

"Your brother will turn up, me beauty." He gave a short laugh. "Massimo has yet to miss a meal." Pevie offered his arm. "Shall we walk?"

Juliana walked until her legs were wobbly, then retired to her cabin to prepare for dinner. The cabins were small but accommodating. It was the one place she could be alone, a circumstance she both welcomed and dreaded. Alone in her cabin, she could escape the feeling that she was constantly under scrutiny from some unseen party—surely Marazzi and Stefano. At the same time, solitude brought no escape from her thoughts, which wheeled in the same unproductive circles. Doubt and worry were her constant companions, and fear rode nearly every waking moment. As the *Ariadne* steamed steadfastly down the coast of Mexico, Juliana's nights had left her wide awake.

A great emptiness filled her, as if Will McKenna were half-a-world away from her instead of trekking happily through the wilds of northern Mexico. Part of her mind jeered at her unhappiness. He might have been in the cabin next door for all the thought he took of her. He had watched her with those cool gray eyes and he had held her in his arms and kissed her once. Just to close her eyes and she could conjure again the feel of his arms, the emotions and longing that swept through her at his kiss. If this was love, she didn't want it.

To Will, she was just a child with whom he had once played. As a man, he'd hired her for her skill: to paint his botanical specimens. She must put him out of her mind and her heart, for although he had made the connection between Juliana and her family, he was gone from her life now. Will was hiking through the wilderness in search of new medicinal plant compounds. For the thousandth time, she admonished herself sternly, she must put away all thoughts of the man and concentrate on the task before her.

Massimo greeted his sister with a quick peck on each cheek at suppertime, then studiously addressed his attention to his meal. Juliana opened her mouth to speak to him, caught Pevie's eye, and closed her mouth resolutely. Massimo looked up at that moment and flashed his sister a cheeky grin. In spite of her worry, an answering grin tugged at the corners of her mouth.

Pevie ate his supper, chewing methodically, lost in thought. Juliana ate without much appetite, although the food was good, and let her gaze wander to the windows that overlooked the deck. Diners from the earlier seating were taking advantage of the calm seas and warm evening air to promenade along the deck, while passengers waiting for the final dinner seating mingled in loose groups. Occasionally a crew member would hurry through the throng.

Back and forth, back and forth her gaze swung across the comings and goings of the strollers along the deck and the knots of people conversing, then drifting apart. Looking down, she found that she had pleated her napkin into a myriad of folds. What flicker of unease was washing over her? Frowning, she identified the feeling: she felt that someone was watching her. Forcing her hands to relax, she picked up her water goblet and drank, letting her gaze rake the view beyond the dining salon windows.

There! By the railing, a man turned away abruptly and slipped away behind a group of men and women lazily drifting away from the salon. Clad in an over-large brown tweed jacket with the collar turned up, and a shapeless hat, the man's features were indistinguishable at the distance between them. Marazzi? Surely not Stefano—his bulk would have been obvious even at a distance. But why should Marazzi lurk about spying upon her? They were all bound for Esmeraldas. She sighed. Would this journey never end?

No dreams came that night to disturb her sleep, and Juliana woke slowly into darkness. Had clouds rolled in during the night? It was still so dark in her small cabin. Then a sound froze her in place. The door handle clicked as someone turned it. Breath caught in her throat, and she eased herself into a sitting position and listened hard. She heard it then, the sound of soft footsteps moving away down the deck. Who had come to her door in the middle of the night? Now that she was fully awake, she realized that it was in fact still night, and the slight sounds of someone at her door had awakened her.

Tired and pale the next day, Juliana kept the news of her nocturnal visitor to herself. Had she told them, Massimo and Pevie would insist on watching her cabin each night until they docked. Neither could afford the added burden.

Instead, she made sure each night they remained aboard ship that her cabin door was securely locked, and, as an added measure, she pushed her trunk in front of the door before going to bed.

And, every night, the same routine was reenacted. Someone came each night to test her cabin door. She began to wonder if perhaps her nightly visitor might not be, in fact, Massimo or Pevie, checking to see that she had secured her door. The routine oddly comforted her, and she found she slept soundly after each incident. Yet she didn't question her companions. If they denied it, then who could it be?

On a hot, muggy morning, nearly three weeks after setting off from San Francisco, the *Ariadne* steamed past the harbor of Esmeraldas. Juliana stood at the rail, squashed between her brother and Pevie, eying the small islands that dotted the harbor. One of these islands was Las Tolitas, the center of the ruins that marked the passing of that ancient culture. Away from the jumbled confusion of the port, mangrove forests fringed the coastline, closed and forbidding.

A day later they steamed into the harbor at Guayaquil. It was midmorning before the passengers were permitted to disembark, and Pevie immediately commandeered a dark-skinned porter to take up their trunks, giving the address of a small hotel the *Ariadne's* steward had recommended. As they waited for their luggage to be loaded onto a cart, Massimo laid a warning hand on his sister's arm. Juliana stiffened as Marazzi came into view and, seeing them, doffed his hat. Behind him, Stefano loomed like a broad shadow, sweating profusely in the tropical heat.

"I will be staying at the *Constitución*," Marazzi said sharply. "You have one month to deliver to me there the treasure of my dear uncle, at which time you and your companions shall be free to take passage back to San Francisco. My *associates*," he said, stressing the word smoothly, "will keep me abreast of your efforts. Good day."

Massimo held tightly to his sister's arm, as her whole body trembled. With an effort she unclenched her jaw and met her brother's eyes.

"He won't beat us, Massimo. We won't let him."

Massimo laughed softly and helped her onto the cart. As they rode through the crowded, dirty streets that fanned out from the dockside, despair replaced her anger and she clutched at Massimo's hand. Warehouses and shacks filled every available inch of space, and the streets about them thronged with people. Brown-skinned *indigenas*, Europeans, and everywhere amongst them the descendants of Negro slaves who had worked the coastal cacao plantations mingled, although they gave way before the fair-skinned European merchants. Cargoes of bananas were being unloaded from carts, big melons and sacks of rice and coffee and cacao beans piled outside warehouses, white men overseeing mestizo workers.

The streets grew more ordered as they left the harbor behind them and made their way into the heart of Guayaquil. Narrow cobblestone streets opened onto small plazas and tall buildings turned their faces away from the busy streets. In the *Calle de la Señora Guadelupe*, they found their hotel, *El Generale*, three stories high above a ground floor of shops. Behind it was a small garden and patio with outdoor dining.

Tired and drained by the unaccustomed heat and the enormity of the task before them, Juliana was content to let Pevie deal with the receptionist as he arranged for their lodging. The hotel offered a small suite of two rooms with private bath and a tiny servant's room. A narrow balcony overlooked the garden below, the doors to this now shuttered against the noon-day heat. Mosquito netting tented the bed and cool water and fresh linen awaited her on a dresser next to the bed.

Massimo came through the connecting door with a worried glance at his sister.

"Mr. Pevie says we should rest midday, Juliana, as the locals here do, then venture out after our dinner to start our inquiries. This is well, *sí*?"

"Yes." Suddenly decisive, Juliana squared her shoulders and managed a smile for her younger brother. "This heat saps one's strength and one's wits! I'm afraid it wouldn't do much good to begin now at any rate, for as you say, sensible people rest midday. You rest, too, Massimo. I'll see you at dinner."

They were seated on the patio, their evening meal beginning with ceviche, raw fish marinated in limes and served with onions and chili peppers. This dish was followed by grilled shrimp on a bed of rice, with wine to drink. Juliana finished her meal with sweet custard apples.

Pevie cleared his throat.

"Before I rested this afternoon, I asked the hotel concierge where one might find shops selling curios and goldwork, as the lady wished to purchase souvenirs." He produced a slip of paper from his jacket pocket. "The concierge obliged me with the names of two well-established shops and noted that there are others nearby."

"You think we might find a merchant who sold the gold mask to Renato Vittorio?"

"I'm thinking it's a start," Pevie said grimly. "I don't believe your great-uncle found a treasure horde and hid it away against his return."

"Nor do I," Juliana agreed. "Shall we go?"

Señor Bartelemo's shop was spotless and well-lit, tucked away on the ground floor beneath the superior *Hotel del Grande* on one of the main streets of the city. His gleaming white moustache bristled as he pulled out a tray of ornate brooches and earrings for a well-endowed Spanish matron and her deferential son.

"*Mamá*," the son, a portly middle-aged man, murmured and waved a hand at *Señor* Bartelemo, who set the tray before the woman and offered her a mirror as she held a pair of earrings to her ears. A gaunt young man stepped out of a backroom and hurried over to greet them.

"May I be of assistance, please?" The assistant's English was serviceable, and again, Juliana let Pevie take the lead.

"*La señorita* is interested in a small gold brooch or earrings, perhaps," Pevie said, indicating Juliana with a slight bow.

"Ah." The clerk's dark eyes smoothly assessed the quality of their clothing and he indicated a tray beneath the glass counter. "We have a beautiful collection here." The tray held ornately worked filigree earrings in gold and silver.

Juliana shook her head slightly and Pevie offered a hand.

"May I, *Señorita* Giuliano?"

Juliana slipped the chain from her neck and lay the gold mask across her friend's palm.

"*La señorita* is interested in purchasing a piece similar to this one." He held his palm before the shop assistant.

"It is most curious," the man began.

"Alfonso!" The shopkeeper waved an imperious hand at his clerk. "Here, please, *la senora's* packages, at once!"

"Excuse me," Alfonso murmured and hurried to retrieve the matron's parcels from the counter while her dutiful son solicitously guided his mother from the shop.

Señor Bartelemo inserted himself smoothly in place behind the counter.

"How may I assist you, *señor, señorita*?" He had clearly been paying close attention to his assistant's efforts. Once more Pevie held out the golden mask for inspection.

The shopkeeper raised a brow and leaned forward.

"May I?" When Pevie nodded, the man took the piece gingerly between thumb and forefinger and examined it with the lens he wore on a chain about his neck. Juliana held her breath as he carefully inspected one side and then the other.

"Ah, no," he said and shook his head dismissively. "A pretty trinket, but I do not sell such here. I have just received, here," he whisked a tray from beneath the counter, "a fine selection of gold brooches from Spain." He read the answer on Juliana's face before Pevie thanked him and took Juliana's elbow.

Outside, Pevie grinned at her.

"We didn't think it would be that easy, now, did we?" Consulting his slip of paper, he pointed to a small square a block away. "That way, I think."

Juliana tugged at his arm.

"Wait, Pevie." She looked back at the shop they had just visited. "Where's Massimo?"

A sharp glance up and down the street showed no sign of the young man.

"On some errand of his own, for sure. That one," Pevie declared, "keeps his own counsel. Don't worry, he's probably ahead of us. We'll meet up in one of the shops, wait and see."

As the hotel receptionist had promised, they found a half-dozen shops clustered around the square before them. Within each, Juliana produced her necklace and scanned the trays of each shop's offerings carefully, but in none of them did they come across any piece that resembled the tiny golden mask.

"Perhaps in the museum at Quito," the last shopkeeper said, offering the same suggestion they'd heard from nearly every shop owner. He shrugged, politely covering his disappointment at the lack of a sale.

Nor had they come across Massimo, although one clerk reported another man had come asking for such an object before them. "Another men, a man— another man," he had repeated, his English halting. When he switched to Spanish, the shopkeeper had frowned and intervened.

On the sidewalk once again, Juliana faced Pevie with a frown.

"When I get my hands on my brother!" She stopped in exasperation.

Pevie took her arm. "Let's go back to *El Generale*. You'll see, Massimo will be waiting for us. We'll have a cold drink and plan for tomorrow."

Scanning the busy streets, Juliana reluctantly followed Pevie back to the hotel. Ensconced at a small table on the patio, she sipped gratefully at her glass of lemonade, leaned back in her chair, and closed her eyes against the waves of fatigue that washed over her. Their search was worse than a needle in a haystack, she admitted bleakly to herself.

They could not even be sure that they were looking in the right haystack. She opened her eyes. Pevie stared off into the hotel interior beyond her, lost in thought. Then his gaze shifted and he beckoned the waiter.

"Another lemonade, *por favor*," he requested as Massimo slid into the seat next to Juliana.

"Massimo!" she began, then held her peace as he gulped down half his glass of lemonade. "Where've you been? Please don't disappear like that again!"

Her brother ducked his head at her scolding, but seized her hand in his.

"My sister, I went where you could not go."

Pevie leaned forward.

"Tell us," he ordered quietly.

"You recall the clerk in the first shop? When he saw your necklace?" Massimo's dark eyes gleamed in the lamplight. "The sight of it seemed to surprise him. I waited, when you left the shop, to ask him why." Here her brother stopped for a moment as if to choose his words. Instead, he reached into his pocket and pulled out a handful of coins.

"On board ship, I made friends among the crew. At night, we play cards for a few pennies." At his sister's frown, Massimo hastened on with his tale. "It was a way to see into other areas of the ship," he turned to Pevie, "and to have friends if we should need them."

Juliana gave her brother a rueful smile. "A good plan, Massimo, although you might have told us." Did his 'friends' explain her nightly visitor? A friend of Massimo's keeping an eye on his sister? Massimo grinned.

"Sometimes I lose a little, but sometimes I win." That quick grin flashed again, and Juliana had the unsettling feeling that her brother had lost only because he wished. "And so, I have money to buy the clerk, Alfonso, a meal, a drink."

"And?" Pevie prompted gently.

Massimo sat forward eagerly and lowered his voice.

"According to Alfonso, twice he has been asked about such an item. Once three-four weeks ago, again two days ago. Both times by *norteamericanos*."

"Did he know their names? Could he describe either man?" Pevie's voice betrayed his anxiety, but his hopeful expression deflated as Massimo shook his head.

"I tried, but it was no good. 'Neither too young, nor too old. The first with dark hair, the second with light hair. Then he said, no, both men had dark hair. Neither too tall nor too short,'" Massimo shrugged eloquently, palms up. "That was all he could tell me."

Juliana griped her brother's hands and met Pevie's disappointed gaze.

"Don't you see, Pevie? We're on the right track. And at least, so far, no one seems to have learned anything we haven't."

Pevie nodded slowly.

"'Twas always a long-shot we'd find any answers here," he said. "I'm thinking we should move on to Quito." He ticked off his reasons on his fingers. "One, the museum is there. Someone there may know if a cache of Las Tolitas' artifacts came to light around the time that Renato Vittorio left Ecuador.

Two, I can't see your great-uncle living here in the sweltering lowlands, when there are mountains like those of home. And, three, if we go now and make our inquiries there, we'll still have time to return to Guayaquil if Quito doesn't furnish any leads."

They sat in silence for a long moment, digesting that bleak possibility. At length, Juliana rose.

"Let's give ourselves another day here to see if anyone recognizes Renato Vittorio's name, then we'll make preparations to travel to the capitol."

In the darkness of her room, she lay beneath the mosquito netting that surrounded her bed and drifted into an uneven sleep. No nightmares came to trouble her. Instead, she dreamed of a slow journey into the mountains, the air thinning and cool, the heat and humidity of the coastal lowlands left far behind. And in the heart of the mountains lay a high green valley perched atop the world. Grasses stirred at her booted feet, and she leaned back against a hard torso, strong arms wrapped around her, savoring the soul-stirring view that opened before them.

Them. Juliana opened her eyes to an early morning in which the sun already clamored behind the barred shutters of her room and moisture-laden air settled heavily about her. A headache threatened and the fleeting images of her dream faded, although she closed her eyes a moment to recapture the feelings of joy and contentment that had enveloped her in her dream-state.

How would Renato Vittorio have made a living in Ecuador? Juliana asked herself that question as she sat sipping a glass of lemonade at a small café facing a plaza and waited for Pevie and Massimo to join her. She could see Pevie's tall figure in a shop across the plaza, but Massimo was nowhere to be seen. Renato Vittorio had followed an uncle to South America, but where had they lived, at what had they worked? His uncle had returned to Italy; his descendants still lived in the old country.

Her own father, Juliana knew now, had returned to the same village in Italy with enough money to purchase a farm with enough land to feed his family. The land adjoined his cousins and he farmed with them. But even that success had not kept him from returning home to San Francisco. Home! What force had been strong enough to make Renato Vittorio turn his back on Italy? To make him believe that he could convince the Giuliano patriarch to leave Italy and settle in Ecuador?

But not here. Not in Guayaquil. She was certain of that. Wherever he had retrieved the golden mask, it was not here in this city. Her grandfather's words came back to her, how he had come to San Francisco to work and send money home, but, how upon marrying Nana Angelina, he had made San Francisco home. He had never returned to Italy, not even when Renato had taken Katherine to live there. Had Renato Vittorio done the same as her grandfather? Had he left a wife, a family, in Ecuador waiting for him to come home? Because he had fully intended to return. Then why had he gone home? She was back to her original thought. Knowing his father as he did, what argument had Renato Vittorio deemed powerful enough to persuade the old man to leave his homeland?

As Pevie joined her at the café, Massimo materialized tableside. Both men looked tired and discouraged. They retreated to the hotel dining room for dinner, and after their orders were placed with the hotel waiter, Juliana shared her thoughts with her brother and Pevie. As one born and raised in Italy, Massimo shrugged.

"Such a man as great-grandfather Giuliano," he responded slowly, "would not have been persuaded easily. If Renato Vittorio had taken a wife, his papa would have told him to bring her home to Italy." He paused for a moment, "and there is this, no letters ever came from South America after Renato Vittorio died." His dark eyes gleamed. "If it was money, Renato Vittorio would have shared it with his parents. But, land is what makes a man truly rich. If Renato Vittorio had acquired land—enough land— he might have believed he could convince his papa to come back with him."

They stared at one another, as they digested that idea.

"'Tis something we can ask about in Quito. If a man bought land, where would it be recorded?" Pevie's brow furrowed. "And what do we do if Renato Vittorio's treasure is property?"

"We take a copy of the land deed to Marazzi. He can break the news to his silent partner." Juliana rose stiffly. "We've a long journey ahead."

The journey from Guayaquil to Quito took ten arduous days out of Guayas Province in the Costa into the highland province of Pichincas in the Sierra. The Avenue of the Volcanoes spread before them in a breathtaking display of natural wonder, but Juliana could only press her mount on, ever upward to the high mountain valley that contained Quito. Time pressed heavily on her. Ten days to Quito and ten back again. Twenty days of their allotted month eaten up just by this trip. She barely ate the food set before her and only made the effort of eating to keep one less worry from her brother and Pevie.

She doubted, now, the conclusions they had drawn—that Renato Vittorio might have purchased land in Ecuador. How could he? The *peninsulares* and *criollos* owned most of the land in the country with the mestizos making up artisans and merchants. The *campesinos* or *indígenas* were no better off than European serfs. How could an Italian immigrant with no status or position in Ecuadorian society have purchased land? This journey would prove fruitless and then what would become of her family? She did not doubt the power of the silent Marazzi partner to carry out his threat.

Señor Rodriguez, the man they needed to speak with at the National Museum of the Centro Banco in Quito, was a trim, gray-haired man of nearly seventy whose energy belied his age. He spoke excellent English. "Princeton," he remarked as he examined Juliana's golden mask under a magnifying glass for several long moments. Moving to a row of wooden cabinets, he proceeded to the middle of the row, opened a door, and hesitated a moment before pulling out a drawer which he brought to a work table.

"Genuine Las Tolitas, no doubt whatsoever." He picked up a mask from the drawer, alike enough to be the twin of Juliana's, but bearing a careful museum catalogue number. "I remember *Señor* Giuliano quite well."

Juliana felt light-headed with relief. At last!

"Please," *Señor* Rodriguez waved to some chairs, "it is a long story." Massimo grasped his sister's hand as they seated themselves. Pevie's features were impassive.

"I was a very young man," the professor began, "just beginning my studies here with my predecessor, *Señor* Estevantes. As part of my education, Professor Estevantes allowed me to be present whenever someone brought in an artifact for sale.

"*Señor* Giuliano was one of many such persons. He brought the very piece I hold here and asked if the museum would be interested in acquiring it." He tapped the museum's golden artifact absently. "Such an artifact would have been part of the burial offerings of a person of some importance. You can imagine," he shrugged, "how the discovery of such a grave would mean its destruction. Those who stumbled upon it would seek only to recover the gold and give no thought to the scientific value of an intact grave.

"Imagine our surprise when *Señor* Giuliano offered us a bargain—if we would pay him an agreed-upon price for the grave's gold cache, he would lead us to it—for it remained undisturbed, hidden away. A man of much honor!"

Juliana's mouth was dry. She had to wet her lips before she could speak.

"And did you? Agree upon a price?" *Señor* Rodriguez flashed her a smile and waved at the drawer. "*Sí*. The museum agreed to *Señor* Giuliano's terms, after we could see the site and verify the contents of the cache. You see for yourselves, he was a man of his word. Although," he pointed at

Juliana's mask, "in the end, he kept at least one of the artifacts for himself."

A small fortune! One that Renato Vittorio had not brought home to Italy. What had become of the money? Pevie cleared his throat.

"*Señor* Rodriguez, where was this grave site that *Señor* Giuliano found?"

"Ah," his dark eyes gleamed, "that was the most interesting part of *Señor* Giuliano's story. The grave shaft was located here in the highlands—far from the coast. So it was extremely important to find such a site relatively undisturbed. But," he held up a hand as Juliana and Pevie exclaimed aloud, "he would not reveal the location to us. Indeed, we traveled southeast from Quito for most of a day, when we made camp. On the second morning of our travels, we were taken blindfolded from our camp on horseback. By mid-morning we arrived at a large shallow cave in a strange highland valley. There we camped in the cave and excavated the grave shaft for one week, then the journey—complete with blindfolds—was repeated. Once in Quito, we paid *Señor* Giuliano the agreed upon sum and that was the last I ever saw of him. And I told the same to *Señor* Dutton when he came asking."

"Mr. Dutton?" Juliana repeated in bewilderment. "Here, in Quito? A young American, fair-haired?"

"*Sí, un norteamericano*. He came a week ago, asking about *Señor* Giuliano. I told him the same as I tell you now—we recovered all of the artifacts from the gold cache. There was only the one grave and we excavated it completely. No treasure remains to be found, and even if there was, as I have told you, we never knew exactly where we were."

"But," Pevie said, eying the museum curator frankly, "I'm thinking you must have a fairly good idea of where to find that grave site."

Señor Rodriguez nodded curtly in assent and pulled a map across the table to them.

"*Señor* Dutton said it was a debt of honor. He asked the same as you, and I will show you what I think." The map had a small penciled circle southeast of the capitol city. "I cannot say for certain, you understand?" He shrugged. "Nothing else ever came to us from that area."

James Dutton had come to Quito before them. Why? Juliana worried at that puzzle, keeping Massimo close in the Mercado, Quito's open-air market, as Pevie bartered for guides and horses to take them on their trek southeast of Quito. Numbly, all she could think of was yet another three to four days gone, then the inevitable return to Guayaquil. Biagio Marazzi would not believe them when they told him that there was no treasure waiting to be recovered.

Massimo tugged at his sister's arm.

"Katerina," he pointed at a stall displaying colorful sweaters and hats, shawls and gloves. "Shall we look for warmer clothes? It will be cold on the trail."

The sweaters were beautifully worked in colorful patterns, although other garments were of dark gray and brown and creamy white colors, wonderfully lightweight. As Juliana handled these, a young woman smiled shyly at her and spoke in Spanish. Juliana caught the word 'alpaca' and 'llama' and nodded to show that she understood. The wool for these garments had come from the pack animals of the Sierra. Pevie joined them, and as they each made a selection of sweater, hat, scarf, and gloves, the young woman waited patiently. Dark-haired with black eyes, she wore the traditional skirt and shawl of the *campesinos*.

While Pevie gathered their selections together and turned to bargain, a man slipped past them and spoke brusquely to the young woman, who cast one swift glance at her customers, then faded into the interior of the stall. The newcomer, who looked to be in his mid-thirties, addressed Pevie in Spanish. In a few short minutes, coins changed hands, and they made their way out of the Mercado with their purchases.

"Curious," Pevie remarked, "that *campesino* barely bargained for a price on his merchandise. 'Tis worth twice what we paid." Beside them, Massimo halted.

"He wanted us to go away quickly. Did you not see, Katerina, how like Lucy the young woman looked? Not like," he pointed discreetly at a group of *indigenas* nearby, "these native women."

"Renato Vittorio wasn't the only Italian immigrant to this area. Pevie," Juliana clutched his forearm, "do you suppose James has been here before us, asking questions in the market? Let's go back. If there's an Italian immigrant community here...." She left her hope unspoken.

But the stall, when they reached it again, was closed up and none of the nearby stall owners appeared to know anything at all about the people who had left. It was only as they left the Mercado that a beggar approached and addressed Pevie in halting Spanish. Pevie replied sharply, and dropped a coin onto the man's outstretched palm.

"He says that the stall's owners come from San Cristobel, higher in the mountains," he paused and excitement colored his voice, "about a day's ride southeast of Quito."

Massimo whistled and Juliana's fingers tightened on her brother's arm. Perhaps this trek would be fruitful after all.

She repeated that hope like a prayer over and over on the long hours of their journey, scarcely noting the trail or the terrain through which they traveled. They woke after a night on the trail to find that their guides refused to take them further. Pevie was furious, but no threat or offer of more money made any difference. If the *norteamericanos* wished to continue, they must do so alone. In the end, the head guide, Raul, agreed to wait two days at the camp for them to return.

Juliana followed Pevie along the trail, Massimo close behind her. The refusal of the guides to continue worried at her. Ecuador was a country precariously teetering between democracy and dictatorship. The liberal Costa region centered on Guayaquil was at constant odds with the conservative Sierra region. Was some political unrest brewing? Or were they in danger of attack by brigands? Pevie called a halt mid-morning to rest, for the thin air was tiring and a hot drink was welcome. Juliana rested her back against a boulder and closed her eyes.

"Juliana," Pevie's voice warned her, and Juliana's eyes flew open. They were surrounded by *campesinos*, their intent unmistakable. Several men were armed, and in no time at all, Juliana, Massimo, and Pevie were riding again. It was mid-day, she guessed, weary to the bone, when they were led into San Cristobel and secured in a stone hut on the edge of the village. Their gear was deposited within and a guard posted outside the door. Dusty and cold, Juliana leaned her head against the door and bit back tears of frustration and fear. Behind her, she heard Massimo's voice, "Katerina?", followed by Pevie's quick intake of breath. "By God!"

She turned about, beyond surprise.

James Dutton smiled crookedly at her.

"Hello, Juliana, I see you wouldn't listen to the guides either. I'm afraid I can't get up to greet you properly." Even as he spoke, his face paled and he held a basin to his face and vomited. Hastening to him, she caught then the sour smell of sickness in the room, but noted that he was heaving up only bile. A pitcher of water stood on a rough table near the cot where James Dutton lay. She doused the end of her scarf in the water and used it to wipe her cousin's face as he fell back on his cot. This, the table, and two rough wooden chairs and a bench by the table were the only furniture that the hut contained.

Pevie and Massimo dropped their packs on the floor and shrugged off their overcoats, laying these on the bench they pulled up before the fire in the hearth. The fire burned just hot enough to take the chill from the room. As James Dutton lay back, his eyes closed, the two men sat. Juliana met the gazes of her companions and shrugged helplessly, sitting on the edge of the cot and holding James' hand. As if his strength had been spent in their short exchange, Jimmy sighed and seemed to sleep.

As the three of them stared at the still form of James Dutton without speaking, voices could be heard outside their hut. Before Pevie could translate the rapid Spanish, the door swung open and Juliana froze in the act of rising from James' bedside. Surely she had taken leave of her senses at last. She put the back of her hand to her mouth and felt the world spinning away from her.

CHAPTER TWELVE

Will McKenna reached Juliana's side before her brother or Pevie could rise from the bench at the fire, taking her hands and chafing the warmth back into them. "Juliana, *cara*." His voice cracked and the world around her steadied and came into focus again.

"How?" Pevie was nearly speechless as Massimo stared and shook his head. Will released Juliana and looked down at the still figure of James Dutton. He ran a hand distractedly through his hair as he gathered his thoughts.

"Henry Dutton asked me to come to Ecuador to see if I could find Renato Vittorio's treasure," he said. "Jimmy told his brother some rambling story about a lost treasure in Ecuador, one he could use to repay some debt he owed. At the time, Henry assumed his brother was drunk, but when Jimmy disappeared, he was certain that Jimmy was here, searching for it."

Juliana caught her breath in dismay.

"No, not Henry!"

Will glanced sharply at her and gave a bitter laugh. "No, not Henry." He pulled a chair from the table and straddled it backward. "Henry was worried and upset, Juliana, after that attack on you. He was even more agitated when he learned there'd been an earlier attack." He took a deep breath. "You see, he was afraid that it might be his brother."

Juliana exclaimed in disbelief, and Will smiled briefly. "Jimmy wasn't himself after the *Alycegee* sank, after his head injury. Henry began to be worried his brother was in some kind of trouble, so he had a private investigator follow him. He discovered Jimmy was frequently seen with a disreputable Italian dockworker called Stefano. "And then James disappeared," Juliana said.

"Exactly. Henry was certain Jimmy was on his way to Ecuador to search for a treasure which might not even exist. But he couldn't go after his brother and abandon Sarah to their father." Will shifted restlessly. "With their father pressuring Sarah to go to New York for eye surgery, Henry couldn't go away and leave her to deal with him alone. We decided it would be best if no one knew I was going after Jimmy, and so we told everyone I was prospecting for new plant specimens. I've been here before, so it made sense I should come."

Juliana remembered their dinner with Rico Peña, when he had so adroitly glossed over the question of Will's travels in Mexico. She glanced at the pale form of James Dutton as he slept uneasily beside her. "Jimmy may have come here seeking Renato Vittorio's treasure, but I will not believe that he ever tried to hurt me. He's sick, Will. We've got to get him back to Quito."

Pevie gestured at the door. "So what do you know about these *campesinos* who brought us here? Why are they holding us? What do they want from us? Money?"

Will's gray eyes darkened, and he ran a hand through his hair again. "I came through this way last time I went through the Sierra. I'd been in Peru collecting specimens and someone suggested I continue into Ecuador. I hired local guides from San Cristobel, and I met a village *curandero*—healer," he explained with a grin for Massimo. "This time around, I managed to pick up Jimmy's trail in Guayaquil and follow him to Quito. I finally met up with him at his lodgings. He refused to explain himself and gave me the slip, laying a false trail for me to follow, north out of the capitol. By the time I got back to Quito, it took me several days to find out he'd gone to San Cristobel. *Señor* Hector, my *curandero* friend, says that Jimmy walked into the village two days ago. I found him like this when I arrived."

Before Will could continue, Pevie stood up impatiently. "But why are the villagers holding us? What is it that they want from us?" He gestured at Juliana in frustration. "Show him," he said.

She pulled the necklace from under her dress. "The attacks on me were an attempt to retrieve this," she said. "My father's uncle, Renato Vittorio Giuliano, brought this and a similar piece back to Italy, where he died before he could return to Ecuador. Father's cousins believe Renato Vittorio left a treasure hidden away here in Ecuador. Along with a partner"—she glanced involuntarily at James—"they threatened Lucy Katerina if we didn't find it for them." She nodded at her traveling companions. "When we reached Quito, we learned Renato Vittorio had found a tomb with a cache of gold. The museum excavated the site and paid Renato Vittorio for his finds. We were told—and Jimmy before us—that the gravesite was somewhere in this area."

She paused and Massimo spoke for the first time. "There is this also, Dr. McKenna. We saw an Italian immigrant merchant in El Mercado. When we went to ask him about Renato Vittorio, the stall was closed up. We were told he was in San Cristobel."

Will shook his head. "Someone misled you, Massimo. There are no immigrants in San Cristobel." He looked at their weary faces and his gaze lingered for a moment on James Dutton, who was stirring restlessly beside Juliana. "*Señor* Hector—the *curandero* opened his home to me. He told me there's been another stranger in the village recently, someone who told the villagers to watch for three *norteamericanos* who were on their way and were bringing trouble with them."

Pevie exclaimed, "Marazzi!"

Will held up a hand. "There's more. Villagers were paid to keep you here until the stranger returns."

"Surely your friend can vouch for us," Juliana protested, but Will shook his head, pointing at James Dutton.

"The *campesinos* are superstitious, Juliana. When James wandered in, ill, the stranger laid the cause of that illness—*la brujería*—at your feet."

Pevie swore softly. "Witchcraft?"

Bile rose in Juliana's throat. How could they fight such a charge? Will rose and came to sit next to her, taking her hand and putting an arm around her shoulders. His look included Massimo and Pevie. "Jimmy stumbled into San Cristobel, half-frozen. God knows how he came there. *Señor* Hector fed him and gave him a bed, but when he woke in the night, sick, the village men who'd been paid by Marazzi brought him here to keep his sickness from infecting the villagers." He stroked Juliana's hand.

"I've checked Jimmy myself. He has no fever, no bites, no cramping—there's nothing that can account for his chills, his vomiting. But *Señor* Hector has had other patients sick like this—sick from *mal aire* or *espanto*."

"Bad air?" Pevie was baffled.

Massimo listened intently, his dark eyes alert, and Juliana guessed that in the village he'd come from there might have been similar superstitious beliefs layered under centuries of Catholicism. She leaned against Will's solid form and felt herself warming from his nearness and his concern.

"*Mal* refers to a bad force in nature. The *campesinos* believe it can accumulate anywhere, in rock outcroppings or abandoned houses or gravesites, and infect a person's body, making them physically ill. More serious is *espanto*; that means soul loss. The symptoms for both are the same—loss of appetite, coldness, paleness, vomiting, headache."

Pevie made a movement of impatience and Juliana squeezed Will's fingers. "James Dutton is sick at heart," she remarked softly, looking sadly at the pale restless face beside her. "Something is eating away at him—something he won't confide to Sarah or Henry or even to you, Will."

"Yes," Will agreed. "The *curandero* is also known as *el limpiador*—the cleaner." He grimaced. "So here's what I've done: I paid *Señor* Hector to perform a ceremony to cleanse Jimmy of his sickness, of *mal*. If he succeeds in driving out the *mal*, then the charge of *brujería* will hold no weight, and the rest of the village will allow us to leave."

"And if he's unsuccessful? If there's no change in Dutton's condition come morning? Nothing good, I'm thinking." Pevie's blue eyes were somber.

Massimo's face clouded at his words, then cleared abruptly. "There is this," he said, nodding at the fireplace. "If all else fails, I'm small enough to climb out the chimney. I could go back to our camp and get help."

Will nodded and might have spoken, but the door opened to admit a short, wiry man wearing the felt hat, vest, and jacket of the highland *campesinos*. Will stood up and strode forward to clasp his hand and speak urgently to him. He turned to the others. "*Señor* Hector speaks no English, but he asks me to tell you all to please be seated and to concentrate your prayers on his patient."

The *curandero* drew bundles of plants from his bag and laid them out carefully on the table. Will fingered them curiously, directing a series of questions at *Señor* Hector. Juliana suppressed a small smile; the scientist in Will couldn't be quashed even by the urgency of their situation. In spite of the uncertainty of the moment, an unfamiliar lassitude crept over her. Will had come. Somehow, they would make it all come right.

The *curandero* was smiling at Will's questions and responded gravely, touching each plant as he spoke. Will translated. "These are his *material medica*—medicinal herbs. *Eucalipto, romero*—a kind of rosemary, *pumin*," he sniffed, "a kind of mint, *chilca, capulí*." Will glanced up. "He'll diagnose Jimmy first, then decide which plants to use. If you'll help me, Mr. Pevie, we need to strip off his shirt and trousers."

Massimo held a blanket as a screen between the cot and Juliana to preserve the patient's dignity. She met Will's amused glance, remembering the times she'd nursed strangers in the lighthouse keeper's quarters. *Señor* Hector produced an egg from his bag and a glass, which he half-filled with water from a jug on the table. Egg in hand, he approached James Dutton and began to rub the egg gently across his cheeks, his nose, his chin, his forehead, his scalp, his neck, then down his chest and abdomen, across his arms and legs, then feet. At a gesture, Will and Pevie rolled the patient over and *Señor* Hector rubbed the egg methodically across his back. The *curandero* took great care as he performed this procedure, murmuring softly. Will didn't attempt to translate.

Juliana sat watching and worrying. James wasn't responding to the treatment: his eyes remained closed and he lay limp, as if he had no strength or awareness left. At length, *Señor* Hector motioned for his patient to be turned again and pulled his blanket gently over him.

Next he moved to the table and deftly cracked the egg into the glass of water. Massimo and Pevie joined Juliana on her bench. Will commented softly as the *curandero* pointed at the egg and pursed his lips, frowning. After several long moments, he spoke in rapid Spanish.

Will translated. "He's considering the color of the egg, its shape—or configuration in the water, and its buoyancy—how much of it is floating. That will tell him whether it's a case of *mal aire* or something more. Ah," he said and nodded as *Señor* Hector tapped at the glass. The yolk was sinking beneath the water and settling at the bottom. From where she was sitting, Juliana could see the color was not the bright yellow of a fresh egg. "He says it is as he suspected, our friend is suffering from *espanto*. He'll prepare his *escobita* now for the cleansing ceremony."

As they watched, *Señor* Hector selected branches of the *eucalipto*, the *romero*, and the *pumin* and began to weave them deftly together.

"It is like a little broom," Massimo observed quietly and Will's teeth gleamed in a quick grin.

"Yes. The *curandero* will take this broom of healing branches and sweep away the *mal*, the cause of the sickness, from the patient's body. Then he'll dispose of the *escobita* far from any human habitation."

"Why not burn it here?" Pevie suggested, eying the *curandero* as he held the finished *escobita* above the fire. The pungent scents of eucalyptus, mint, and rosemary wafted from the *escobita* as he gently shook it back and forth over the fire. Will asked *Señor* Hector a question; he jerked his head in a gesture that they all understood and replied at length. Will raised his brows thoughtfully and summarized for their benefit.

"*Mal* is a natural force. It can't be destroyed. So he'll take it far from here, so it will be released back to nature far from people."

Taking his warmed *escobita*, *Señor* Hector returned to James Dutton and began to brush his body from head to toe in long, slow strokes with the bundle of plants. He chanted under his breath as he worked, stopping only once to direct his assistants to roll the patient over. Juliana found herself breathing deeply, her spirits reviving as she inhaled the crisp clean scents of the *ramos benditos* or healing branches of the *curandero*. When he was finished, Massimo held the blanket again as Pevie and Will redressed James and then tucked the blanket carefully about him. The patient yawned once, like a child, rolled on his side and slept on.

Señor Hector wrapped the *escobita* in a worn piece of blanket, then packed away his *material medica*, disposed of the egg in the fire, and rinsed the glass and put it in his bag. After a few brief words with Will, he nodded shyly at the others, then accepted a handful of coins from Will and took his leave.

Will sat down next to Juliana.

"*Señor* Hector will return in the morning to check his patient. In the meantime, he will send his wife with food for us. If Jimmy wakes in the night, we're to see if he can take something to eat."

As soon as *Señora* Hector brought their food—potato soup with bread and a pot of hot coffee—and they had eaten, Pevie and Massimo made up their bedrolls by the fire. Juliana followed suit.

"We can take turns sitting with Dutton." Pevie's blue eyes were dark with fatigue and worry. "I'll will take the midnight and early morning shifts with Massimo." He was careful not to glance from Juliana to Will as he spoke, and Juliana nodded gratefully. She pulled the bench to the table and sat with a cup of hot coffee between her hands. Will joined her, and they sat in silence as he put his arm around her and held her close. There would be a time and place for words, but just being here together was enough for the moment.

Juliana, leaning drowsily against Will, caught her breath when she detected a movement from the bed. James had opened his eyes and smiled at them. She hastened to get the soup, kept warm on the coals of the fire, as Will helped his friend into a sitting position. Jimmy drank some coffee first and heaved a sigh of relief when it stayed down.

"How do you feel?" Will asked him, taking the cup as Juliana handed Jimmy the soup. He gave a short, rueful laugh.

"As if I'll live, by heaven! Better than I've felt in weeks." He rubbed his hand over his face.

"Oh, thank heavens, you had us worried!" Juliana set his emptied soup bowl on the table and came back to sit beside him.

"Why did you come to Ecuador, Jimmy? And why here, to San Cristobal?" Will put the questions quietly, and James Dutton sighed again and shook his head.

"I'm not being secretive for no reason, Will," he said with a quick glance at Juliana. "I haven't known what to do, but coming here was a fool's errand. I see that now. I talked with that man at the museum—I'm guessing you did the same. Hired a guide and horses only to have them run off in the night by bandits." He ran a hand through his fair hair. "I'm not quite sure they weren't friends of that guide, you know. And then I walked and walked some more and then when I didn't think I could walk any more, someone found me."

He rubbed his jaws hard.

"I was a fool, Will. I'm going home to talk with Henry. If I'm wrong, then no one ever needs to know how silly my fears were. But if I'm right," he looked grimly from one friend to the other, "then Henry will know what to do."

"I see," Will responded neutrally, and Juliana thought she saw a glimmer of the truth. James suspected someone of wishing harm to the Giulianos, and coming to Ecuador to search for Renato Vittorio's treasure had been his solution to buying their safety.

Jimmy clasped Will's shoulder. "Thank you, Will." He handed his bowl to Juliana. "But what are you doing here, Juliana? You and your brother and Mr. Pevie?"

As quickly as she could, she told him why they had traveled to Ecuador and why they were all together at this moment in San Cristobel.

"Then I'd better rest now," he replied determinedly, "so the villagers can see I'm no longer ill as soon as possible. I've taken all the soup I can for now."

He roused himself once more before midnight and took a little more nourishment. Both stayed down and his face lost some of its pallor. Pevie awoke as James drifted off to sleep. Juliana crawled thankfully into her bedroll and Will stretched out in Pevie's. She lay on her side facing Will and fell asleep with her fingers interlocked in his.

A wan gray light feebly lit the interior of the hut when Juliana sat up from her bedroll the next morning, roused by a knock at the door. *Señor* Hector and his wife entered. She was bearing hot potatoes and salt and more hot coffee. The *curandero* listened attentively as Will gestured at James, who was awake and propped up on an elbow. His alert features and the gusto with which he devoured the potato and coffee Juliana brought to him needed no translation, for *Señor* Hector was nodding and smiling broadly as Jimmy finished his breakfast. As the door closed behind the *curandero* and his wife, Will crossed to Jimmy's side.

"If you feel strong enough to ride, my friend, I suggest we leave for Quito immediately. *Señor* Hector is informing the villagers you are healed, the *espanto* has been cured. We need to be on our way quickly, before anyone decides to ask for a second opinion."

No one opposed them when they stepped out of the hut. Their horses were waiting, held by the *curandero* and his wife. It was decided that James would share a mount with Massimo, for both young men were slight of build and Massimo's sturdy horse could carry them easily enough for the day it would take them to return to Quito.

Will gave Juliana a leg up, and she settled herself securely in the saddle as the rest of her party mounted. She could feel eyes on her from the villagers' stone houses. It made her uneasy in a way she couldn't put her finger on, and she urged her horse close after Will's as he took the road out of San Cristobel northwest toward Quito.

Massimo and James fell in behind her, and Pevie brought up the rear. Her moment of uneasiness passed as they cleared the village fields. Here they would climb out of the valley, she recalled, and the road would soon fork. Their path lay along the road that continued northwest through the mountains to the pass which would bring them down again into the highland valley that held Quito.

The other fork was little more than a trail, heading northeast and higher into the mountains.

Mindful of James' precarious strength and the stony road, Will set a steady but slow pace. They had ridden nearly an hour, Juliana judged, when the road opened up to the fork. Her horse crowded close to Will's and she glanced back to see that Pevie had drawn abreast of Massimo and Jimmy.

Large boulders had tumbled down from the mountainsides here and there, dividing the road. Will and Juliana rode together around one such massive fall. The going was rough and Pevie and her brother fell behind them as they sought the easiest path for their horses.

A shot rang out behind them and the rock beside Juliana suddenly splintered. Her horse reared in fright and bolted along the north fork of the road. She heard Pevie shouting, then a second bullet pinged from the mountainside beside her and her horse was running with the bit between his teeth, heedless of her knees, her voice. She couldn't risk a backward glance, but held on in terror as her horse careened headlong up the trail. One misstep and she and her mount would plunge to certain death. Then she heard hoofbeats and risked a glance over her shoulder. Will! He caught up with her just as the trail rose in a steep curve and leaned wide to pull her to safety, his arm an iron band around her as he fought to stop his mount.

The momentum took them into the curve of the trail, and as they did so, another bullet ricocheted off stone behind them. Will's horse reared in fright, and Juliana fell, rolling free of the slashing hooves. They could clearly hear someone approaching. Will jumped clear of his horse and pulled his bedroll free, then turned his mount and slapped it hard on the rump to send it galloping back along the trail. Tossing the bedroll aside, he heaved a pile of small rock and soil over the trail edge, grabbed the bedroll and followed after Juliana.

She was making for cover when he joined her and got them wedged between boulders. Will proceeded to scale a rockface that looked sheer to Juliana, then reached down and hauled her up to his perch. Lying flat, he inched his way cautiously forward, Juliana wriggling close beside him. They lay side by side and peered below, Juliana's eyes widening when she noticed the revolver in his hand.

A moment passed, no more, then two riders came up the trail, leading Will's horse. They paused at the rockfall Will had pushed from the edge, the lead rider dismounting to scan the mountainside below. He gestured abruptly up the trail, and his companion rode on while the first man slowly surveyed the mountainside. Juliana tensed and flattened herself onto the stony ledge so close to Will that she might have been part of him.

Marazzi had not been content, after all, to wait comfortably in his hotel in Guayaquil, but had followed them to Quito and beyond. He must have been certain they had retrieved the treasure and were returning with it, but he—or his silent partner—clearly had never intended for them to return to San Francisco. She heard noise and risked another look below to see Marazzi's companion returning. His short quick shake of the head communicated the results of his search. Marazzi raked the mountainside one more time with a searching glance, then mounted and jerked the reins of his horse hard back down the trail to the fork.

Will put the revolver away.

"Will." Juliana's voice was hoarse. She clung to him and there was nothing gentle in the kiss they shared, needing to communicate in that one intense, wordless moment the overwhelming relief that they were yet alive and together.

"Juliana, *cara*." Will was the first to pull away. He pulled her to a sitting position.

"What are we going to do?" she asked. "That was Biagio Marazzi!"

"Listen to me, Juliana. If... if Pevie and Massimo made it through the ambush and down the trail.... You've got porters waiting for you, yes?" Juliana bit her lip and nodded. Will continued. "We can't risk going back. Marazzi will have the *campesinos* from San Cristobel searching for our bodies. He may think we have the treasure. We'll never make it back to the fork and down the trail on foot without being seen." He squeezed her hands, and she pointed with her chin up the trail. "Then we go up?"

He nodded. "This trail must lead to a pass. With any luck, we'll find a trail there to bring us back to the road to Quito."

With Will's help, Juliana clambered back down the slope, and they followed the track northeast in silence. Every nerve in Juliana's body told her to turn around and go back, back to the road that would take them to Quito and from there to Guayaquil. But with Biagio Marazzi between them and freedom, it would be foolhardy to risk returning. The worry continuously battered at her: who wanted her gone? No: who needed her *dead*, so desperately that not even the lure of a golden treasure was enough to keep her alive? No answer came, and she held tight to Will's hand and matched his pace.

Later, as their trail wound higher and higher into the Avenue of the Volcanoes, Juliana wrapped her scarf around her mouth and nose and concentrated on breathing, putting one foot in front of the other, sometimes stumbling on a pebble. She couldn't think any more: carrying all her prayers in her mind was all that she could manage—praying that her brother and cousin and Pevie were truly safe, that her unknown enemy would not strike at her family left behind in San Francisco, that this trail would head down the mountain at some point and lead them to safety. She was conscious only of Will's hand in hers and the sharp cold air.

The light was fading from the sky when Will stopped and cupped her face in both hands.

"*Cara*, we'll get off the trail for the night. It's too risky to keep moving in the dark." He kissed her forehead. They climbed once more up the mountainside until at last Will found a sheltered nook out of the worst of the wind. A rockfall had made a low wall of boulders on a flat ledge and it angled out to give them some meager protection on two sides; sitting, they were out of the worst of the wind. Will slipped his bedroll from his back and laid out the groundsheet against the rockface before wrapping a blanket around Juliana and handing her the canteen of water tied to his bedroll. While she drank, he rearranged some of the rocks in their makeshift walls, chinking the larger cracks.

"Here, *cara*," he grunted and wedged himself into the space beside Juliana, drawing his second blanket over them. A spare shirt, rolled up, served as a pillow. He drank from the canteen and she leaned against him. Putting the canteen away, Will wrapped his arms around her and they lay down, cocooned in the blankets, gratefully out of the wind. Slowly, she warmed, her cheek against the roughness of Will's wool coat, her body stretched the length of him as he held her and rubbed her back gently.

"Will?" Her voice was low, though they might have been alone in the Avenue of the Volcanoes, so far away from any vestige of civilization did they seem.

"Hmm?" His breath tickled her cheek, and she smiled against him.

"I love you."

His hand tightened abruptly on her back, then he sighed and his hand resumed rubbing her for warmth.

She whispered, "From the moment you opened your eyes in the kitchen at Point Lobos. You took my heart with you when you left." She felt his lips on her hair.

"I will always love you, Juliana, *cara*."

"I didn't think you liked me much," she admitted, craning her neck to look into his face. "You seemed to frown every time you looked at me. I thought you must be in love with Sarah."

Will shifted position until they were face-to-face. "Sarah's always been a dear friend, Juliana, nothing more. And if I frowned, it's because John Pevie's a hard man to measure oneself against." He sounded rueful. "You were so clearly at ease with each other, I was afraid your heart was already his. But you were always meant to be mine to love and care for, Juliana, although I was too young to understand." His arms tightened around her as he kissed her gently, then she tucked her head beneath his chin.

It will be okay, she thought sleepily, when we come to the valley. The golden mask she wore beneath her shirt warmed against her skin, like a sliver of sun above her heart.

They were walking close together now for support and comfort, blankets wrapped like cloaks to cover their heads. Juliana was tired and hungry and afraid—afraid that the cold would soon reach so far inside her, she'd die of it. Will never let her go, his arm around her, shielding her body as best he could; but some part of her recognized that his efforts took a heavy toll.

She was no longer sure how long they had walked when Will halted.

"Juliana," he said, putting his face close to hers, "*cara*, look, we've made it through the pass! The trail descends from here. There'll be a village soon. There are horse droppings along the trail."

She clutched his arm and nodded that she understood. In another twenty minutes they had descended far enough down the other side of the pass to a point where the mountainside dropped away, revealing the land beyond.

Staggering against Will, Juliana felt hysterical laughter welling up. She met his gray eyes, now wide and disbelieving as her own. Below them lay a small, elongated valley. A high mountain river was fed from streams on either side of the valley, whose narrowest end lay at their feet. The valley floor held several hamlets strung at intervals along the river and flocks could be seen grazing in the higher pastures. Below the pastures, fields surrounded the hamlets. Wordlessly they began the hike into the valley below.

It took them more than an hour, plodding steadily, now almost stumbling, to descend into the upper pastures. A dog greeted them, tail wagging and eyes bright, clearly not threatened by the pair of them. He danced before them before bounding away again, barking.

The first villager appeared as Will helped Juliana over the low stone wall that marked the upland end of a field. Will's arms tightened about Juliana, and he called out to the man. *"Señor, ayudanos!"*

The *campesino*'s dark features were neither hostile nor welcoming, Juliana saw, but warily appraising, as if assessing them, their situation, and his possible responses. They waited.

At length, he replied. *"Sí, ustedes vienes?"* He turned and they followed. He led them along a stony path between fields that brought them into the center of one of the hamlets revealed from the heights of the pass. He called out as he approached, and a door was flung open. A woman stepped out, a child on her hip, and a girl of about eight peering around her skirts. The woman exclaimed softly at the sight of the two strangers.

The house was warm after the cold outside and Juliana swayed with relief. The woman pushed a bench closer to the fireplace and Juliana collapsed onto it, keeping herself upright by force of mind alone. Will braced her and sat with his back to the fire.

"*Gracias, gracias*," she repeated over and over to the dark-haired young woman, holding her hands to the welcome warmth of the flames. The man—her husband?—had not come in with them, Juliana noted as the woman took thick ceramic bowls from a shelf above a table and shook the coals to glowing in the grate of a stove. She lifted a pot over a burner and spoke rapidly to her daughter, who disappeared outside, then returned almost immediately with a bucket of water. The little girl filled two mugs and brought them shyly to Will and Juliana. Her mother poured water into a kettle and set this too on a burner to heat.

The warmth of the room and the fresh water revived Juliana, as did the smell of stew, and, she thought, amazed, something that was surely not fresh bread. She smiled at the woman. "*Gracias, muchas gracias*," she said again.

"*De nada*," the woman responded and shifted her bright-eyed infant to her other hip as her daughter hid once more behind her skirts.

Beside her, Will repeated Juliana's thanks, but said nothing more, and Juliana was aware of his sharp-eyed scrutiny of the stone cottage. A stone fireplace sat to the left of the front entrance and marked a large square keeping room furnished with chairs that could be drawn up to the fire or to a sturdy wooden table that sat off to one side. Their bench had been pulled away from the table. Above and to the side of the stove were shelves that held the household's crockery and sacks and bins of foodstuffs, while a low cupboard next to the stove provided additional workspace and storage. A narrow bed hugged a wall opposite the fireplace, and beyond this, a door stood open through which Juliana could see the foot of a larger bed.

A window to either side of the entrance and one in the kitchen area next to the fireplace filled the cottage with light. Kerosene lamps graced the kitchen table and small tables were placed on either side of the low bed. Everything was well-scrubbed and well-kept.

As Juliana thawed out, their hostess ladled stew into bowls and gestured at the table. She refilled their mugs with the hot brew from the stovetop kettle, which proved to be strong tea, and placed a goodly portion of a long loaf of bread on the table. Tears of gratitude sprang to Juliana's eyes and she wiped them with the corner of her shirt as Will took a seat beside her.

Then they were eating, the food and tea restoring her strength. When every last morsel of stew had been wiped from her bowl with the crust of her bread, Juliana paused in the act of popping the last bite in her mouth. Will, she saw, had gotten there ahead of her, but before she could speak, the door swung open. The *campesino* who had found them entered behind an elderly, white-haired woman and three other men.

Their hostess hastened to pull a rocking chair close to the hearth, and the tiny white-haired woman lowered herself carefully onto the seat. Juliana looked from one face to the other. The two older men looked so much alike, they might have been twins. And those faces! She stared at the third man and her hand went to her alpaca scarf. He was the *campesino* from *El Mercado*. Her gaze moved back to the two older men—as old, she guessed, as her father, Renato.

"Renato Giuliano!" There was a moment's sudden stillness in the room, and she realized that she had spoken his name aloud.

"Renato Vittorio Giuliano?" The two men eyed one another, then Will spoke in rapid Spanish, pausing briefly to translate for Juliana's benefit.

"This woman is Katerina Giuliano. Her father is Renato Giuliano. Her grandfather is the brother of Renato Vittorio Giuliano."

The old woman's bright eyes studied Juliana's face for several long moments, then she pointed to herself and the men to either side of her and replied. Will again translated.

"I am Maria Giuliano, wife of Renato Vittorio. These are my sons—Renato and Vittorio, and Esteban is the son of Vittorio. Tell me, please, what has happened to my husband Renato Vittorio that he never returned to us?"

Her lined face softened as Will repeated the story of Renato Vittorio's return to Italy, how he'd tried to convince his father to come to Ecuador with him, how the man had died in a terrible accident, leaving behind a golden mask which had been handed down to his namesake nephew and hence to Juliana. Juliana pulled the mask from beneath her shirt and watched as her great-aunt nodded in recognition.

"*Sí, sí*, I knew that he must have died, else he would have returned to us, to his family." Will translated softly as words poured from her. "We met in El Mercado. My family has always lived here in this valley and we took our weaving to sell at El Mercado. He came to our stall one fine morning when I was selling. After that, he came many more times." She smiled, remembering. "One day, Renato came to my papa at the market. He gave him one gold piece, *Señorita* Giuliano, and asked permission that we might be married. After we were married, Renato traveled here to the valley with us." Here she began to speak rapidly and tears filled her eyes. Will blinked and asked her several questions. He leaned toward Juliana.

"Renato came here with Maria and discovered that Maria's family and their people were the only ones who knew of this valley, they were the only people who lived here. As Maria's husband, they made him welcome—to farm, to herd. To raise his family. And shared with him a secret: the tomb with its gold cache. Then Renato conceived a plan. He made a deal with *Señor* Estevantes to sell the treasure and use the money to secure his family's future."

Julia was watching the old woman as Will continued. "Some of the money was given to an attorney to draw up a legal title to the whole valley. This was filed in the capitol," he explained, "during the period when Ecuador had won its freedom and land reform was underway. Part of the remaining money was used here to build better homes and for livestock and tools. And part of it was put by to take care of *Doña* Maria and his sons, in case he didn't return from Italy."

Juliana took in the cottage—a setting in which Nana Angelina would feel at home. Renato Vittorio had recreated home. More importantly, he had ensured this valley would always remain home for his family, for his children and his grandchildren— and, yes, for old Vittorio Giuliano, had he been persuaded to leave Italy. She recalled the orderly pastures, the fields, the stone outbuildings and cottages of the hamlets glimpsed as they came down into this valley. The well-made woven scarves and sweaters, hats, and gloves sold in El Mercado in Quito. Renato's family had prospered because of his legacy and their own hard work.

Doña Maria's shrewd, intelligent gaze swept the two strangers before her. She asked a question and the muscles in her sons' jaws tensed. Will met Juliana's glance of inquiry.

"She asks why we have come to this valley."

Juliana sought Will's hand and squeezed it. "If you will translate, Will, tell *Doña* Maria it's an honor to meet Renato Vittorio's family. Then please tell her we claim no rights in this land."

Pulling the chain of her necklace over her head, Juliana slipped from the bench and knelt before the old woman. Taking the hand of Renato Vittorio's widow, she laid the gold mask across *Doña* Maria's palm. "Our family," she met that wary gaze directly, "is in danger because of Renato Vittorio's gift to his papa." Then she told the story as concisely as she could, with Will translating. When she had finished her tale, the old woman blessed herself and raised a hand, gesturing about her.

"*Sí*," Will nodded emphatically to her comments and spoke to Juliana. "*Doña* Maria says she will pray for her family in America, but this—the land you see about her—is Renato Vittorio's treasure."

"No," Juliana contradicted him softly, "my great-uncle's greatest treasure sits in this room—the wife and sons he wanted to come home to." She raised her voice. "We must find Massimo and Pevie. Ask if they can help us return to Quito—"

A shout reached them. Before Juliana could move, *Doña* Maria's sons and grandson were flinging the door wide, followed by Will, who remained in the doorway. As Juliana joined him, she saw three riders galloping into the village. Pevie pulled his horse up and jumped clear in time to grab the bridle of the horse behind him. Juliana's brother toppled from the saddle and sprawled face down on the ground in front of the cottage door, a red stain spreading across his jacket.

James Dutton flung himself from his own horse and ran forward as Will turned Massimo over, Juliana kneeling beside him.

"Marazzi," Pevie spoke roughly as Esteban Giuliano and James lifted Massimo under Will's eye and carried him swiftly into the cottage where he was laid on the narrow bed in the keeping room.

Will was already easing off Massimo's coat. "I'm a doctor. Is there a *curandero* here?"

Doña Maria rose from her place by the fire.

"*Sí*, I am *curandera*." Will met the elderly woman's gaze without surprise.

Pevie ran his hands through his thick blond hair and took a shaky breath. "We saw Will going after you when Marazzi attacked, Juliana, but we were cut off from following. We made it back to our porters' camp, but by then it was too dark to come after you."

He stopped and gestured at Massimo. "'Twas better, we were thinking, to wait and set out early this morning with fresh horses and rifles. We rode up the pass looking for some sign of you. Marazzi must have followed us.

"He and his thugs attacked as we cleared the pass," James added and Pevie's blue eyes darkened as he nodded grimly toward the mountain pass. "The *campesinos* will find at least two bodies on the trail. I think Jimmy hit Marazzi after Massimo was wounded."

The door opened and a slim, dark-haired youth slipped in and whispered urgently to Esteban. It was like looking at a mirror image of her own brothers, this young man. Pevie's head jerked and he interrupted the men's low conversation, translating for Juliana.

"Marazzi and three men are holed up in the pass, Juliana. We can't get past them to return to Quito."

"*Tio* Renato and *Tio* Vittorio!" Juliana called over to her great-uncles. "Ask them, Pevie, if the tomb their father found is here in the valley." Pevie was answered by a decisive nod. Juliana locked gazes with *Doña* Maria. "Then I will ride up to the pass and tell Marazzi that he can see for himself that there is no more treasure."

Will, cleaning Massimo's wound, looked up sharply. "Juliana, no!"

Her shoulders sagged, and Pevie's arm came around her. "I have to go, Will. He won't believe anyone else." She went to her brother's side, careful to stay out of the way as Will bandaged the young man's wound.

Will nodded at it. "The bullet passed clean through. It missed his heart and his ribs are intact, but he's lost a great deal of blood. He'll mend if we can keep the wound free of infection."

James had sunk into a chair at the table, his face pale; at Will's words, Pevie joined him. Juliana told them quickly how they had, after all, found Renato Vittorio's treasure.

In the end, Juliana, Will, and Pevie accompanied Vittorio and a small band of villagers back up the pass.

Staying well out of firing range, Juliana called out. "Biagio Marazzi, this is the valley where Renato Vittorio discovered the gold in a tomb! It's all gone now. He sold almost all the gold to the Museo Banco in Quito before he returned to Italy. Most of the money he used to buy this land." No answer came and Juliana cried out. "Show yourself! These men will take us to the tomb where the treasure was found and you will see for yourself."

"Ah, no! You take me for a fool!" Marazzi's bellow echoed back from the peaks.

"Yes," Juliana shouted angrily, "you're a fool if you think I would put gold before the safety of my family! Stay in these mountains until you die from greed, but there's no more treasure to be had here! Follow us or not, as you choose!"

Vittorio led them back down toward the valley floor, taking a trail that wound along the mountainside above the highest pastures. Marazzi followed at a distance, and Will was careful to keep his horse between Juliana and the Italian at all times.

Finally Vittorio halted his party on the trail and pointed upslope. The mountainside rose in slabs of rock, stark and gray. Juliana shivered. What a burial place! One felt already in the land of the gods here on the roof of the world. They dismounted, and Juliana didn't look back to see if Marazzi still followed. She knew he'd come, propelled by greed.

One by one they ducked after Vittorio into a low cave mouth, then Marazzi entered, pistol in hand.

"Put that away," Will ordered brusquely. "There is nothing here to kill for."

The cave held a low, linear mound of dirt along one wall with a shaft six feet wide and at least that deep near the back. A dusty wooden ladder protruded from the opening. The floor of the shaft lay exposed to the uneven bedrock and Vittorio gestured at the dirt; Pevie repeated his story in English. "He says the dirt was sifted by the diggers. They took everything they found in the grave shaft—even the bones."

"They lie!" Marazzi moved then. "Papá knew there was a treasure." The sheen of sweat glistened on his unshaven face and his eyes were wild. "Papá said!" he insisted.

"Then look to your heart's content, Marazzi," Will advised coldly. "Juliana has upheld her end of the bargain."

She doubted whether her father's cousin heard, for he stuck his pistol in his belt and darted for the ladder. Vittorio turned an impassive face to his companions and led them from the empty tomb.

Outside, Stefano sat stolidly at a distance with the remaining *campesinos* as they came out into the mountain air.

"Marazzi is inside, see for yourself," Will called. At his words, Marazzi appeared behind them, screaming a stream of Italian at his nephew. As Juliana and her party mounted, Stefano dismounted and trudged uphill.

"*Loco d'oro.*" Vittorio blessed himself.

"*Sí, es la verdad,*" Will responded, and Juliana needed no translation. Marazzi was indeed crazy, crazy for gold.

CHAPTER THIRTEEN

The morning sun came slanting across the foot of the bed, waking Juliana. She raised herself up onto an elbow and saw Will sprawled on his stomach beside her, his bare back free of the quilts. They had all returned from Ecuador nearly two months before—she and Will, Pevie, and James Dutton. At the last moment, his gunshot wound on the mend, Massimo had declared his intention to remain in Ecuador. He would come home again, he assured Juliana, and sent a long letter to his parents. But for now, while he was young and free of family responsibilities, he was content to stay and get to know Renato Vittorio's family. While Juliana missed her younger brother's presence on the trek back to Quito and from thence to Guayaquil and on board their steamer, Will's presence warmed her days. They decided to marry as soon as her parents could be told and arrangements made on their return.

Because Faith and Bernard couldn't leave the Point Lobos lighthouse, Juliana and Will were married by the priest who served the Portuguese fishing village at Point Lobos. Nana Angelina and Papa Nunzio, her parents, Lucy Katerina, and Nunzio had come down to the lighthouse with Juliana on the train. Marthe McKenna arrived with her brother and Frederico Peña, who served as Will's best man. The three Dutton siblings had come as well. Stewart Patterson and his shy young wife Susannah had also attended.

Lucy Katerina, dressed in a lovely pale-yellow frock, served as her sister's attendant. Juliana's youngest brother, when asked to escort her down the aisle, flushed with pleasure and spontaneously threw his arms around her.

"He's so lost without Massimo," Juliana explained to her father. "I hope you don't mind? I want Nunzio to know how special he is to me." Her voice faltered. "And you and Bernard, too," she added.

Renato Giuliano kissed his daughter's cheek. "You must knit together a family from all of your families, my daughter. Your Giuliano family, your Russell family, and now your McKenna family. It is a very loving honor you bestow upon our Nunzio."

After the ceremony, Faith served a light luncheon, followed by cake, champagne for the grown-ups, and punch for Nunzio and Lucy. Henry and James, along with Sarah Dutton, left immediately after for San Francisco, accompanied by Marthe and Rico. Juliana's family had taken rooms at the hotel in Santa Rena for the night.

Juliana changed from her wedding dress to a traveling suit in her old room at the lighthouse, then came downstairs to make her farewells to both her families and to Pevie, who shook hands with Will, then hugged Juliana and kissed her cheek. "Be careful, Juliana, me beauty" he cautioned, his blue eyes sober, "t'would be best to be careful."

There hadn't been time, nor was it the place, to ask James or Henry about James' homecoming. If the brothers had figured out, between them, who Marazzi's silent partner was, they did not say. And Juliana found she no longer cared. The danger which had threatened them was over, in spite of Pevie's caution. Will handed her up into the buggy that would take them into Santa Rena and the train. She lifted her hand and waved goodbye, then turned her face to the road before them.

She and Will traveled south to the small town of Carmel where a friend of Will's had loaned them a tiny cottage overlooking the ocean for their honeymoon. For two weeks they reveled in their privacy, rejoicing in every look, every touch, every shared laugh. Some mornings they spent cocooned in bed, exploring their new physical intimacy. Other mornings, they were up early for long walks along the ocean's edge, talking of everything under the sun, or nothing at all—as long as they were together, their sense of communion seemed to deepen so that it hardly mattered whether they talked or not.

In spite of Pevie's last-minute warning, no sense of unease marred their time in Carmel. They returned to the Queen Anne on Webster Street and soon settled into a routine. Will resumed his study and description of his botanical collections, while Juliana looked after the housekeeping in the mornings after breakfast. Annabelle's cousin Deirdre came in to help with the cleaning and laundry, and once Juliana set the girl at her chores, she would retreat to the spare bedroom where a workspace had been created for her to continue her drawings of Will's plant specimens. She had tried to do this in Will's study, but they had found it too distracting to be in such close proximity. Juliana suggested they separate their working spaces, and Will had laughingly and reluctantly agreed.

"Juliana, *cara*, just please leave the door open, so we don't feel cut off," he'd said as his only condition. They worked most days like this until taking a light luncheon, sometimes with Marthe if she was free. Work resumed in their separate studies until suppertime, when Will would read the evening paper as Juliana prepared their meal. After helping with the dishes, Will more often than not suggested a walk, and they would return home to a quiet evening where Will might catch up on his scientific journals, and she would do the mending or write to Faith or Pevie or Massimo.

Now the sunlight advanced along the coverlet, and Juliana slid across it and leaned over, her dark hair falling forward to pool on her husband's bare skin as she brushed his shoulder with her lips. Will's gray eyes opened, deepening with emotion. She traced the curve of his shoulder along his neck, then he rolled on his side and his arms pulled her down beside him.

"Juliana, *cara*." His voice was husky with desire.

"Shh," she whispered, and the unbidden thought came to her, let this day wait yet awhile before it begins.

Dishing up eggs with crisp strips of thickly sliced bacon, Juliana brought their plates to the table as Will poured out two cups of coffee.

"What would you think of inviting Marthe and Rico and Sarah to dinner next week when Pevie comes up?"

Will lifted a brow. "Marthe and Rico?"

"Yes, darling, and Sarah and Pevie."

His eyes crinkled at the corners and he suggested gravely, "Perhaps we should include Henry and James, so as not to be obvious?"

Juliana stretched a hand out to her husband. "Thank you, darling."

His hand tightened on hers, then she pulled away reluctantly. She wanted her friends to know the same kind of happiness she had found with Will. But Deirdre was coming in the door, and it was time for the day's work to commence.

"Don't forget, *cara*," her husband reminded her, "I'm meeting Rico in the lab for lunch, then spending the afternoon there to go over his latest results. I'll be home in good time for supper."

As Deirdre bustled in, Will kissed Juliana hastily and retreated to his study. Deirdre, a large-boned lass with gorgeous red curls and a dimple in her right cheek, winked at her mistress. "Aye, and it's best if they know their place and keep to it, missus."

Deirdre was beating the parlor rugs in the back garden as Juliana stood in the pantry and took stock, thinking ahead to what she might prepare when Pevie came to San Francisco next week. He had written to say that he would be helping out at the Angel Station lighthouse for the next month due to a fall by the current assistant there. Reading between the lines, Juliana felt there was more to it than Pevie was sharing.

Stewart Patterson, his wife and young child now thriving, had proven an able assistant to Bernard while Pevie traveled with Juliana to Ecuador. The young man and his family seemed well-content at Point Lobos. If a permanent position in San Francisco opened up, Pevie could in good conscience accept it, knowing that Bernard wasn't alone. And, Juliana mused, a permanent position for Pevie in San Francisco would provide her dear friend and Sarah Dutton ample opportunities to see one another.

The doorbell interrupted her musing, and she hurried to the front hall to answer the bell before Will was disturbed. A tall, gangly young man stood before the door, his sandy hair wind-blown. She noticed a bicycle at the curb.

"Mrs. McKenna?" She nodded and he produced an envelope. "I'm to deliver this to you, ma'am, and wait for a reply."

Juliana tore the envelope open and scanned the contents of the paper within.

Dearest Juliana, I have some startling news to share, but please do not say a word to anyone.

It is to be a surprise. I will be attending a meeting this morning at the Bay City Bookstore on Russian Hill. Just pop in about noon and we'll have lunch. Please send a reply by return messenger. Your friend, Sarah

Juliana read through the message again, then told the errand boy to step inside while she scribbled a hasty note assuring Sarah that she would be able to meet her. Tipping the boy before he sped away on his bicycle, Juliana stepped along to the rear garden to check Deirdre's progress.

"I've just these to finish, Mrs. McKenna, then I'm done for the morning."

"Excellent, Deirdre. I've a basket in the larder. If you would take it over to Dr. Marthe and Annabelle, I'd be much obliged." The basket contained a loaf of moist lemon-herb tea bread she had baked the evening before, one she knew Annabelle would serve Marthe during her afternoon break and that Marthe would insist on sharing with both Annabelle and Deirdre.

She found Will deep in thought as she stood in his study doorway. His eyes brightened when he saw her. "My dove, my darling, my dearest, have you come to dally awhile, sweet temptress?" He rose and leered hopefully.

Juliana laughed and went to him. "Not now, but maybe later." She kissed him swiftly. "Sarah's invited me to lunch. I'll see you later for supper, love." She kissed him again, this time with a promise of later, and Will let her go slowly.

Checking the watch pinned to her shirtwaist, Juliana saw that it was not quite a quarter to noon. She paused outside the shop to wait for Sarah, knowing from experience how Sarah's committee meetings could run on. The bookstore was surrounded by secondhand shops, some selling clothing and toiletries, others paper and tobacco. Sarah had said, plainly enough, to come along in if the meeting ran late. When fifteen minutes had passed with no sign of Sarah, Juliana entered the bookstore.

The shop was stuffed full of books, so much so that the interior was dimly lit. As she approached the clerk, a dour-faced gentleman with a narrow mustache, she realized that Sarah had not told her what kind of meeting was being held here—or where.

"Excuse me, sir, but is there a meeting on the premises?"

The man eyed her without curiosity for a moment, then jerked his head at a door at the rear of the shop. "Through there."

Thanking him, Juliana opened the door to find herself in a short, poorly lit hallway. A flight of stairs led up, and at the foot of the stairs doors opened to the right and left. Now which way? Juliana, turned, exasperated, to return to the bookshop and its taciturn clerk. She had a fleeting glimpse, as she turned, of a door opening behind her, then an arm came around her neck and a damp cloth was pressed against her nose and mouth. A sharp odor gagged her, her knees buckled, and she knew no more.

A bumping noise woke her.

Juliana opened her eyes and fought waves of nausea. There was enough light to show her that she lay bound and gagged on a pile of thick ropes. Dampness filled the air and she realized that she was moving—that she was in the hold of a boat moored somewhere. It was bumping against the wharf or another boat.

She tried to think coherently. Had Biagio Marazzi returned? They hadn't seen him or Stefano since leaving them in the empty tomb in Ecuador. If not Biagio, then who? Marazzi's silent partner? But why? Why? Surely, Marazzi had reported that there was no treasure.

Juliana tried to push away the overwhelming despair that threatened to engulf her. This was like that other time, the sickly smell of chloroform, the rocking of the ship when she had been kidnapped as a child. She closed her eyes against the dizziness and tried desperately to work her hands free of their binding. Forcing the panic away, she listened. No other sounds reached her, no movement of the boat from someone else on board. Alone, for now. Until nightfall. She had no doubt that under cover of darkness she would be taken out of the bay and disposed of permanently.

If she could sit up, perhaps the nausea would abate and she could think more clearly. Rolling over, Juliana drew her knees beneath her, then slowly, by degrees, wriggled until she raised herself into a kneeling position. Panting from the effort, she took several deep breaths to steady herself.

Who had sent that message to lure her away from home? Who knew about her friendship with Sarah? Surveying the area around her, she searched for anything that could be used to loosen or cut the bindings on her wrists. There was nothing. Just the ropes. She sagged against them and fought back tears. She would not allow herself to cry. When her abductor returned, she would make one last effort to reason with him, to bargain for her life if she could, but she would not let him see her despair.

She set herself the task then of recalling each kiss she had shared with her husband, beginning with the first, when he had held her in the moonlight on the porch of the Point Lobos lighthouse. And the second, when they had sheltered together on the trail to the hidden valley. And the next....

The light was dimming and she had dozed off when the boat rocked violently and she jerked awake, her heart pounding, her mouth dry in the gag. Someone had jumped aboard. Footsteps sounded above, then a hatch cover was slid open above her and a lantern lowered within the hold. She heard an expletive and a grunt, then the light was withdrawn and a rope ladder dropped down.

As a dark figure started down the rope, the lantern was once more thrust through the hatch. "Hurry!" The man jumped the last few feet and then knelt beside her.

"Juliana, *cara*!" It was Will's voice, strained almost beyond recognition as he jerked the gag from her mouth. She gagged and retched and couldn't speak, her mouth and throat dry and parched. "Here," her husband said, cutting her hands free as he spoke, making quick work of the bindings at her ankles. He pulled her to her feet. "Hurry, darling, we've no time to talk."

He half-carried her to the rope ladder, then clamped her hands on it. "Can you climb? Good girl!" He followed right behind, the light above her withdrawn and half-shuttered as she clambered clumsily onto the deck.

"Juliana." An arm reached out to help her to her feet and she stumbled, recognizing James Dutton as she wobbled on her feet. Will's arms came around her. "Quickly, now," James began, when a voice spoke from the shadows.

"I think not. Put your hands up where I can see them, or I shall shoot Mrs. McKenna where she stands."

James Dutton froze in the act of raising his hands as his father stepped from the shadows. Juliana felt Will stiffen beside her.

"It is most unfortunate, James, that you had to meddle in something that does not concern you."

Richard Dutton jerked a gun at his son. "Leave now and return home. Wait for me in your room."

His son paled, but shook his head. "No, Father. It's over. Henry knows the truth. You must stop this."

His dark eyes glittering, Richard Dutton pointed the gun squarely at Juliana again. "She should have stayed dead. Don't you see? If he had known, her grandfather would never have let Aunt Alyce leave her own money to a granddaughter he despised! I need that money for Sarah—to make her whole. *Herr Dr.* Mueller has agreed to come to San Francisco and do the surgery here." Richard Dutton's face twisted. "It is all I ever wanted, all I have ever wished for, to make my little girl whole again!" His hand shook as he pointed at Juliana. "But she had to come back from the dead, befriending my Sarah, making her believe there was no hope for her!"

The pressure of Will's hands warned her as Juliana drew breath to speak. James Dutton held out a hand, pleading with his father. "Please, Father!"

Richard Dutton took aim, and as he did, Will shoved Juliana. She heard two shots as she struck the deck, Will's body across her. Had he been struck? Oh God, had Richard Dutton killed her husband? Sobbing, she cried out, "Will! Will!" and tried franticly to struggle free even as the weight lifted from her and Will crushed her to him. "Shh, Juliana, *cara*, I'm here!"

He helped her to her feet, and it was then that she saw James Dutton cradling his father's head on his knees. Richard Dutton's eyes were open, but it was clear that he was beyond seeing ever again. Two police officers approached and, behind them came the unmistakable figure of Samuel T. Jones. He tipped his hat gravely in Juliana's direction, but did not speak.

Will took off his jacket and laid it across Juliana's shoulders as she shuddered in his arms. "I don't understand, Will. How did you know where I was?"

His voice husky, Will turned her away from the sight of Richard's lifeless body. "Jimmy guessed long ago that his father was behind the attacks upon you. When he came home from Point Lobos, he found his father in the drawing room one evening, staring white-lipped at his sketchbook. Dutton must have been struck by your resemblance to Katherine and set out to discover who you were and how you had come to be at Point Lobos."

He took a deep breath, tightening his arms around her. "Richard rifled through James' other work to try and destroy any other drawings and came across Jimmy's paintings of Katherine and Lucy K. done in Italy. He knew that with you out of the way, there would be almost no chance of anyone learning about your inheritance from your grandmother Alyce—even if Katherine Dutton should return to San Francisco."

His voice softened. "Poor Jimmy," he said. "He couldn't make himself believe such a thing about his father, but Henry is made of sterner stuff. He sent me to find Jimmy—I never went to Mexico—but he eluded me in San Francisco. Then Mr. Jones found out he'd taken ship for South America, and Henry sent me to Ecuador to find Jimmy and the treasure, hoping it would be sufficient to stop the attacks on you. When we returned home, Jimmy confided his suspicions to Henry. Henry was able—with very little effort—to find that your grandmother had left you a sizable inheritance, one that his father had been dipping into for years. He set Mr. Jones to keep an eye on you without our knowledge."

His voice broke. "Thank God he did! Samuel saw you go into the bookshop. When you didn't come out, he went in and realized you'd been taken. He contacted Henry immediately. And Henry called me. We searched everywhere but you weren't on the property. Henry went through his father's desk and came across a recent transaction. His father had purchased this boat."

Juliana felt like his voice was receding. "I'm taking my wife home, officer," she heard him say. "She's in no condition to be questioned. You may come around to Webster Street when you're finished here, and I'll speak with you then."

Dinner was a greater success than Juliana had dared hope. She served oyster stew, followed by a roast with potatoes and peas. For dessert, she'd made a flan from a recipe Faith had given her during her years at the Point Lobos light station.

Sarah was flushed but composed when Pevie tapped his wine glass with his knife. Henry and Will left off their dissection of the city's mayor, and the rest of the table fell silent.

"I'd like to thank our host and hostess for a memorable meal."

"Here! Here!"

"And," Pevie took Sarah's hand. "I have the honor of announcing that Sarah has consented to become my wife." He kissed her hand and Sarah blushed.

A moment of stunned silence greeted him, then both Henry and James rose at once to kiss their sister and shake Pevie's hand. As Juliana and Marthe kissed Sarah, she held onto a hand of each. "We thought, with everything that has happened...." Her voice faltered for a moment, then she rallied. "That a quiet ceremony with just our dear friends and Aunt Katherine and Uncle Renato would be enough for us."

"That will be lovely, dear Sarah." Juliana hugged her friend's thin frame. Will opened a bottle of champagne and Juliana's attention was caught by Frederico Peña. Rico was raising his glass as Henry proposed a toast to his sister and Pevie, but his eyes were on Marthe McKenna, who stood with an arm around her brother. Marthe blushed under Rico's steady gaze, but her chin came up. At the same moment, Will sought Juliana's eyes and winked. She laughed, champagne bubbles tickling her nose.

They would heal, all of them, from the long shadows of the past. Will came to stand beside his wife, and Juliana saw Rico touching his glass to Marthe's in a toast. Love would be their sanctuary, as the Point Lobos light station had once been hers.

MW01241739